INSTRUCTION MANUAL FOR SWALLOWING

INSTRUCTION MANUAL FOR SWALLOWING

ADAM MAREK

ECW Press

Published by ECW Press
2120 Queen Street East, Suite 200, Toronto, Ontario, Canada M4E 1E2
416.694.3348 | info@ecwpress.com

First published in Great Britain in 2007 by Comma Press
3rd Floor, 24 Lever Street, Manchester M1 1DW | www.commapress.co.uk
Published by agreement with Comma Press.

LIBRARY AND ARCHIVES CANADA CATALOGUING IN PUBLICATION

Marek, Adam, 1974–
Instruction manual for swallowing / Adam Marek.

Short stories.
ISBN 978-1-77041-080-0

I. Title.

PR6113.A74167 2012   823'.92   C2011-906942-3

Editor: Michael Holmes / a misFit book
BackLit editor: Jennifer Knoch
Cover and text design: Ingrid Paulson
Typesetting: Troy Cunningham
Printing: Friesens   1   2   3   4   5

MIX
Paper from
responsible sources
FSC® C016245

This book is set in Adobe Caslon

"Batman vs. The Minotaur" was first published as "Batman vs. The Bull" in The British
Council's New Writing 15 (edited by Maggie Gee and Bernardine Evaristo, Granta
2007). "Tamagotchi" was first published in The New Uncanny (edited by Ra Page,
Comma Press 2008). "Testicular Cancer vs. the Behemoth" was first published in
Parenthesis (edited by Ra Page, Comma 2006). "The Forty-Litre Monkey" appeared in
the Bridport Prize Anthology 2003. "Robot Wasps" appeared in the Bridport Prize
Anthology 2005.

PRINTED AND BOUND IN CANADA

For Naomi, who keeps my head in the clouds.

CONTENTS

The Forty-Litre Monkey . . . 1

Belly Full of Rain . . . 11

Jumping Jennifer . . . 35

Testicular Cancer vs. The Behemoth . . . 49

Sushi Plate Epiphany . . . 65

Boiling the Toad . . . 75

Robot Wasps . . . 83

The Centipede's Wife . . . 97

iPods for Cats . . . 111

The Thorn . . . 125

A Gilbert and George Talibanimation . . . 133

Cuckoo . . . 155

Instruction Manual for Swallowing . . . 173

Meaty's Boys . . . 183

Acknowledgements . . . 221

THE FORTY-LITRE MONKEY

I once met a man with a forty-litre monkey. He measured all his animals by volume. His Dalmatian was small, only eighteen litres, but his cat, a Prussian Blue, was huge — five litres, when most cats are three. He owned a pet shop just off Portobello Road. I needed a new pet for my girlfriend because our last two had just killed each other.

"The ideal pet," the owner told me, "is twelve litres. That makes them easy enough to pick up, but substantial enough for romping without risk of injury. What did you have?"

"A gecko," I replied. "I guess he was about half a pint."

"You use imperial?" The man smirked and gestured towards a large vivarium in the corner. "Iguana," he said. "Six litres, and still growing."

"Oh right," I said. "I also had a cat. She must have been four litres, maybe more."

"Are you sure?" He asked. "Was she a longhair, because they look big, but when you dunk them they're small, like skinny rats."

"She was a short hair," I said.

"How old?"

"Four."

"That volume would have dropped anyway, unless you mixed tripe with her food. Did you do that?"

"No," I said. "She ate tuna fish."

"No pet ever got voluminous eating tuna," he smiled, almost sympathetic.

"What's the biggest thing you've got?" I asked.

"That would have to be my forty-litre monkey," he smiled.

"May I see it?"

"You doubt my veracity?"

"Not at all. Is it a secret monkey?"

"No, he's not a secret monkey. I've shown him in South America, Russia and most of Western Europe."

"What sort of monkey is it?"

"He is a baboon," he said, raising his eyebrows.

"A baboon? What do they usually scale in at?"

"Twenty-three litres."

"How did yours get so big?"

"I won't tell you. Have you any idea how many thirty-litre monkeys I got through before I hit on the right combination?"

I shrugged my shoulders. The man rubbed his brow between his thumb and forefinger, as if wondering why he was even talking to me, the owner of a dead half-pint gecko. I was getting claustrophobic and started to leave, when he grabbed my arm and said, "Would you like to see my monkey?"

I nodded that I would. He locked the front door and led me up a narrow staircase. Names were written on every step, and alongside, a volume: Edgar 29 litres; Wallace 32 litres; Merian 34 litres. Also on every step were paper bags of feed, books and files, stacked up against the wall, so that I had to put each foot directly in front of the other to walk up, and I kept catching my ankle with the edge of my heel.

"So how did your pets die, anyway?" the man asked.

"The cat managed to slide the door of the gecko's tank open. She tried to eat him whole, and he stuck in her throat."

"Hmph," the man laughed.

The man took me to a door, which was covered in stickers of various animal organisations I'd never heard of: Big Possums of Australasia, American Tiny Titans. The door had a keypad, which he shielded with one hand as he punched the code with the other. A pungent stench of meat and straw and bleach poured out of the room, and I heard a soft sucking noise, like air drawn into a broken vacuum, but I may have imagined this.

Being in the room felt like being suffocated in an armpit. Something was shuffling about in a cage in the corner, grunting softly. The perimeter of the room was like the staircase, with books, files and bags of dried foodstuffs piled up the walls. The floor was covered in black linoleum, and the section in front of the door was rough with thousands of scratches. Opposite the door was an archway, which led into a bright bathroom. He had a huge glass tank in there with units of measurement running up the sides and extra marks and comments written in marker pen.

"He's over there," the man said. "Stay here, and I'll let him out."

"Does he bite?" I asked.

"Not any more."

The man took a key from his back pocket, which was attached to a chain and belt loop. The lock undid with a satisfying click. He opened the cage door a little and crouched in front. He whispered something to the baboon, but I couldn't hear what he said. He nodded his head, as if receiving a response from the monkey, then moved back, staying in his crouched position.

The bad air in the room was making me feel sick.

"Why is it so dark in here?" I asked.

"Light makes him too active. He burns off all that volume when the light's on," he replied.

The man stayed crouched down, and began to bob his backside up and down, as if he were rubbing an itch up against a tree. He patted the floor with his hands, staring all the while into the cage.

A shape shuffled out. I'd never seen a regular-size baboon, so had no point of reference for his size, but he was big, big and greasy.

"Why is his fur all slicked down like that?" I asked.

"Vaseline," the man replied. "Baboon hair is slightly absorbent. If he soaks up water that makes less volume."

"So you grease him up to make him waterproof?"

"Yes."

"Is that legal?"

The man looked at me like I was an idiot.

The baboon came further out of the cage. The man put something in his own mouth. The baboon shifted back nervously at first, but then skipped in and took the food from his lips. He looked at me while he ate. His face seemed to be saying, "I know I look ridiculous, but if you say anything, I'll pull your arm off."

"What's his name?" I asked.

"Don't speak so loudly," he whisper-spat. "He's called Cooper."

"So what's next," I asked. "A fifty-litre monkey?"

"You can't get a baboon that size. Not without steroids."

"Do they make monkey steroids?"

"Are you mocking me?" The man stood up. The baboon raised his arms and hooted. The man squatted down again and bowed his head, looking back at me and suggesting I do the same.

I squatted down. The smell became worse. It hung near the floor like a fog.

"Do many people do this, grow big monkeys, I mean?"

"Not many. In this country anyway."

"How many would you say there are around the world?"

"It's hard to say," the man said. "Not everyone competes, but there are about sixty regulars I guess."

"And is this a record monkey?"

"By half a litre."

"So have you got like an arch rival? An enemy monkey grower?" I couldn't help smiling when I said this. The man seemed to be having a crisis. He didn't know whether to be angry, or to be excited. I think this must have been the first time anyone had wanted to see his monkey.

"There's a guy from Thailand. He claimed he had a forty-three-litre monkey, but he'd put putty in its armpits and stuffed golfballs up its bum."

"You're kidding."

"It's quite common. They're a lot stricter about it now though."

The baboon settled close to the man and allowed him to stroke its greasy head.

"Who's they?" I asked. "Is there some kind of governing body?"

"Yes, the BMG."

"What's that stand for, the Big Monkey Group?" I laughed.

"Yes. They're a part of the Big Animal Group. People compete with almost every animal you could think of. I specialise in baboons, but I dabble in cats and guinea pigs too. They're cheaper to transport long distance, and they take less time to grow."

I was glad that it was dark because my eyes were watering.

"Do you want me to measure him?" the man asked.

"What, now? In the tank?"

The man nodded.

"No, don't worry. You're okay. I wouldn't want to get Cooper all wet for nothing."

"It's no trouble."

"No really. It's fine," I said.

"But how do you know I'm not lying to you?"

"I trust you."

"Would you know a forty-litre monkey when you saw one?"

"No, but at a guess, I'm sure that he's about . . ."

"Not about. Exactly. He's exactly forty litres. I'll show you."

The man scooped Cooper up in his arms. The baboon wrapped his long arms around the man's neck. His blue shirt became smeared with Vaseline.

"It's really okay. I believe you," I said.

The man ignored me and went into the bathroom. He pointed to the water level, which was exactly on the zero position, and then lowered the monkey in. I expected him to freak out, but instead, he went limp, as if dead.

"How come he's like that?" I asked.

"If he moved around, he might splash water out of the tank. Instant disqualification. Getting them to be still can be even harder than getting them large," he said.

Cooper grasped the man's index fingers and remained still as the water covered his throat, his mouth, and then his whole head. When the water level cut a line across the baboon's forearms, the man let him go. Cooper pulled his arms down below the surface. The water made a soft plopping sound. The man ducked down to look at the monkey through the tank. He clapped his hands twice, and Cooper stuck his arms out to either side, pressing against the glass and holding himself below the water.

His hair stayed flat against his body. Air bubbles clung to the corners of his eyes and to his nostrils. His black-ringed eyes darted around while his head stayed still, as if the monkey was just a suit, and there was something alive inside it, something that didn't like water.

"There, you see?" the man said.

I looked at the water level. "It says thirty-nine," I said.

"Don't be stupid," he snapped, but then he looked at the meniscus and gasped. It was a sound of pain, of betrayal. His intake of breath and the way he stared at the baboon were loaded with hurt.

The baboon stayed beneath the surface of the water. The man looked him up and down and around the tank, looking for a reason for the reading. He walked around the tank, looking for spilt water.

"Is he waiting for some kind of signal to come up?" I asked. Cooper's eyes were frantic.

The man ignored me, still trying to see a reason why the reading would be low. He scrambled around the tank, his hands wrestling each other.

"Should I clap or something?" I asked.

The man looked at me, and then at the monkey, and clapped twice. The baboon let go of the sides of the tank and rose up. His head broke the surface and he wheezed for breath, panic over his face, as if he knew he was guilty of something awful.

The man grabbed his wrists and dragged him out. He was being much less delicate with Cooper than before he went in the tank.

"What did you do?" he snapped. "What did you do?" The baboon shook some of the water off of his oiled skin. "Did you make yourself sick?"

"Bastard monkey," he spat.

"Surely it's not his fault," I said.

"Oh, you think?" The man smiled, and then turned nasty. "What the hell do you know about monkeys, huh?"

I shrugged my shoulders, and the man turned his attention back to the monkey. He dropped Cooper to the ground, and the baboon bounded across the room. The man muttered to himself as he grabbed a paper sack from the floor. He poured something that looked like muesli into a bowl, and then squeezed a bright yellow liquid over it. He dumped the bowl on the floor while he used both hands to unscrew a large tub, out of which he scooped two spoonfuls of a gelatinous substance. He mixed this into the bowl, all the while muttering to himself. He took the bowl to a cabinet, which was full of droppers and bottles like a medicine cabinet. He put drops of this in and a sprinkling of that, and popped a capsule of something else in, then stirred it all up and slid it across the floor to the baboon.

The baboon looked at the bowl, and then at the man. He turned away and slunk into the cage.

"Oh, you're not hungry," he said. "Maybe you're happy being a thirty-nine-litre monkey? Is that what you're telling me? Why are you doing this?"

The man looked like he was caught between crying and bleeding from his ears.

"I should probably go," I said. "Thanks for showing me your monkey."

"Is that some kind of joke?" The man turned to me. "Thanks for showing me your thirty-nine-litre monkey? Is that what you're trying to say?" His fists were bunched.

"I'm not trying to say anything. I think you've got a lovely monkey, whatever volume he is."

I don't know what I'd said to him, but he went crazy. His face flushed bright red and the tendons in his neck went taut. He actually reached his arms out towards me and stretched his fingers, as if he were going to strangle me. I backed away towards the door, preparing myself to sprint.

But then a cloud seemed to pass behind his eyes. He began tapping the side of his left palm and whispering to himself. And this had an immediate calming effect. He took a deep breath.

"I apologise for displaying inappropriate emotion," he said.

"That's . . . okay," I said.

The man locked up Cooper's cage, shoulders hunched, and his posture repentant. He spoke to Cooper in a soft voice. I could not hear the words, or see the baboon's face, but the shuffling sounds in the cage calmed, giving me the impression that they were making their peace. "Let us sort out a new pet for your girlfriend," the man said as he stood up and ushered me to the door, huffing air through his nose.

The air in the shop, which had been thick when I first entered, was fresh compared to the poisonous fug of Cooper's room. "Look around," he said. "I'll give you a very good deal."

I paced around the shop, sidestepping to get through the tight spaces between display shelves, and looked at the eyes of cockatoos and kittens and rabbits and snakes. Nothing made an impression on me. My mind was blank. I couldn't shake the image from my head of Cooper beneath the water, his hands pressed against the glass sides of the tank.

"I don't know," I said. "You're the expert. What do you think my girlfriend would like?"

At this, the muscular plates of his face slid around an expression of pure delight. "Yes. Yes!" he said, jabbing a triumphant finger into the air. "I have it." And he went through a beaded curtain into a back room, coming back moments later with a small cage covered in a thick, dark cloth.

The man lifted up the corner of the cloth and urged me to peer inside. I could see nothing in there at first, but as I pressed my nose against the metal bars, my eyes adjusted and I could see, sat on a smooth branch, a small possum-like creature. Its long tail was wrapped around the branch, and as I inhaled, it turned its enormous eyes to me.

"Wow," I said. "What is it?"

"She is a Madagascan nightingale lemur. Very rare. At dusk, she sings a song that would send lions to sleep."

"That's perfect," I said. "Thank you."

We were discussing the price, when the man put one palm up in the air, and the index finger of his other hand to his lips. "Wait," he said. "Do you hear that? She is about to start singing."

BELLY FULL OF RAIN

Brendan knew why Doris was grumpy. It wasn't just the hormones. Fear makes people snappy, and Doris was terrified. Even more than he was. On the way to the hospital she complained about all kinds of irrelevant things: the state he'd left the bathroom in before they left, the Mexican wrap packaging he'd left in the footwell of the car.

"You're no help at all around the house," she said. "I hope this isn't what it's going to be like when the baby comes."

"All I do is work. Do I get *any* time for myself?" And the argument degenerated into a poisonous bicker about money and their lack of it. Brendan only realised as they were pulling into the maternity car park, screaming at each other, that Doris wasn't really concerned about any of the things she was arguing about. She was just scared, and this was her way of dealing with it. He'd seen her do this dozens of times before. Meanness was her coping mechanism. In the seven years that they'd been together, he'd never been able to get past his pride and allow the argument to fizzle out in her favour. They checked in to the ultrasound section swearing at each other.

"I'm not getting a very good picture," the trainee ultrasound nurse said, looking round at her mentor for reassurance.

The mentor frowned and said, "Keep trying, apply a little more pressure. Work it round this way." She took the trainee's hand and gently guided it across Doris's slick belly.

"Did you drink plenty of water before you came in?"

"I'm busting for a pee," Doris said. "Do you have to push so hard?"

Brendan was watching the mentor's face. She was a powdery old lady, severe looking. Her mouth rested slightly open, tugging at the slack skin on her cheeks. With these pendulous features she made an expression of befuddlement that terrified him. She was now completely controlling the scan, cupping her pale old hand over the fleshy fingers of the trainee. "I'd like to call someone else in," she said, not waiting for a response before leaving the room.

Doris's mouth was open, like she couldn't breathe properly. Images were rushing through Brendan's head. Something was wrong with the baby. Maybe it had two heads, or was missing various pieces. In the seconds that it took for the consultant to come into the room, Brendan had imagined what life would be like caring for a child that people would have trouble looking at, and he felt a protective surge welling up inside that was his first taste of fatherhood.

The consultant was almost bursting the buttons on his shirt, and his hand was the hairiest Brendan had ever seen. He took the ultrasound scanner and used it to gather up gel from the sides of Doris's stomach. "Just try to relax," he said. "How many weeks is she?"

The consultant worked the gel around Doris's stomach and asked the mentor questions, which she answered with the help of their notes file. Brendan didn't understand half of what the consultant was talking about. He just squeezed Doris's bony little hand and told her that everything would be fine.

And then the consultant put the ultrasound scanner back in its holster and gestured for the trainee to give Doris some tissue to clean herself up. "Well," he said, as if he'd just pulled his head out of a hole into the fresh air. "You seem to have an unusual number of foetuses."

Brendan pictured himself and Doris with a bespoke pram that was three seats wide and three high to house the nine children he expected to be in there. "Unusual' couldn't mean two or three. It had to be at least four.

"I have to admit I've never seen anything like this," he continued. "I'm not sure how it's possible."

Brendan and Doris squeezed each other's hands as if this moment of plummeting would pass and they would soon be coasting on a level track once more.

"How many?" Brendan managed to ask.

"Too many for them all to make it, I'm sorry to say. The human body can rarely hold more than eight safely. You have at least thirty foetuses in there."

Over the next week, Brendan watched many people stick their hands up Doris and scan her phenomenal belly. They were transferred to the Windsor-Hegel private hospital on Baker Street in London. It was a beautiful facility, with velvet curtains, soft carpets and nurses that smelled of fresh flowers. But these comforts did little to divert their fears.

Mr. Branje was their consultant. He emitted waves of calm confidence, giving the impression that he dealt with this kind of thing every day, even though he admitted that Doris's pregnancy was unprecedented.

Doris transformed over that week. Her belly swelled rapidly, as if the knowledge of what was inside it gave her womb licence to explode. She lost weight from the rest of her body, particularly her face, which showed her bone structure more clearly than before. Even her eyes seemed smaller, like she was retreating into herself, rather than face the reality of her belly full of babies. She wouldn't say anything for hours, and would then demand attention and conversation at three in the morning when Brendan was asleep.

Brendan too was looking ill. He'd been sick with fear since the first scan, but was now getting high on the situation — it was so ludicrous that he couldn't take it seriously anymore. There was no way to pre-empt what life with thirty-seven kids (because that is how many foetuses they found in Doris's womb) would be like. He would just have to go with the flow. He'd reached a kind of stoic calm about the whole thing. But trying to keep Doris together and affirm her ability to go through with the pregnancy was draining him, and his skin was looking thin.

Mr. Branje sat down with them in his plush office one sunny afternoon when they'd been in the hospital for a week. He rubbed the end of his nose with his index finger and tweaked the lobe of his left ear.

"We're not sure what to do," he said, and paused, as if waiting for Brendan or Doris to come up with a suggestion. "Your pregnancy is unique."

Brendan was rubbing his nose and ears too. Doris's hand found his and begged to be held.

"What's going to happen as they get bigger?" Brendan asked, looking at his already bloated wife.

"This is the problem. Your body isn't designed to carry anywhere close to that many foetuses. If we don't do something within the next couple of weeks, there's a chance that none of them will make it."

Doris's hand throttled Brendan's. He tried to pull free, but her fingers were a vice. "That's not an option," she said.

"Of course, of course," Mr. Branje said. "What I suggest we

do, is remove most of the foetuses so that a few have the best chance of making it to full term."

"Where will they go?" Brendan asked. He imagined for a moment that they would be transplanted into other women, women who were having trouble conceiving and would be grateful for this unearthly bounty.

"I won't terminate any of them," Doris said.

Mr. Branje looked into his lap before speaking again. "There really isn't a choice. If we were to leave all thirty-seven foetuses in you, they would fight for space and nutrients until they killed each other, and then you."

Brendan looked at Doris. His eyes felt like they had grown too wide for their sockets. "Honey," he whispered. "We have to let them do something."

"I won't terminate any of them," she reiterated.

Mr. Branje patted his legs with the palms of his hands. "It's a lot to take in," he said. "Go home and get some rest. See some normality. You're both shattered. Come back here in two days and we'll discuss what we can do."

They spent the two days eating take-out and watching DVDs, mainly comedies, trying to delay thinking about what they were going to do. When they did catch each other's eyes and start to talk about the situation, it would quickly break apart, as if the issue were made of some friable material that could not bear investigation. At the end of the two days, they had come no closer to reaching a conclusion.

"We have to take out most of the foetuses within the next week," Mr. Branje said when Doris called rather than returning to the hospital. "After that, they'll be fighting to get enough nutrients from you. Come in tomorrow."

Doris dropped to the floor beneath the telephone, wrapped

her arms around her waist and bawled. She cried with such force that Brendan was afraid to approach her. He reassured her from the other side of the room that she would still have more babies than they could cope with, but her protective instincts had kicked in and she wanted to save each of the thirty-seven babies. To lose even one was not an option.

"Why can't they do anything?" Doris said again. "With medicine the way it is, why can't they do something?"

"What would they do? Rear them all in test tubes?"

"Well why not?"

Brendan watched Doris searching on the Internet for anyone who had been in a similar situation. He squeezed her shoulders and allowed her persistence of hope to drain the feelings of responsibility from him.

The next night, when the phone rang, Doris flinched. Brendan was sure it must be Mr. Branje again, asking why they hadn't come to the hospital that morning. He bit the tip of his thumb, at first relaxing as he realised that it was not Branje, but soon grew nervous, as Doris was wandering deep into a discourse he couldn't translate from one side of the conversation.

"Who is it?" he mouthed to her. She batted him away with her hand.

Hillman August was an obstetrician-turned-clinical researcher at a small facility based in Devon. He said he'd helped a woman from Switzerland deliver ten babies only last month, and he promised to help Doris carry her thirty-seven foetuses to full term.

It was exactly what Doris wanted to hear. She agreed to travel to Devon the next day without even consulting Brendan.

"Who the hell is this guy?" Brendan said after Doris related her conversation with Hillman. "What about Branje — he's the top specialist in London. No one's going to know more than him."

"I don't know why," Doris said, "but I have a good feeling about him."

"You're out of your mind and you can't see it because you're up to your eyeballs in hormones."

Doris flared a nasty red colour, and the muscles in her face rippled. "You just can't stand the thought of having a big family."

"A big family. You're fucking joking right? We are not having thirty-seven kids, and that's that."

Hillman August's private hospital was an art deco building on a grassy cliff. The white sides reflected the late afternoon sunshine and looked just like a Hopper painting. Gulls moved in the air above the hospital, and a breeze blew in from the ocean. It looked more like a plush hotel than a hospital.

"How are we going to pay this guy?" Brendan said as they pulled into a space in the almost empty car park.

"He didn't mention anything about money."

"Of course he didn't."

"If he does want a lot of money, we'll just sell our story to the tabloids."

Brendan looked at her as if a stranger had just materialised in the passenger seat. "Fine," he said. "We can go on Oprah. She can video your vagina for the whole world to see."

"Don't be so melodramatic, look, someone's watching."

A man in a v-neck sweater with a shirt collar poking over the top was looking at them from the front step of the hospital. He pushed his long blond fringe across the top of his scalp and leaned down, as if this would help him see through the window.

Doris opened the car door, and the man ran across the car park, weakly concealing excitement.

"You must be Doris," he said. "I'm Hillman."

Hillman August held out his hand to Doris, and when she

took it he helped her to her feet. Looking over the top of the car, Hillman caught Brendan scowling. "Mr. Stirling?" he said. "Pleased to meet you."

Hillman's grin was full of gleaming straight teeth. He looked like he should have an American accent or be advertising designer underpants. He treated them like a concierge might treat a wealthy guest, smiling and making comforting sounds, gesturing to the sea with broad strokes of his hands.

"You have nothing to fear," he said. "I'm going to take care of you all."

Doris visibly relaxed at these words. Her cheeks were ruddy again, rather than the pale yellow she'd worn for the last week. Brendan followed behind, the suitcase handles digging into his palms. He had a terrible feeling that he would be leaving this place with more children than any man on earth.

Their room was better than their honeymoon suite had been. It had cable television, antique pine furniture, marshmallow quilts and a wall of windows that overlooked the ocean. There was even a room service menu.

Hillman had told them to unpack their things, have a cup of tea and something to eat, then come down to see him in a couple of hours. He didn't seem to be in any rush, and Brendan couldn't help thinking that this meant they might be here for a long time. Surely he wouldn't keep them there for the next seven months?

"You're unique," Hillman began. "I'm confident I can help you keep more babies to full term than any other person on the planet. Multiple births are my speciality. Janice has a scrapbook, which I'm sure she'll be glad to show you, with cuttings of all the families I've helped."

Brendan opened his mouth to say something, but Hillman pre-empted his question.

"You needn't worry about expenses. You won't pay a penny. In fact, I can help you make a substantial amount of money from this pregnancy, and if you're going to have thirty-seven kids, you're going to need a lot of cash." He made a laugh that was all mouth.

"Are you suggesting we sell the story to the papers?" Doris said.

"Not just the papers. The TV networks will fight to get hold of this story. They'll bid each other so high that all your expenses here will be covered and you'll make enough on top to ensure that you and Brendan won't need to work ever again."

Brendan pictured himself living a life of leisure, but in a room with terry towelling nappies hanging from the ceiling like vines.

"How is Doris going to carry all those babies?" Brendan said. "It can't be done."

Hillman placed his palms together in front of his mouth. "We're going to have to try something radical. It's an experimental technique, and I'm the only person in the world that can do it. It's my concept. I'll be honest with you, I'm going to have to push the technology much further than it's ever gone before, but I'm positive we can do it. It's going to involve you both being patient and making some big sacrifices." Hillman paused as if contemplating how best to construct his next sentence. "There's no easy way to break you in gently with this idea. I'm just going to lay it on the table. I promise I'm going to be straight with you the whole way. It will sound unorthodox to you at first, but please take a few days to think about it. I'll answer all your questions."

Janice, Hillman's secretary, entered the room with a tray of teas in china cups. He smiled at her before continuing.

"Okay," he said. "Your body cannot support anywhere close to thirty-seven babies."

"But I thought . . ." Doris said, but Hillman silenced her with a raised finger.

"Not how it is at the moment. Your womb won't be able to contain them all for much longer."

"So you're suggesting we put them all in test tubes?" Brendan said.

"No, no, definitely not. No, they'll stay in Doris, but I'm going to help her body adapt."

"How?" Doris asked, her mouth wrinkling at the edges.

Hillman clasped his hands together, his fingers interlocked, then he slowly pulled them apart, making a ball shape that increased like a slow explosion. "As your stomach and womb expand," he said, "I'll insert grafts to allow you to stretch and stretch."

"You're joking, right?" Brendan said. "Where's the skin going to come from?"

"It's manufactured. It's animal skin that I've grown specially in the lab."

"What, like pig skin?"

"The original skin cells are porcine, yes, but I've cultivated them in a way to make the immune system accept them."

"How big will I get?" Doris asked.

"I'm not sure," Hillman said. "But there's no limit to how much I can expand your womb and stomach. Capacity won't be a problem. I don't think there's any chance of you carrying these babies much past the six-month mark. We'll deliver them early via Caesarean and we'll give the babies steroids to develop the lining of their lungs. They can spend the first month or two in incubation chambers, where they'll have the best chance of survival."

"What about all the other problems?" Brendan said.

Hillman gave him the briefest of glances, then returned his attention to Doris. "We'll have to hook you up to a blood cleaning machine — a bit like kidney dialysis. This will help take out all the waste the babies produce, and it will also help your heart and arteries cope with the increased pressure."

"How long will I have to be on the machine?"

"We'll have to put you on it in about a month, and you won't come off until after they're born."

Doris dropped her face into her hands and rubbed her eyes with her fingertips. Brendan stroked her back. "This is crazy love," he said. "We need to go home and talk about this."

"I want to stay," Doris said.

"You can't be serious. Look," he said, leaning in close to whisper in her ear. "I don't want to have this conversation here."

"I'm staying," Doris said. "And I'm having these babies."

"Well don't I get a say?"

"No, you don't."

Brendan stood up, and without looking at Doris or Hillman, he walked out of the room.

Brendan needed to walk, as if motion would keep him safe. Mr. Branje was recommending that they terminate most of the babies to allow a viable number to survive. Hillman was talking about turning Doris into a human balloon, her insides crawling with tadpoles. Both options were horrific. He bounced between these possibilities, every time ending up at the same thought — he wished she'd never become pregnant in the first place. But he knew that kind of thinking was futile.

He kept walking until he was outside the hospital following a sandy path down the cliff to the beach. He felt so powerless. For one guilty second he wished that Doris would miscarry the lot of them, and then they could go home and return to their real life, but he drove the thought from his mind as soon as it came.

Brendan just wanted one kid. One boy he could play rounders with on a Sunday afternoon, share a box of popcorn with at the movies, read stories to. He couldn't possibly have thirty-seven children. It was ridiculous. They wouldn't even be able to fit in the same class at school. They'd probably have to go to different schools, or even have a special school built for them. And again he came back to wishing Doris had never got pregnant in the first place. He couldn't leave Doris, and he couldn't stand to have thirty-seven kids to look after. He was screwed whichever way he turned.

Brendan started to wander back to the hospital, but stopped and returned to the beach before he got there.

Brendan couldn't watch Doris being hooked up to the machines. He held onto her right foot, but turned the other way, listening to the sticky tearing sound of nurses pulling lines of surgical tape off a roll. They talked kindly to her, their fingers silent against her skin as they teased giant needles into her. The plastic tubes made sucking and popping sounds as the nurses assembled an array of artificial veins and arteries and connected them to the machines. Doris bunched her toes, and squeezed them.

The machines made alarm noises when they were first switched on, but the nurses did not seem concerned. "They always do that," they said. Brendan listened to the hum and wheeze of the machines, and knew that he would dream about those sounds, associate them with smells of sweat and sterilising tissues. He turned to smile at Doris, carefully keeping the tubes outside the periphery of his vision, knowing that sooner or later he'd have to look.

Brendan stared at himself in the mirror. He had a green pallor, the white of his eyes a similar colour to the skin around them. His forehead was oily. Black bristles erupted from his face.

He chewed on his toothbrush for a minute before realising he'd not put any paste on there.

Brendan had felt even more detached from the situation since he'd been sleeping alone. Hillman had taken Doris into a special room two months ago, one that was large enough to accommodate her and all the machinery keeping her and the babies alive. She liked Brendan to be around and presentable at seven thirty, when she was woken, but for the last few weeks he'd had trouble willing himself to her bedside much before nine. He shuddered as he pictured her. Hillman had transformed his wife into an alien.

Brandy, the young TV journalist who was recording the pregnancy for a show on BBC3, had arrived before Brendan, as she did most mornings now. Today she was wearing a dark brown skirt-suit and high heels. Brendan could fall asleep looking at her calves. The way they slid out from the hem of her skirt then dipped into the shoe strap around her ankles made him melt.

Shaun, her cameraman, squatted on a silver tripod box at the side of the room slurping coffee from a polystyrene cup. Brendan wondered where he'd got this cup from — you could only find china at Hillman's hospital.

The air pressure in the room felt stronger than outside. Brendan's legs had to work harder to keep him standing. This feeling grew worse the closer he got to the bed. Maybe Doris had her own field of gravity.

"Pass me a thingy," Doris said. "I need a wee."

Brendan found a cardboard urine bottle in the cupboard. He knew where everything was in the room now. He passed it to Doris and looked away. She was a bloated creature, her stomach a Frankensteinian beach ball of sutures and pig skin. She had become translucent, showing all her veins, like roots burrowing through her. Her stomach bulged with the babies moving within it, like an animated blackberry. She was red around the eyes and lips, and her ears were yellow-green. No longer able to stand, she wore constricting tights that prevented her from getting blood clots. Tubes went into her one colour and came out the other side a different colour. She was at the mercy of these babies and these machines. And he was at the mercy of her.

"I can't reach," she said. "You do it."

Brendan pushed the cardboard bottle between Doris's legs and felt the cup growing warm and heavy with her urine. She was always thirsty, and always peeing. If her water jug was empty for more than a few minutes she would grunt and bark. The bin at the side of the bed was filled with Lucozade bottles. And she wanted sweets all the time. Mainly fizzy cola bottles. Sugar and water, she just couldn't get enough to satisfy herself.

"Kiss me," she said, after he'd taken out her urine and handed it to a nurse.

Brendan leaned over her. She smelled sweet and musty, like an expensive mushroom, and her face was sticky. He did not linger on her lips, but pulled away, and looked at Brandy's calves for comfort.

At six months, one week and three days, the machines were no longer able to stabilise Doris's blood pressure. She'd turned a blue colour, but raved like she was red. "You're never here," she screamed. "Why don't you just go home? It's what you want to do."

Brendan had been able to take this barrage of insults

through most of the pregnancy. He knew that she was a water balloon filled with hormones, and couldn't control herself. He kept calm by convincing himself that one day soon the balloon would burst and all the hormones, babies, sutures and pig skin would come out, leaving the real Doris behind.

But now he'd had enough. He'd got drunk last night and stayed up late talking to Brandy — she was now living in the hospital full-time. They'd sat on the steps outside. Her concern had seemed real. She felt sorry for him. She could see his plight. She was wearing a strappy crop-top that showed her smooth young navel. She rested the underside of her arms on her bent knees, her delicate fingers dangling, then flicked her hair behind her shoulder. When it fell back to the same position, Brendan reached out and pushed her hair away from her face.

It was a simple gesture, but he may as well have stroked her bare tummy, or licked between her toes. His intent was obvious, and she stood up mid-sentence and went back into the hospital, leaving Brendan emptier than ever.

So when Doris began spitting vitriol at him that morning, he couldn't cope. There was no calm left within him. All his reserves were depleted. "You're a fucking monster!" He screamed, not caring that Shaun had his camera pointed at him and that Brandy was on the other side of the bed. "I can't take this any-more. It's a nightmare. I've made the biggest mistake, and I'm going to spend the rest of my life paying for it."

Doris didn't even pause to take breath before launching a retaliation. Her mouth moved independently of the rest of her face, growing wide and manufacturing insults with teeth and flailing tongue. They came so fast and loud that Brendan could barely hear them. He went deaf, and his eyes received the full blast of this attack, like her words were solid manifestations of hate launched through the air from the cannon that was her mouth, and he felt real physical pain as they smacked against his body and dissolved into his blood, making him weaker with every blast.

Doris's eyes were bulging like they were going to pop out of her head, and her fingers became claws that raked at the sheets. Her stomach, which was now more pig than human, wobbled on the bed, and the babies within it gambolled against each other. She moved one leg off of the bed, and Brendan took a step back. The machines started bleeping like a game of space invaders.

The doctors came rushing in, including Hillman, who placed a hand on Doris's forehead and was able to calm her with alarming ease. Hillman decided that now was the time for Doris to give birth.

The Hillman Institute usually seemed quiet and empty. It was possible to go a whole day without seeing another patient, adding to the illusion that this was a private residence. But on Tuesday 2nd August (the day when Doris gave birth), the place was throbbing. White coats flashed everywhere. Thirty-seven incubators were wheeled into the room and arranged in neat lines, awaiting the squadron of babies that was impatient to get out.

Doris's anger collapsed under the weight of her fear, and she summoned Brendan to the head of the bed, where he stroked her face and whispered, "It's going to be okay. You're doing really well," over and over.

The surgeons put a green screen between Doris's boobs and belly, so that she couldn't see what was happening. The screen had to be three feet high to eclipse her line of sight. It was so tall that Brendan had to stand on the tips of his toes to peek over — something he didn't do often, as she was a horror movie behind that screen, her belly ladled with dark yellow iodine.

Anaesthetists arrived and stuck needles in Doris until she could feel nothing behind the screen, like she was a magician's assistant with her lower half removed.

Trays of silver knives and clamps and claw-like devices lined both sides of the bed. Brendan tried not to look at these, but couldn't help it. He saw the tail of a doctor's white coat flick up a ball of dust and fluff on the floor. It rolled under the bed, and his confidence in Hillman plummeted. What if Doris died during the operation? He stroked her forehead again and said, "You're going to be fine. You're doing really well."

The preparations took hours — almost half a day. Brendan was exhausted before it had even begun. He was thirsty and his legs and back ached from hunching over Doris's head.

Doris was wearing a fake smile when Hillman asked her if she was okay. Brendan hated seeing her terrified like this. He knew that if he were in her position he would be insane by now.

After waiting for so long, when one of the surgeons finally held a knife at Doris's stomach, it seemed too soon. This was it. In a few moments, Brendan would be a father. The father of the biggest family the world had ever known. He was shaking. He'd been having nightmares that there would be something wrong with them, and until that moment could have been happy if they never came out. Doris's stomach was so monstrous that he couldn't imagine it creating anything human.

"You're doing really well," he said and smiled at Doris. She smiled back, then grimaced. "What is it?"

Doris shook her head and tried to push a smile through. Tears ran out the sides of her eyes and trickled down to her ears.

"Are you in pain? You shouldn't be feeling anything," Brendan said.

Hillman pulled his mask down to his chin. "Are you okay Doris?" Doris nodded. "You're doing really well," he said before returning his attention to her belly.

Shaun stuck his camera in Brendan's face, then tripped over a wire as he tracked down the bed to film Doris's stomach. He moved back and forth, trying to find a view between the doctors, but they were gathered so tightly and in such numbers around Doris's stomach, like a herd of thirsty cattle at a puddle, that he couldn't get a clear shot.

A few seconds later, Hillman held up the first of the babies, a girl.

"Would you like to cut the cord, Dad?" Hillman's grin leaked out the edges of his mask. It was the first time that Brendan did not find that smile irritating.

Brendan shuffled to the business end of the bed and took a pair of scissors from one of the surgeons. He nearly vomited when he saw Doris opened up. She looked like a butcher's shop.

Hillman held the baby, and another surgeon presented the cord horizontally. "Do I just cut?" Brendan asked. Hillman nodded. Shaun found a window into the scene by pushing the lens of his camera against Brendan's elbow. Brandy was peeking round the side of the screen, an expression of horror on her face. The surgeons were poised, ready to get in and pull out the others.

"Quickly, Brendan," Hillman said.

Brendan cut into the cord, expecting it to snip in two easily, but it was tough and sinewy, and it took three cuts to get through. While Brendan was lost in the grotesque flower of Doris's opened up womb, a nurse clamped the cord and took the baby from Hillman.

She moved up the bed and held the baby in front of Doris. Brendan was glad to be able to move behind the screen again and focus on their first child.

"Look what you made," he said.

Doris grinned and cried and held her arms out. The nurse helped her open up her gown, exposing her chest so that she could hold the baby's bare skin against hers.

So this was it. The big moment when Brendan saw his first child. He'd heard other dads talking about the experience and saying things like "it's the best thing in the world," "your whole life changes," "it's the most wonderful thing ever." But Brendan just felt empty and fearful. The baby didn't seem like his. He grinned and tried his best to act the proud father that he was supposed to, but he could find no connection to the baby. She was covered in white goo, and beneath that her skin was blue and pink. She had thin black hair on her wrinkled head that was plastered down with blood and muck. Her eyes were swollen and shut. She shuddered and let out a scream. Brendan dug deep. Where was this magic feeling? What was wrong with him?

Doris held the baby out to him. "Do you want to hold her?" she smiled.

Brendan took the baby in his huge hands. A nurse wrapped a blanket around the baby and helped ease her into Brendan's arms. He rocked her a little. She whimpered and shook. "You're my little girl," he thought, but he didn't know what it meant.

"Here's number two," Hillman said, holding up a boy.

The babies came out every couple of minutes. Doris's belly was a factory. Girl, boy, boy, boy, girl, boy, girl, girl, boy, girl, girl, girl, girl, boy, girl, he could only keep count because the less important personnel in the room chanted the number aloud as they came out.

Each time, Hillman passed the baby to the nurse, who pressed it against Doris's bare and bloody chest for contact, then passed it to Brendan, before it was taken away and placed in one of the waiting incubators. They were on a conveyor belt.

Brendan watched the tiny creatures in the plastic boxes. He couldn't comprehend that these things had been inside Doris. It seemed impossible. Doris was so excited with the appearance of each new baby that her fear had dripped away. Five nurses had gathered by her head, and they cheered her on. "You're doing really well, dear, really well, keep going."

The atmosphere in the room was one of celebration, but Brendan didn't feel like he had any ownership of it. It felt like a party he'd gatecrashed.

The mood in the room was so elevated that he easily sensed the wave of concern that spread out from Doris's stomach when baby number twenty-nine came out wrong.

Baby twenty-nine was too small, and blue. It was curled like a shrimp and did not hold its arms out like the others had done. The nurses' and doctors' movements slowed. The huffing and bleeping machines grew louder in the gloom.

Hillman took this baby to Doris himself, and the conveyor belt stopped while this rejected one was examined. "I'm sorry, Doris," Hillman said. "This one didn't make it."

Doris looked at the small blue thing and her face flared minutely before the tears leaked out. She reached out to the baby and squeezed it against her chest. When she felt the lifeless thing against her skin, she sobbed, and that gave way to a convulsion of tears, and a sound of pain that made a cramp in Brendan's stomach.

Doris held this baby the longest. She was reluctant to let it go when the next baby came out, alive and well. The nurse took the blue baby from her and approached Brendan. She invited him to hold it by doing something subtle with her eyebrows. Brendan lowered his head. He didn't want to watch to see where they'd take it.

So many babies came out of Doris that it seemed strange when the last one was held aloft and a great cheer went up from the medical staff. Maybe there was another one hiding in there? It would be easy to misplace one among so many.

Thirty-seven incubators containing thirty-six wriggling babies formed a phalanx along the side of the room. Brendan's fear vanished in the face of this absurdity. He couldn't possibly look after so many babies. They would have to hire ten nannies. He looked at Brandy, who was talking to Shaun's camera, pointing over her shoulder at the Stirling army. Brendan felt a pang of longing. It had been too much. He felt frazzled inside, his nerve endings numb and exhausted. He wanted to lay his head in Brandy's lap and sleep.

"We did it," Doris said.

She looked deflated. Her face was ruddy and slimy with tears. Brendan kissed her salty forehead and hugged her until she winced and asked for space.

"Thank you," Doris said. "You did really well."

They gave Doris a general anaesthetic and operated to remove all the pig skin and re-join the parts of her own body. It was like trying to put a peeled orange skin back together. She would never wear a bikini again.

While Doris was in the operating theatre, Brendan drank tea from a china cup and walked up and down the rows of babies. Some were sleeping, some looked up at him with glassy-black eyes as he passed. The midwives had cleaned them up now, and freedom from Doris's cramped stomach had allowed their blood to circulate freely around their bodies, changing their skin colour to a rosy pink, like real babies.

Brendan wondered how they were going to name them, and how they were going to tell them apart and how they were going to remember their names. Maybe a coloured clothing coding system? He counted them again. Thirty-six. Twenty-one girls and fifteen boys.

He was feeling quite relaxed. The nurses smiled at him as they moved from one incubator to the next, checking the babies like bees attending flowers. They looked at him like he was something special, and he supposed that he was. He was the most prolific man in history. A totem pole of fertility. What wonders would his offspring achieve?

A feeling of unbearable emotion, like a great body of water forced through a geyser, rocketed through him and caused his face to make strange shapes of pain, and his body to convulse with tears. Brendan almost broke his cup as he put it on top of a medical cabinet and fled to the corridor. Baby twenty-nine was somewhere else and he could not protect her. She was alone, floating in space, drifting forever, and he would never reach her.

He crouched on the floor, and the sobs made squealing sounds, which he struggled to silence, but these sounds were escaping him at high pressure and he was powerless to stop them.

Doris had been stitched back together. The hormones that had made her monstrous for the last few months were flowing in the opposite direction, and her mood was light. The television company had to enter a bidding war to retain its exclusive rights to the Stirling story. The negotiations were managed by Art Wendell, a pin-striped man who moved like he weighed nothing. He was Doris and Brendan's agent and business manager, because that is what they had become, a business.

Art clawed in enough money to make sure that they would never have to work again. They had fat trust funds set up for each of the kids, so they'd all be going to the best schools, and would always wear good clothes and enjoy the benefits of a private tennis coach.

One sunny afternoon, when the Stirling brood (as it had come to be known) was three months old, Art arranged a press event back at the Hillman Institute. All of the nurses and midwives were there, plus Hillman, Brandy and Shaun, and the

Stirling entourage, which consisted of fourteen full-time nannies and many members of Doris and Brendan's family.

They posed for a photo in the garden of the Hillman Institute. The babies were arranged on the floor, like a horde of white mice, with the adults encircling them. In the background was the hospital building, and then the tall grass at the edge of the cliff, and then the sea. It was a bright day and everyone carried their jumpers and squinted in the photograph.

Brendan smiled from the middle of this photo as Emily, baby seventeen, shat her nappy in front of him, because he knew that someone else would change it.

JUMPING JENNIFER

Today started right at the beginning of the day, at 12:02 a.m. Most of the other students in the halls were already asleep. I'd brushed my hair one hundred times and only managed to read a page of *Norwegian Wood* before my eyes started blurring. I fell asleep with my thumb trapped in the book. I woke up just three minutes later from a dream where I stumbled off the edge of a kerb. The moment I hit the ground in the dream, I was awake. In those three minutes, today became yesterday, and tomorrow began. There was a strange thickness to the air, as if a part of me could already sense the tumult that was approaching and feel the relative quietness of this moment. So I was already tensed for something to happen. And then the first scream shot out of a window across the campus.

I jumped up, disoriented, because I'd just started to get into the rhythms of sleep. My window was already open to let cool air in, but I opened it wider for a better view. The grass quadrangle in the middle of the campus was lit by large floodlights, almost too bright. They flooded every corner. The university had hacked back all the large shrubs as part of their drive to protect students from attacks, of which there have been none since I started here a year ago. The campus looked like a sports playing field. On the third floor, almost opposite my room, a girl in a blue t-shirt was leaning out of a window, shouting for help, pointing across to my side of the quad. Below her, a cigarette she must have dropped was releasing a thin tree of smoke, undisturbed by any breeze. I leaned further out of my window and noticed other people doing the same. More screaming started.

Jennifer Banks was on the ground.

The way her hips were twisted over made my stomach turn. Her beautiful blond hair was fanned out over the paving, and a thick ribbon of it curled over her face. There was something else strange about her shape. It took me a moment to notice that one of her arms was bent back the wrong way.

When my friends and I bitched about Jennifer Banks, about how gorgeous and vacuous she was, we called her Barbie. Right then, she looked like a Barbie doll thrown out of a window by an angry kid.

Ralph Connolly, one of the teachers, ran across the grass in his pyjamas. You get so used to seeing people in certain kinds of clothes that you hardly recognise them when they wear something different. Ralph Connolly reminded me of my dad as he ran towards Jennifer.

Most of the windows were now filled with faces staring down at the commotion. Female students' long hair trailed down towards the ground like hanging baskets. There was a hum of excited chatter and crying. The hallway outside began to thunder with footsteps as students ran to each other's rooms. Heads would disappear from one window, then appear alongside someone else in another window. A boy I didn't know looked up towards me, and I thought how strange that the body had only been discovered a minute ago, and already he was bored of looking at it.

The thundering in the hallway got louder, and then my door

flew open. Karen and Issy came in, grinning and gawping at the same time.

"Can you believe it?" Karen said. "Look what the silly cow's done now."

"She's such an attention seeker," Issy added.

I nodded in agreement. I was relieved they felt like that, because secretly, when I'd seen Jennifer lying on the ground all twisted, I felt excited. Jennifer was a real bitch. She hadn't acknowledged my existence in almost a whole year. She avoided looking at me at all. Why should I suddenly feel sorry for her because she tried to kill herself?

Karen and Issy stuck their heads out of my window.

"I didn't see that coming," Karen said.

"Why would Barbie jump out of a window?" Issy said.

"Maybe she was pushed," I said.

We all looked out of the window. About ten students had now joined Ralph Connolly hovering over Jennifer's body. Rita Williams from the Student Union office shuffle-ran across the grass in her slippers, clutching her dressing gown closed about her chest while calling someone on her mobile. One of the guys, whose name I didn't know, placed a blanket over Jennifer, covering her head and everything except one of her feet. His blond bed-hair looked perfect sticking up everywhere. This was just the kind of guy that fawned over Jennifer.

"Who's that?" I asked.

"Darren something," Issy said. "He transferred from somewhere last term. Shall I call him for you?"

"Don't you dare!"

"Darren, Darren," she whispered, teasing me.

"He's looking," Karen said.

I was too busy thumping Issy on the arm to notice that Darren was looking up at me. When I looked down, we shared a gaze for half a second before I dived inside.

"Issy!" I said, thumping her bum. "Barbie's dead on the ground and you're making me laugh in front of the whole place."

"He's still looking up here," Karen said. "I think he wants you to come back."

"Oh shut up," I said.

Karen said she was serious, and that made it even worse. I couldn't go back to the window, even though I was desperate to see if he really was looking for me. I just couldn't believe that someone who looked like that would find me attractive. Issy and Karen say I'm gorgeous. They say that without my port wine stain I'd be the most beautiful girl on the campus. With it, I'm just in the top five. But I can't believe they're telling me the truth. I just can't see it.

I don't like the phrase "port wine stain." It implies that the mark on my face was caused by a drunken accident, maybe my mum laughing so hard at one of my dad's jokes that she sloshed her glass of wine down her front, and somehow it seeped through her stomach onto my face. It's not the kind of thing you can scrub off with salt and water. I don't like to think of it as an accident, but as something with a purpose, something that will lead me somewhere. That's why I call it map. Sometimes I have to talk about it, and I hate saying "my mark" or "my stain" — all the words most people could think to call it are negative. Map is fine. My map.

Everyone says I have beautiful eyes, and I agree. They're my favourite thing about myself. They're so dark brown, they're almost black. When people talk to me, their eyes don't flit to my map, because my eyes captivate them.

When Issy and Karen call me Princess, which I love, I wonder whether the second looks I often get aren't actually looks of horror. Maybe my beauty has disarmed them, and they feel compelled to look again. But then other days, days when I comb my long hair in front of my face and wear sunglasses, I feel like this can't be true. I feel like Quasimodo. On days like this,

Karen might say something like, "It doesn't matter how you see yourself, it doesn't affect the way you look to the rest of the world. I wish I looked like you."

I couldn't believe Karen would ever want to look like me, even though I loved the idea that someone was jealous of my looks. Karen is pretty in her own way. Her hair is straight and brown, in a bob and a little dry. She has freckles and a wide nose. Her mouth is small. She doesn't have any features that would make people look twice, for any reason. In that way, I guess I'm lucky. On days when I'm feeling self-conscious, I wonder whether I'd rather look like Karen, and have no one notice me. Someone once asked me whether, if I had the choice, I would rather live a long and safe and average life, or a thrilling life full of deep troughs and high peaks. Given the choice, I'd go for the rollercoaster, although I don't remember ever being given the choice.

"They're telling everyone to go back inside," Issy said. "But no one's moving."

I poked my head out of the window again. There were now six teachers around Jennifer's body, and about thirty students. The windows were still full of heads leaning out. Two of the male teachers were talking with the students, pointing up at the building, trying to work out which window was Jennifer's. Jennifer's window is usually easy to spot. It's the one with the pink flowers on the sill. She's the only student I know that can afford the luxury of cut flowers. The smell is so alien in this place. You can sense it when you walk past her room. It makes everyone else's rooms smell of feet and rubbish bins and stale soup-in-a-cup.

Two teachers left the body to come into the building. We brought our heads back inside.

"Maybe you were right," Issy said. "Maybe they do think she was pushed."

"Yeah, why would someone like Barbie kill herself?" Karen said.

I flicked the kettle on. "Do you guys want some tea?" I felt like doing something mundane. I was filled with nervous energy. The cups in my room contained dregs of tea. Usually I would chuck them out the window at night. We decided to go and wash the cups in the kitchen instead, as it was almost opposite Jennifer's room and we could eavesdrop.

Along the corridor, most people had their doors open, and from them we heard snatches of conversation.

"I thought she'd seemed down for a couple of days."

"Jackson said she was acting weird."

"I saw her at lunchtime and she was fine."

"Did you tape *Friends*?"

We paused outside Jennifer's room. There was an almost tangible field of magnetism flowing from it. The hairs on the back of my arms stood up, and I felt a tingle up my spine. I wondered what might be in the room that would explain her state of mind. Maybe a suicide note, maybe some enigmatic clue, like a half-eaten piece of cheesecake.

The male teachers, whose names I didn't know, would be on their way up the stairs. Six flights. The lift hadn't worked at all since I arrived. I washed out the cups. Karen shook them dry, as the drying cloth was rancid.

"I would have thought you could survive a fall of six floors," I said.

"Maybe she landed on her head," Issy said.

I pictured Jennifer diving headfirst out of the window and shuddered.

There were footsteps in the hall. The male teachers were approaching Jennifer's door. They looked at us with serious, unbreakable faces. It reminded me of my grandma's funeral, when I'd smiled as I arrived, because I always smile when I see people, but no one could smile back.

We lingered outside the kitchen, waiting for them to open Jennifer's door, then walked past once we could see in.

The teachers hovered in the doorway. Through the negative spaces between their body parts — the irregular triangle made by hand on hip, the tall arch of legs, the half-vase of hips and doorframe — we peered into Jennifer's room.

Jennifer's lilac bed was made, and there was a line of shoes just poking their toes out from underneath. Her bedside table, the same one we all have, was covered with a deep purple cloth, hiding the graffiti scratched into it and the felt tip scribbles. The books on her shelf were arranged in order of height. On the wall was a poster of Robert Smith. I'd never have thought she would be a fan of The Cure. I really wanted to see the windowsill, the last thing she touched before she died, but the teachers were in the way. I caught a half-glimpse, so brief that I might even have imagined what I saw.

Back in my room, I re-boiled the kettle and dropped teabags into our cups.

"Did you notice the pills on her windowsill?" I asked.

Karen shook her head. "All I saw were her colour-coded timetables pinned above her desk. I didn't think she actually did any work."

"I didn't see the pills," Issy said, "but I saw a puddle of wine on her windowsill. I thought maybe it was blood."

"Oh don't be so Hammer," Karen said.

"If she jumped out, wouldn't she have moved the glass of wine first?" I asked.

"Why would she care about knocking over a glass of wine if she were going to kill herself?" Karen said.

The room filled with curls of steam. I poured hot water into the cups, then spooned in dried milk and sugar. "She was fussy about everything," I said. "I can't imagine her kicking over a glass of wine on her way out of the window. I reckon she would have crept up there carefully and perched for a few minutes, waiting to see if fate would throw someone her way to stop her jumping."

"So you think she was pushed?" Issy said, slurping her tea and wincing as it burned her tongue.

"I don't know."

"If she was pushed," Karen said, "there would have been a struggle, and her room looked immaculate, except for the wine you saw."

We all blew the little islands of dark brown tea skin around the ponds in our cups. There were more footsteps outside. It sounded like about six people. One of them asked another if he should dye his hair. Maybe they were going downstairs to get close to the action. I wanted to go there too. I wanted to be close to all the people outside, to share this moment with them. Even though we'd only been sipping tea for a minute, it felt like we'd floated miles away from everything, that we were isolated. That was the only time I've ever felt lonely when I've been with Karen and Issy.

I was about to ask them if they wanted to go outside, but the words faltered in my mouth. I'm not sure why. I looked around my room and couldn't help comparing it to Jennifer's. My bed smelled stale. The duvet cover was the black and grey striped one that I've had since I was ten. It had never occurred to me that I was expressing something about myself with my choice of bedding, and then I felt ashamed. I had just three pairs of shoes, one with little heels, pink DMs and Converse All Stars. Unlike Jennifer's, they were in a jumble at the bottom of the wardrobe, where I toss them when I take them off. Above my desk, there were no timetables or work plans, just photos of me and my old school friends, whom I write to every week. My desk was too messy to work on. I usually work on my bed, and rest the books on my knees. I thought how strange it was that Jennifer might actually work harder than I do and get worse results.

Outside, there was a sound, like a hundred people drawing breath at the same time, then a burble of excited voices. We heard people jumping onto beds the whole way down the corridor to see what was happening. We did the same.

On the ground, the people around Jennifer's body were leaning over her, obscuring our vision.

"What's going on?" I said.

Before either Karen or Issy could reply, Ralph Connolly shifted position, and we were able to see that they'd uncovered her face. Connolly was talking to her.

"She's still alive," Issy said.

"Oh my God," Karen said. "She's been lying there for what, ten minutes, with a sheet over her face as if she was dead?"

"Isn't Connolly the biology professor?" I said. "And he couldn't tell that she was alive?"

We heard sirens approaching, and then saw blue light spinning in the archway at the far end of the quad. There was nowhere for an ambulance to come in, so the ambulance people had to run across the grass. They carried a stretcher and a big box, like a tool box. One of the teachers sprinted towards them as soon as he saw the light.

"The guys in the ambulance must have thought they were coming to collect a body," Issy said.

"I can't believe she's alive," I said. "Her body was all over the place. Is that the kind of thing you can recover from?"

Issy and Karen shrugged their shoulders.

"My dad broke his knee in a motorbike accident when he was fourteen," Issy said. "And he limps when the weather's cold. I think there's a limit to what the body can repair."

"Just think," I said. "When she comes back in days or weeks or however long, she's going to be a different person. Something like that has got to change you."

"Maybe she won't be such a bitch," Karen said.

The ambulance crew scampered over Jennifer's body with their fingers, sussing out what was broken. They put splints and braces on both legs and one arm and her neck, and manoeuvred her onto the stretcher with great care. The circle of people around her pulled back to let the ambulance crew work. The excitement of the moment was draining away. There was a palpable release of tension, and in its wake flowed an emptiness. I felt bad because I was almost disappointed she wasn't dead. I'd never wish anyone dead, but for the ten minutes that Jennifer had been, we'd all been really excited, and now I missed it.

"So what do you think happened then?" Karen asked.

"I reckon she was posing in her window and slipped," Issy said. "That's the most simple explanation."

"I definitely saw a bottle of pills on her windowsill though," I said.

"Let's go and look," Karen said.

"Don't be dumb," I said.

"What if the police come to check the room out?" Issy said.

"We could pretend we're putting an overnight bag together," Karen suggested.

I thought it was a stupid idea, but Karen and Issy seemed to think it was okay, so I went along with them. We went out into the corridor, pretending to be going to wash our cups again, and checked whether the two teachers were gone. Jennifer's door was closed, and there were no sounds coming from it. I hovered there for a moment, and then Karen just opened the door.

Her light was on and the window was open.

We stayed away from the window, so no one outside could see us, but crept close enough to see the bottle of pills on the windowsill. They looked like sleeping pills. The bottle was in the middle of a pool of spilled wine, which had run under the sill and streaked down the wall. Issy was right, it did look like blood. The empty glass was on the carpet beneath the window. Jennifer's vase of cut freesias was on the bedside table.

"I've found it," Karen said, hovering over Jennifer's dressing table. The lights around the mirror shone through a ring of plastic flowers. The pink light made our shadows green. On the mirror was a Post-it note. "It's a suicide note."

"You're kidding," Issy said.

Issy and I skipped over to the dressing table, crouching low so we couldn't be seen through the window. We could all read the words, but Karen read them aloud anyway, and I followed along as she spoke.

"Leap and the net will appear."

"What does that mean?" Issy asked.

"That's not a suicide note," I said. "That's an affirmation, Deepak Chopra or Oprah or something." I almost laughed. I did laugh, and the more morbid I found it, the more I laughed.

"Where's the bloody net?" I said, flailing my arms around, pretending to be Jennifer sailing down past the windows.

When Issy laughs, she draws air in through her nose like a snore, and this cracks me up even more. We set each other off.

"I'm so beautiful. I'm leaping," Karen said. "Hang on a minute, there's no . . . aaaagh!" Karen was nearly wetting herself. We laughed so much my chest hurt. I caught my reflection in Jennifer's mirror. Laughing like that with my friends in the pink light, I could hardly see map, and in a strange way, it didn't look like me.

When we'd calmed down, we looked around Jennifer's room some more. I found a diary, and tempted as I was, it would be going too far. I put it back in the drawer and looked through her wardrobe instead. She had more clothes than I've ever owned in my whole life. I tried to remember if I'd ever seen her wear the same thing twice, but right then, the only thing I could picture her in was the blanket covering her when they thought she was dead.

I looked through Jennifer's collection of books, and was surprised to find several that I had on my own shelf: *On the Road, Steppenwolf, Brave New World.* I didn't think Barbie would read that kind of stuff.

In the middle of Jennifer's bookshelf was a fish bowl, and in it was a single fish. It was one of those black goldfish with the bulgy eyes. It was swimming with lazy flicks of its tail, picking flakes of food out of the water as they floated down from the surface. There were a few flakes still sitting on the meniscus.

She'd fed the fish before going out the window.

I don't know why, but knowing that she'd fed the fish moments before falling out of the window made me certain that it wasn't an accident.

We heard footsteps in the corridor outside. Karen threw down the magazines she'd been flicking through. Issy stood up and put her hair in a ponytail. I remembered that I'd seen an overnight suitcase in the wardrobe and darted for it. Flinging it open on the bed, I went into Jennifer's underwear drawer and grabbed a fistful of knickers and chucked them in. I was shaking.

Jennifer's door opened. Rita Williams and Helen, one of Jennifer's friends, came in. Karen explained that we were packing an overnight case because we felt so awful about what had happened. I was shocked at how easily she could lie. I'm a terrible liar. Helen frowned at us and looked around the room to see if anything was out of place. She looked at the underwear in the case, and then at me. I looked back into the suitcase. I couldn't meet her gaze. Although neither Rita Williams nor

Helen said anything, I could tell they didn't believe us. Or maybe I just imagined this because I felt so guilty. We left the room with our heads down.

Issy, Karen and I sat in my room for a while afterwards. I lit a stick of Tibetan incense to calm me down. I felt like I was eight years old and had been told off by my mum. I felt contaminated. I kept thinking about the fish with the bulgy eyes and decided that I'd ask Rita Williams if I could look after it while Jennifer was away.

We all attempted to make jokes, but we couldn't dispel the bad aura. None of us wanted to go to bed in that mood, and so we stayed up until dawn, drinking tea and talking about junk. When the sunlight streamed through the curtains, it had the most amazing curative effect. Like in a horror movie, when the vampire gets fried by the first ray of dawn, the fog of bad feeling we'd sat in for most of the night was vaporised by the sun. We all had lectures at nine, so there was no point going to bed. We drank more tea, and the shaky scaffolding of caffeine held us together for the day.

Rita Williams said it was fine for me to look after the fish. I put it on my bedside table. It felt good to have another living creature in my room. I didn't know what Jennifer called the fish, so I called it Barbie, because it looked nothing like Barbie.

TESTICULAR CANCER
VS. THE BEHEMOTH

The ground shook, and a sound like thunder shot through the city. Austin felt the vibrations travel through the floor beneath his feet, and up the legs of the chair on which he sat. He'd never been so afraid. My world is ending, he thought.

The doctor looked around, as if the source of the tremor could be found within his office. "You should have come as soon as you noticed the lump," he said. "I'm not a specialist, but your cough and backache indicate that the cancer may have spread from your testes to your lungs and lymph nodes."

Austin looked at him, and the beginnings of a word formed on his lips, but the rest of his body was inert, and no sound escaped him.

"I'm sorry, Mr. Weaver," the doctor continued. "I'll make an emergency appointment for you at the clinic. In these circumstances, they'll fit you in tomorrow. I'll call you later at home to confirm a time."

Austin stood up from the chair, and the ground wobbled beneath him. He ached. He could feel the cancer dissolving him. He thanked the doctor and left. The people in the waiting room stared at him as he walked through, and he wondered whether they'd heard what had been said. Why couldn't it have been one of these people? he thought.

Outside, the sun was baking the street, melting ice-lollies, making people crazy. Austin watched the pavement as he walked. He was half-aware of people running past him, of screams and exclamations. Two cars collided, and then a third drove into them, but Austin barely noticed. The ground shook again, and he stumbled.

The pain in his balls was unbearable. He had another hour until he could take pills again, but he couldn't wait. He saw a hotdog vendor racing his cart along the street, looking back over his shoulder. Austin chased after him.

"Can I have a bottle of water please?" he asked, struggling to free his wallet from his pocket while keeping up with the vendor.

"Are you crazy?" the vendor said. "Get out of my way."

"I just want a bottle of water, come on, stop a second, I'm dying here."

"Get out of here," the vendor said, then huffed to himself and opened up the freezer compartment, still running, and pulled out a Coke.

"I can't take painkillers with Coke," Austin complained.

"I don't care," the vendor coughed. "Take the whole lot."

The vendor pushed the cart off the side of the pavement and then broke into a run. Austin followed the cart to where it rolled into a parked car. He fished around in the ice and found a bottle of water. The ice compartment smoked in the hot air. He wanted to crawl into the compartment and switch himself off. He fished a blister pack of pills from his back pocket and unscrewed the lid of the bottle. A woman in high heels ran into him, glancing off his side, spinning round and hitting the floor. She yelped as she fell, and one of her heels pinged off.

"I'm sorry," Austin said. "I didn't—"

The woman picked herself up before Austin could stoop

down to her. She kicked off her shoes and ran barefoot. He watched her weaving through the hundreds of other people running in the same direction, but the sight meant nothing to him. Nothing made sense anymore. He looked at the woman's shoes on the pavement. A man in a dark suit, tie loose around his neck, jumped over them as he ran to the car that Austin stood beside. He stabbed his key into the lock and looked at Austin.

"Is that your cart?" he said, climbing into the car, sweat and panic all over his face. Austin shook his head. "Get it out of the way, now, move it." The man gesticulated with his arms. Austin just stood there, watching reflections of people moving across the windscreen in front of the man's face. The man honked his horn, and Austin stepped back onto the pavement. The man slapped the steering wheel with both hands. He turned the ignition on and pushed the cart out of the way with the car. He made a five point turn, crashing into a parked car and a lamppost alternately until he was free and sped off in the same direction that everyone was running.

Austin popped two pills. He thought about Margot, his sister. She lived about ten blocks from there. As soon as he thought about her, he needed to be with her. Margot would make sense of it all. Margot would bring comfort.

Austin floated down the street, while the stream of people flowed around him, often bumping into him in their desperation to get past. The booming sound continued every couple of minutes, like the slow heartbeat of the city, shaking the ground, making Austin flinch. The sun was right above his head, its rays frying his blond hair, cooking his pale skin, making freckles. His face leaked sweat, and his shirt was wet against his neck. He guzzled the remainder of the water. Looking up at the sky, he wished it would rain. He wanted the sky to crack open and wash away the heat and sweat and rinse the cancer from his body, flush him out and make him new again.

This can't be happening to me, he thought. It's some grotesque mistake.

Austin had first felt the lump six months ago. He had been in the bath, holding his balls for comfort, when he'd felt something irregular, like a dried pea. He rolled his balls between his thumb and fingers and felt it again, a hard lump on the side of his right ball. He'd felt sick all day thinking about it. He knew if he went to the doctor, he'd have it chopped off. And he wondered what would happen to his sex drive if he only had one ball, or no balls? What if they had to remove both? So he left it. He would go next week when things weren't so hectic at work, when he'd been with Molly for a little longer. They'd been together for less than a year. It was too soon to be going to her with things growing on his balls. She would be disgusted. There never seemed to be a right time. There was Christmas, and then the cluster of family birthdays that occurs in February. In March, the pain started, first a dull ache, then getting worse every week. The pain terrified him. He suspected that he had testicular cancer, but he didn't want to go to a doctor and have it confirmed. While he didn't know for certain, he might not have it, and every day that he might not have it was a luxury.

A month ago the pain became unbearable. He was taking paracetamol and ibuprofen pills together every four hours from the moment he awoke. He couldn't concentrate at work, and it was difficult to pretend that everything was all right when he was out with Molly. After six months, he decided that he couldn't wait any longer and made the appointment. But now it was too late.

Margot Weaver, Austin's sister, lived on the seventh floor of an apartment block. The corridors were full of people charging about with suitcases and the sound of television sets blaring from open doors. Someone had stuck chewing gum to the floor outside Margot's door, and he kicked at it while he waited for her to answer, releasing a stale minty smell.

"Austin," she said, her eyes wide. "What are you . . . thank God you're alright. Have you just come from outside? Did you see it? It's all over the news. I've been worried sick. Mum and Dad are here too."

Margot was still in her pyjamas. He felt a spring of tears begin to form in his eyes and blinked and blew at them to hold them back. How was he going to tell them all?

The apartment smelled of coffee, and there were half-full cups and packets of biscuits all over the table. Mum and Dad were sitting on the sofa, perched over their knees, the faint flicker of television light shining on their eyeballs. They flashed him a quick glance as he stepped into the room, then returned their attention to the television.

"Can you believe it?" Dad said. Austin hadn't seen Dad for a couple of months, and he looked older than he remembered him. A wisp of white hair evaporated off the top of his head. His checked trousers were too short and riding high up on his calf, revealing thin ankles, but the way he hovered on the edge of the couch, and the way his hands massaged each other made him seem full of energy. "They say it's heading this way. I just hope it gets full before it arrives."

"We should go," Mum said. Mum was wearing a powder blue jogging suit, which she always wore around the house, but Austin had never seen her wear it outside her home. She smiled at him briefly and looked back at the television.

Margot touched Austin's elbow and smiled sympathetically. "Would you like some coffee?" she asked.

"Sure, and a big glass of water. It's baking out there."

"You've been outside?" Mum asked.

"Yes, I just came in," Austin said, perplexed.

"How far did you come? Did you see it?"

"I've just come back from the doctor. It's been a rough morning. I got—"

"Doctor Stewart's?" Dad said. "That's quite close; did you see anything?"

Margot shuffled back into the room in her pink Muppet slippers. She fixed her eyes on the television as she handed Austin his coffee and spilled some down the back of his hand. Austin wiped his hand on his trousers. He cradled the hot cup in his palms and stared into the milky surface of the coffee, watching the reflection of the ceiling light ripple and break apart.

"Why are the lights on and the curtains closed?" he asked. "It's the middle of the day out there." They all ignored him, transfixed by the television. Austin looked at the screen. There was a monster movie on. A giant lizard was tearing up the city. Why are they watching this? he wondered.

"Is Molly on her way?" Mum asked.

"Molly? No. She's at work."

"I doubt she'll be working. She's probably on her way home. You should give her a call."

Austin's brain turned in his head. He couldn't make sense of things anymore. Maybe the cancer already had its feelers in his brain. He looked at the television again. Why are they watching this stupid programme? The film was done in a real-time docu-drama style. Jerky camera movements, shot on video to make it look like the news. Icons in the corner of the screen. Panicked anchorwoman. Everything. The cameraman was set up on top of a building about half a mile away from the monster. The monster was barely visible within the cloud of dust and smoke. Buildings had been smashed to rubble around it, twisted spires of metal poking through the devastation. A flat-roofed factory was punctured where the monster had stepped straight through it, and from the hole sprang orange fire and black smoke.

The streets around the monster had been emptied, and military vehicles had moved in. The soldiers looked tiny against the backdrop of the giant lizard, which stood upright on its hind legs, slapping buildings into powder with its enormous tail. The soldiers were setting up a tall barrier in a perimeter around the monster. They had missile launchers and heavy machine-guns pointed at its scaly belly.

"Why would Molly be on her way home?" Austin asked.

"Are you drunk, Austin?" Dad said. "She works over that side of town. People have been fleeing in this direction all morning."

"Fleeing?"

"The monster."

Reality flickered for a moment, as if his sister's apartment was on television, and a spike of electricity had rippled the cathode rays. He looked again at the television screen, and at his family glued to it. It couldn't be real. And then he remembered the people running on the street, and the loud booming he'd heard from Doctor Stewart's office. He felt pain in his head as he understood, as if the mental leap he'd had to make had snapped a few synapses. His ears fogged up, and he could hear his heart coughing blood around his body. He retreated inside himself. Saw his organs pulsing and jiving, fluids rushing around, and his genitals, blackened and swollen, wheezing.

"The monster, Austin," Dad repeated.

The monster.

Austin looked at the television screen again with new eyes and saw familiar landmarks. The sign of the Halcyon Hotel, which was visible from Molly's office. The golden dome of the mosque. Peppard's toy store. And amongst them, the monster, muscled and green, a crest of short spikes running from the top of its head to the end of its tail. Its skin, like an iguana's, hung in saggy folds around its armpits and thighs, a suit of armour, and the military's bullets appeared to have little effect.

"This is real?" Austin said.

"Get this boy some more coffee, Margot," Dad said. "Yes, it's real. How could you have missed it?"

"I had other things on my mind. So how did it happen?"

"It came up out of the sea, just crawled out and started smashing up the city. They think we're safe over this side though. The military say they can take it down when they've cleared the area."

Austin's muscles twitched with excitement. His balls, which had been like infected melons, dragging him down, shrank to peas. In the light of the monster, they were almost insignificant. And for that moment, he was released from their burden. Thanks to the monster, he stopped dying for a second.

"So what distracted you so much that you couldn't see a giant lizard?" Mum asked.

"Is everything okay?" Margot asked. "You look green."

"Everything is fine. Can I borrow your phone?"

Austin dialled Molly's mobile number. It rang six times before she picked it up.

"Where are you?" Austin asked.

"I'm downtown," she yelled. "In Osma's."

"You're downtown?"

Mum and Margot shifted close to Austin and clung onto his elbows.

"Can she see the monster?" Mum asked.

"Can you see the monster?"

"I can't hear you," Molly said. "The monster is just behind the Sony building."

"Tell her we're at Margot's," Mum said.

"Are the military there?" Austin asked.

"I'm trapped," she said. "I couldn't get through the exits. There were too many people. Some of us tried to find another way out, but the monster blocked us off. We're hiding out. My battery's almost dead. I've got to go."

And then she rang off.

"What happened?" Margot asked.

"She's downtown, in the kosher bakery on Beazely Street."

Mum put her hand to her mouth and her eyes went watery as she looked at Austin. Dad looked at him for a moment, then turned back to the television. They all looked at the screen. A camera mounted in a helicopter moved around a column of smoke to reveal the monster. It was thrusting its arm into a tall building and pulling out handfuls of people, desks and light fittings to eat.

"I'm going there," Austin said.

"You can't," Mum said.

"Don't be so stupid," Margot said. "You'll be killed."

"You'll never get past the barrier anyway," Dad said.

Austin looked at them and listened, but his whole body felt tugged by the magnetic force of the monster. He had to get close to it. If anything could cure his testicular cancer, then standing in the presence of the monster would do it, like standing in the shadow of a mountain, his own shadow would be obliterated. He guzzled the remainder of his coffee, kissed his family goodbye and ignored their protestations as he left.

The city was twitching with panic. Now it all made sense. The people were fleeing, migrating uptown. He climbed into Dad's black Saab, swooning in the heat. The leather scorched his back, and he leapt out, opening all the doors to let the small breeze that flowed through the city carry away some of the heat. He watched the heat distortions pouring out of the open door, and listened to the sound of gunfire in the distance, and a great booming sound, like a landslide, like the monster had pulled a whole building down to its foundations.

The inside of the Saab had barely cooled when he got in, and he wound all four windows down. The steering wheel burned his palms. The cold fans blew hot for a few minutes until air rushing through the front of the car cooled the machine. The only good thing about the heat was the driving seat — the warmth flowing from it soothed his aching balls and allowed him to concentrate on the road.

The journey downtown was like swimming upstream. Cars and people flowed uptown, away from the monster. A couple of times, when the roads were wide enough to allow two cars to pass, he had a clear run, but most of the time the streets were narrow with cars parked on both sides and people driving away from the creature. They hooted and gesticulated at him as he tried to bully his way through them. No one wanted to give way. At first he was careful of Dad's car and leaned out of the side window to check he had room to squeeze between the cars, but he was conscious of how much time it was taking him to get downtown, and he began ploughing through, popping the head-lights and drawing scrapes in the black paint. When he could see the military barrier ahead and tried to get out of the car, the door was so buckled that it wouldn't open, and he had to climb through the window.

Downtown was devastated. The air was full of smoke and brick dust. He ripped the arm off his shirt and tied it around his face. Powdery grains of fallen buildings collected on his eye-lashes. The gunfire was loud and punctuated by explosions as the military fired missiles at the monster. Above this though, was the sound of the monster. Its roar hadn't come through on television. It sounded like a rusted iron ship being dragged across an enormous blackboard. It bypassed his ears and went straight to the centre of his brain, where it reverberated and made him feel nauseated.

The barrier was ten metres high, shining grey in the sun. People ran, tearful and dirty, through three doorways within it. Soldiers in helmets and goggles with big guns shooed them through, one at a time. When they emerged they were weak from struggling against one another, and stumbled as they ran for safety.

Austin wiped the sweat from his forehead. His feet were swollen in his shoes. His shadow was small around his feet, like he'd started melting and leaking out the bottom of his trousers. He skirted around the edge of the barrier, looking for another way in. He found more exits, but they were the same as the first three — packed with people trying to escape. The barrier broke at one point to allow the shops of Hayman Street to pass through it. This section of barrier had no exits and no guards. The barrier stopped half way through Brannigan's sports store. The lights were out and the doors were locked. Austin picked up a wine bottle, which sat in a doorway, and hurled it into the display window. The point of impact veined out and fell back, like a net catching the bottle. Then the top section of the window dropped down in one sheet and smashed the bottom section into frag-ments. It was so loud that the silence afterwards was startling. Austin leapt through the broken portal before anyone came to investigate. He kicked footballs and trainers out of the way, jumped down to the shop floor and walked through to the other side of the shop, on the inside of the barriers. He grabbed a baseball bat from a tub and hurled it at the window. A huge keyhole-shaped section collapsed, and he nicked his shoulder as he slipped through it. Blood fanned out across the shoulder of his shirt, fuelled by the sweat-soaked material. Salt in the wound stung.

Hayman Street was deserted. Dust and ash and smoke filled the corridor of shops. Austin knew the way to Osma's: he and Molly used to meet there for lunch when they first started dating. Austin walked because the heat was too oppressive to run. He took the smaller streets, where the shops and offices were closer together and gave more shade.

He was only two streets away from Osma's when he ran into a patrol of soldiers. They were dead, crushed by a lump of concrete the size of a van. Austin grimaced when he saw their blood sprayed outwards, mingled with the dust. The soldiers' guns were pinned beneath the rock with them, but one had been thrown out across the ground. A soldier's arm stretched out towards it, as if he were reaching for it, or had been throwing it to safety the moment the rock fell. Austin picked up the big gun. He swung the shoulder strap over his head and held the gun like he'd seen in the movies. He felt great with it, a little cooler, in control, sharper.

Osma's was deserted. The shop door was wide open. The smell of bagels and rye bread was intoxicating against the smells of smoke and gas outside.

"Molly?" Austin walked towards the back of the shop.

"Austin? What the—"

There were sounds of bare feet climbing a short flight of stairs, and then Molly appeared through a doorway. Her dark hair was messy and stuck to her face. She held her high-heeled shoes in her hand.

"What are you doing here?" she said as she hugged him. Austin linked his arms behind her back, but only for a second. It was too hot to hold each other. They kissed, and Molly's face tasted salty. She touched the blood on his shoulder with concern.

"I came to rescue you. Look, I have a gun and everything."

"Where did you get that?"

"I found it. We should get out of here. There's a route through Brannigan's. We don't need to queue for the exit."

"Austin, I can't believe . . . what did you—"

The monster bellowed, and Austin's brain quivered in his skull. The beast's scaled foot slapped down outside and threw the bakery into shadow. Austin was mesmerised. The three front toes were truck-sized, with talons that raked up the tarmac.

"We've got to get downstairs," Molly said.

"It'll crush the whole building."

"We can't go out there. There's nowhere to run."

The building shook as the monster tore a chunk out of the roof. Plaster dropped down around them. The monster shifted its weight about and the ground trembled, making them dizzy. The sound of helicopters came.

"The soldiers will be here in a minute," Molly said. "We've just got to wait it out, downstairs."

"We won't be safe there. The monster could bring the whole building down into the cellar, and the military are going to bomb the crap out of this area. They think they've cleared the zone, so they can do what they like. You make a run for it, and I'll distract the monster for a moment."

"Don't be ridiculous."

"What's going on?" a man said, climbing to the top of the stairs and stepping out onto the shop floor. Two other men and one woman were behind him, peering out fearfully. One of them shrieked when he saw the foot outside.

"We're going to make a run for it," Austin said. "The whole place is coming down."

"We can't go out there," one of the men said.

Everyone ducked down and threw their arms over their heads as the monster tore down another chunk of the building.

Half the ceiling crashed around them, filling the air with dust, setting off electrical sparks. The monster seemed to have sensed that there were people in the building, and was poking one of its long green fingers through the roof, probing. Austin turned to face the door, and using the shield of his back to stop people seeing, he massaged his balls. The painkillers were wearing off, and the ache was returning, flowing out of his groin, washing against his stomach and his legs.

"We have to go," Molly said.

"Brannigan's is only five minutes from here," Austin turned to face the group again. "You can climb through the broken window and then out the other side of the barrier."

"You lead the way," Molly said.

"I've got the gun. I'll hang back and make sure it doesn't follow."

"A gun is useless against that thing. Put it down, Austin. You look ridiculous."

Austin felt a pang of embarrassment explode in his stomach. He'd been running on adrenalin since he left his sister's house. He had felt like a hero. He'd gone to rescue his girlfriend from the monster. His shirt was torn. He was covered in dust and blood. He had a gun. Could Molly not see that? He thought about kissing her on the mouth before they left, but her comment had soured him. He didn't feel like kissing. He wondered whether he should have come for her at all.

Molly and the others shuffled through the rubble to the door, careful not to step on any fallen wires. A helicopter, buzzing overhead, had captured the monster's attention. The group seized the moment and ran from the shop.

Austin ran with them a little way, but the pain in his groin was too much. It was making his legs weak. He couldn't run. He watched Molly from behind as she ran away, her curly hair bobbing on her shoulders, her calves tensing and flexing, her feet bare. He wanted her to turn around and see what he was about to do, but maybe it was better that she didn't. She'd only try to stop him.

The monster slapped the helicopter. It spun round, a mangled heap, and exploded before it hit the ground a few blocks away. Austin walked back towards the monster. He raised the gun up to eye level, but it was too heavy. He held it down at his side, with the strap round his shoulders supporting the weight. His finger was wet against the trigger, and almost slipped as he squeezed.

The gun rattled and shook as it spat bullets, but he held tight. The noise shook his eardrums into numbness. The vibration shot all the way up his arms, into his head, making his vision blur. It rattled his stomach too, and soothed his aching balls. He had the gun aimed at the monster's groin, and he kept the trigger depressed. A constant stream of bullets fired out of him, into the monster. Ribbons of blood spattered out from between the monster's legs. The monster tried to advance on Austin, but he stepped back and kept on firing. As his body shook, it became one with the gun, one with the monster, one with his testicular cancer. Nothing mattered anymore. Years of anxiety, all the things he'd ever worried about, were shaken out of him. His sister and his parents fell away from him. His job. The city. His car. The time he'd spent working for things that would never reach fruition. His unhappy schooldays. Everything came apart and dropped away, leaving him pure and fresh and empty.

SUSHI PLATE EPIPHANY

Gilby wanted to have sex with Tori. Staring at her across the table, he could think of nothing else. His feet moved of their own volition, banging against each other and scuffing the floor, because he couldn't keep them still. Everything about the night, about the restaurant, was part of his conspiracy to finally see her naked, to feel her bare tummy pressed against his, the soles of her feet rubbing against his calves, to have her hands moving around his back and her breath on his throat.

"What are you thinking about?" she asked him, leaning on her elbows on the table. Her black dress hung on her gentle lines in rills and ripples, reminding Gilby of wind moving through sails. The dress had a sheen, and a pattern of small pink flowers. It was cut low, so that he could see a tantalising glimpse of the place where her Wonderbra pushed warm shadows over her sternum. He'd never seen so much of her flesh. Even in suits at work she drove him crazy, here at the sushi bar with her body so exquisitely draped, Gilby found himself needing to swallow often.

"You," Gilby said. "Us. Here. It's great."

She pushed her silky black hair back behind her ears and smiled. The sushi plates chinked every so quietly as they moved past on the conveyor belt. Gilby and Tori were silent enough to hear this. Gilby was thinking about what to say. He knew that he wouldn't stand a chance with Tori if he mentioned work. He wanted her to ask him a question, something to get things going. He couldn't break the inertia of this conversation. The air was still enough for him to be able to hear his own breath struggling in his nose. He was recovering from a cold, but didn't want to sit there with his mouth open looking moronic. He couldn't go to the toilet to blow his nose, not yet, when there was no conversation. That would look terrible.

"I'm not sure if I fancy that one," Gilby said, pointing at a circle of seaweed filled with orange fish eggs. Tori screwed up her face and stuck the tip of her tongue out.

"I only really like the salmon and tuna on rice ones," she said.

"Would you rather eat somewhere else?"

Tori shook her head, and ribbons of her hair fell in front of her face. She seemed much shyer outside the office.

"They do soup here too," Gilby said. "It's got monster-sized noodles in it."

"I'll be fine with a bit of sushi. I'm not really that hungry anyway."

The Japanese waitress came to the table. The simple starched folds of her shirt rolled up at the elbows and her plain black apron made Tori's outfit look like underwear. The waitress poked a strand of hair behind her ear and aimed her biro at a notepad.

They both ordered the six-plate meal and Kirin beer. The waitress ticked boxes on a pre-printed sheet of paper on her pad, then slid it under the soy sauce bottle with practised ease.

Gilby had only eaten two plates of sushi when he began to feel full. Tori was on her third plate, but she'd left most of a plate of salmon on rice. The only ones she was eating were the slightly sweet rice rolls. Gilby watched the plates going past, and waited for one to appeal, but he'd suddenly gone off sushi. He ended up eating the rice rolls too. They only ate six plates between them.

"I'm sorry," Gilby said. "I should have taken you somewhere else."

"Don't be silly," she blushed. "I'm having a nice time. I don't want to eat too much anyway. It might spoil my appetite." Tori grinned, showing her lovely white teeth, and bit her lower lip.

"Where would you like to go after we've eaten?" He asked.

"Anywhere. We could go for a walk, or find a little café somewhere."

Gilby smiled and glugged down the last third of a bottle of Kirin. It was his second, and he was feeling a bit drunk because he'd eaten so little. He was grateful for the feeling though. It was lubricating the words in his mouth, and he wasn't so self-conscious about the silences.

"You look amazing," Gilby said, resting his cheek in his palm for a second, then returning his hand to the neck of his bottle.

"I like your shirt too," Tori said. "Is it new?"

"I bought it just for tonight."

"Sweetheart," she smiled. She leaned across the table, and gestured with her fingers for him to lean forward too. She poked her tongue out of the corner of her mouth before searching out his ear with her lips. "I'm wearing my naughty pants," she giggled, then slumped back in her seat, laughed loudly and took a big gulp from her beer.

Gilby slid down in his seat and laughed, a big, dirty, open-mouthed guffaw. Excitement bubbled deep in his stomach, and he sat back up in his seat because he had to keep moving.

The waitress brought over fresh beers, cold and wrapped in condensation. Gilby's phone vibrated in his pocket. He covered it with his hand as if to calm it. "I'm just going to powder my nose," he said, stumbling as he shuffled out of his seat.

The toilets were down some curving stairs and along a thin corridor. Gilby had to turn sideways to allow a waiter to pass. He smiled at the waiter but the waiter did not smile back. The corridor was tight with a low ceiling, illuminated by small yellow lights that you would usually see in porches. The floor was dark concrete and gave the impression of being wet, although it wasn't. It felt like a back alley, in stark contrast to the clean elegance of upstairs. There were two toilet cubicles, just signed as "toilets' with no male and female differentiation. The door opened into a tiny cubicle, reminiscent of an aeroplane toilet. The ceiling was so low Gilby had to tilt his head, and his knees pressed against the sink when he sat down.

Gilby pulled his phone from his trouser pocket and could see that he'd missed one call, and that there was a text message. The missed call was from Vicki, as was the text message. "When are you coming home?" She wrote.

"V busy," Gilby wrote back. "Late. G."

Something large rolled over in his stomach, or that was how it felt, and Gilby was suddenly firing hot liquid shit into the toilet bowl. It came so fast that it hurt. When the movement passed, the last few bits bubbling out as if escaping a pressure cooker, a spasm of pain rocked his guts so hard Gilby had to press both feet against the sides of the toilet bowl for stability.

The phone vibrated in his hand.

Gilby read the message while another explosion of diarrhoea burned his arse. "Fitz and bella throwing up," it said. "Pse come home."

Gilby looked between his legs at the inside of the toilet bowl and grimaced. He urinated a little, then blasted one more round of foam into the bowl. He started thumbing a reply into his phone: "Sorry. Stuck," then cancelled it. Gilby put the phone back in his pocket and began mopping up. The toilet paper was scratchy cheap stuff. He was worried about blocking the toilet, and so flushed while he sat on there. The rushing water soothed his burning rectum.

It felt like he'd been in there an hour when he was finally clean. His bum was swollen inside his trousers, and he imagined that he was walking funny. He wondered for a paranoid moment whether the whole restaurant had heard him.

Gilby was sticky with sweat inside his shirt, but he didn't want to take his jumper off in case he had damp patches under his arms. His face felt prickly with sweat. Something rolled in his stomach again, and he squeezed his buttocks and stomach muscles to get the creature under control. He sat opposite Tori. Two couples came in, dressed for the theatre. The cold air that came through the door chilled the sweat on his body. He wanted so badly to lie down.

"Are you okay?" Tori asked.

"Fine, yes fine," Gilby said, squeezing every muscle below his chest to stop himself from firing in his trousers. "I need some air, I think. Shall we go?"

The cold air outside was soothing, but Gilby couldn't stand upright. They walked through Soho looking in the windows of clothes shops, staring at people in cafés and restaurants, inhaling smells of coffee, cigar smoke, a skip behind a Chinese restaurant.

"Are you feeling okay?" Tori asked again. "You look like you're sweating."

"No, yes, I'm fine," Gilby said. He was leaning forward, one hand on his stomach, the other dangling at his side in case Tori should feel the desire to hold it. "Let's sit down somewhere. How about the brasserie? On one of the outside tables."

"But it's freezing."

"You can have my jumper," Gilby said. "I'm quite warm."

They ordered coffee, and when it arrived, Tori ordered a

cinnamon muffin too. Gilby hunched over his coffee. The thought of taking a sip made his whole body shake. The collar of his shirt was wet around his neck. He had to take his jumper off, even if his shirt was soaked. He needed some cold air on his body. He needed to dry out.

"Here you go," Gilby said, passing Tori his jumper. She smiled and draped it over her shoulders. She picked at her muffin and it crumbled in her fingers.

"How are you supposed to eat these things?" she asked.

Gilby smiled at her, but was in too much pain to speak. If this wasn't his first date with Tori, he would have just lain down on the pavement. He was desperate to be horizontal.

"I bet no one's allowed to serve these to the Queen," Tori said. "You know, like spaghetti, but I heard she has to eat whatever she's served because it's rude not to. Once, I think she had to eat a curried goat's head, but don't quote me on that. Oh god I'm waffling, sorry."

Gilby smiled that it was okay. He hadn't heard most of what she'd said. Her voice sounded like it was muffled by a pillow. The lights in the brasserie were swirling. The candle on the table was too bright. All around, the sounds of cups clattering on saucers and cutlery scraping plates bombarded him. He had to get out. He had to be somewhere quiet. His mind was so consumed by the pain and nausea that he hadn't realised Tori was talking to him. He looked at her and pulled his lips back from his teeth in what he hoped looked like a smile. Tori's mouth was moving, but Gilby couldn't hear what she was saying. It was like his head was below water. She was looking all around her while she talked, pointing at the ivy leaves wrapped over the supports of the awning they sat beneath, pointing at the shiny black Harley parked alongside them, pointing at her earrings. She stopped and furrowed her eyebrows, looking concerned. She said something, but Gilby couldn't hear. He guessed she'd asked if he was okay. He tried to say that he needed to leave right away, but he couldn't even hear his own voice. Inside his ears was the ocean, the sound of his guts rolling. He put a twenty-pound note on the table and couldn't wait for change.

As they walked, Gilby couldn't fake it any longer. He was bent right over, both hands around his stomach. Tori had her arm round his shoulder. He kept saying, "I'm sorry, I'm sorry." Tori rubbed his back. Somehow they ended up at Soho Square, and Gilby staggered to a bench to lie down. He lay on his back, staring at a streetlight through the branches of a London plane tree. As soon as his head touched the cold wood, his head cleared, as if all the liquid had flushed out of his ears.

"Do you want to go home?" Tori asked.

"I'm sorry," Gilby said. "I wanted this to be so perfect."

Gilby wanted her to somehow say, "It has been." But she didn't. She said, "Don't worry."

The branches of the tree above him were swirling, but he was feeling a little clearer lying down. He hung his legs over the side of the bench, so the arm was digging into the underside of his knees. Tori sat beside his head. Her perfume and the smell of her dress were soothing enough for him to be able to tilt his head back to look at her.

"You look so beautiful tonight," Gilby told her. He reached his hand round the back of her head. His blood ran quicker as she allowed him to pull her close, and their lips touched.

He'd been dreaming about this happening for months. Her lips were softer than Vicki's. Her lipstick was gooey and sweet, like strawberries. She exhaled over his cheek and pushed her tongue into his mouth. Gilby hadn't kissed anyone but Vicki in five years. An alien tongue in his mouth was exhilarating. Her tongue was cold and hard, thinner than Vicki's. He moved his hand through her hair, which fell about his face, tickling him.

Tori's breathing deepened, and she let the weight of her

head relax onto his face. She nibbled at his upper and lower lip in turn, then licked the tip of his tongue as he reached it out towards her. He was so excited he wanted to move, to kick his legs, to grab her with his arms, to be fully animated, but he restrained himself. He felt no guilt. He could only think how amazing it was to be kissing a foreign mouth, how thrilling it was that another woman wanted him. Gilby hadn't felt this happy since he was a teenager. It was a virgin experience, something new and precious. It felt like he'd been sloughing around in a torpor for years and had been awoken. His senses were fresh and alert. He could almost feel the end of each of her hairs tickling his cheek. He could have floated up to the sky right then.

Tori pulled her head back from Gilby's a little and smiled. She stroked his face. This was what they both wanted. Gilby rolled onto his side, and his body pushed out a fountain of vomit at high pressure. He had no warning, just a sudden convulsion in his stomach. All he could do was try to point it as far from Tori as he could, but she was sitting right beside him. The vomit splattered over the grass, spraying the bottom of her dress and her shoes. She leapt up with an audible noise of disgust. Gilby barely had time to take a breath before his guts clenched again and emptied onto the grass. He rolled onto the ground, hugging his stomach, the sick on the ground soaking into the knees of his trousers. He didn't want to be sick again. He sipped breaths through tight lips. It took all his willpower to try to control himself, so he had no attention to give to Tori, no ability to talk to her, to apologise. Gilby kneeled on the floor with acidic burps honking in his throat.

His stomach clenched again, and this time it hurt. The retch lasted too long and Gilby couldn't breathe. Nothing came out at first, but his insides squeezed until they found solids at the bottom of his stomach. Bits of rice and raw tuna fired out through his nose and scratched his throat. He could still feel these particles in his mouth when the retch finished and he made disgusting noises trying to spit them out.

After this third vomiting spasm, Gilby felt a little better, enough to look up at Tori. He couldn't read the expression on her face. There was some concern there, but more revulsion.

"I'm sorry," Gilby said, for what felt like the hundredth time that night.

"It's okay," she said. "Are you okay?"

"I'll be fine, yes. I just need to get back up here," Gilby crawled onto the bench and lay on his side. A gentle breeze blew the branches of the London plane tree and wafted the foul smell up to him. He belched and spat again, but was not sick.

"I'd better get cleaned up," Tori said. "Are you coming?"

The way she said it required him to say no. She wanted to get away. Gilby had become abject. It was over. She'd never be able to kiss him again without thinking of this moment. In a strange way, it was almost a relief, but maybe Gilby was just relieved to have stopped vomiting.

"I need to stay here for a few minutes," He said. "Will you be okay?"

"Yes, yes," she said, smiling with half of her mouth. "I'll see you."

She hopped across the grass of Soho Square in her high heels, holding her dress away from her legs. Gilby watched her scuttle along the path and out through the iron gate.

He pulled his knees up higher for comfort and shivered because a cold breeze had picked up. He watched car headlights moving through the small gaps in the hedge. Every minute he felt a little better. He took his phone out of his pocket and wrote a text message to Vicki. "Im ill," Gilby wrote. "Coming home."

A minute later, his phone vibrated. Vicki's message said, "Ill tuck u in with the kids."

He felt a little better as he walked back to Leicester Square tube station. He could walk upright at least. His head felt clearer as his senses widened to take in the lights and whirr of cars and people. On the platform, a train was there waiting for him.

Gilby put his feet on the seat and wrapped his arms around his legs, resting the side of his face on his knees. He thought about Vicki and the kids, and warmth spread through him. He closed his eyes, and the rocking of the train became so soothing that he started to drift off.

BOILING THE TOAD

Audrey wanted to play the bum rape game again last night. It's starting to concern me. At first, it seemed to happen by accident, but then she began adding layers of complexity, so that now it's almost a ritual. There are even rules. It makes me think that she planned the whole thing all along. I feel like one of those toads that will leap out of hot water when dropped into it, but will sit in slowly heating water until it boils.

Audrey doesn't seem like the kind of person to devise something like the bum rape game. She's sweet, even shy. She drinks Ovaltine before bed. I can smell it on her breath when she's lurching behind me, grunting in my ear.

We met four years ago on a training course. We were learning how to be assertive — I've always had a problem saying no to people. I still do. I guess it wasn't a very good course. Audrey was my partner on the first day. I'd watched her all morning while we did introductions and went through some basic individual exercises. She was pretty, and her face flushed whenever it was her turn to speak.

"I have an artificial foot" was the first thing I ever heard her say. The course leader had asked us all to reveal something about ourselves that the others didn't know. Little did I know then the intimate relationship I would come to have with that wooden appendage.

I could tell from the way the other delegates raised their eyebrows and looked at each other that they thought she was a bit of a kook. They all revealed things like, "I'm learning to speak Spanish," or "I like Woody Allen movies." They weren't really giving away anything. I felt sorry for Audrey. So when it came round to my turn, I said, "I'm a virgin," which was a lie.

Audrey gave me the warmest smile when I said that. I assumed she realised that I'd said it to usurp the group's attention from her foot, and was thankful. Thinking back now, maybe it was the idea of a twentysomething virgin that appealed to her depraved mind.

I smiled back. I was so naïve.

At the end of the course, we were both travelling home on the same tube line. We had plenty to talk about. We both had low rank jobs in big publishing houses. We compared the similarities and differences in our work until Tottenham Court Road, where I had to change to get on the Northern Line. Audrey had to change here too, and I was glad to be able to continue our conversation.

"Which stop do you have to get off at?" I asked.

"Any," she said. "It doesn't matter."

"But where do you live?"

"South Ken."

"But that's in completely the opposite direction."

I'm sometimes kind of slow at reading people. It took a couple more stops and a strange question and answer session before I understood that she had got on my train because she wanted to spend time with me.

"Don't you ever just do impulsive things?" she said.

"Like what?"

"Like, whatever you feel like at a given moment, no matter how abstract it might seem."

"No. I've never done anything like that."

"You should. It's good for you. If you can do anything, then anything can happen. If you keep doing what you've always done, you'll keep getting what you've always got. I learned that on the last course I went on."

And then Audrey leaned over me. I thought she was trying to kiss me and missed by a couple of face lengths, but then she pushed out this ridiculous fart. A high pitched toot that rippled and went flat at the end.

I was too embarrassed to say anything. And so were the other people in the carriage. A few people looked at her for a second, as confused as I was, and then they looked away quickly. Maybe afraid to make eye contact. There must be something wrong with her, they probably thought. I was thinking the same thing.

"Nobody really cares what you do," she said. "See. You can do anything you feel like. None of these people is going to say anything. They're all sheep. You're all sheep aren't you?"

"I'm not," said a guy a couple of seats down. He had a beard on his face and a book in his lap.

"Okay. Except him," she said.

I couldn't believe this was the same girl I'd spent the last two days with. She'd seemed so introverted, fragile almost. She'd totally transformed. She frightened me, but I wanted to be around her for a bit longer. So when we got to my stop, I asked her to come and have a drink with me.

"Fuck drinks," she said. "Come on, let's do something different. Something we'll always remember. To make a day stand out in your head thirty years into the future, you have to make some pretty big waves in it."

"What do you want to do?" I said.

"I don't know. You decide."

I hadn't a clue what to do. What she would like to do. What I felt comfortable doing. I was panicking. Now it felt like she might fly away at any second. Somehow, between Tottenham Court Road and Hendon Central she'd managed to make me need her.

"Okay," I said, improvising, and not really sure where I was going with it. "I've got about eight quid in cash in my pocket. Let's get in a cab and tell him to take us as far as that will get."

"That's good!" she said, her face full of delight.

The cab got us as far as Highgate Cemetery. Audrey bought a bottle of wine and a pack of tortilla chips, and then we climbed over the fence and sat behind Karl Marx's tomb.

The momentum of our conversation kept going until about two thirds of the bottle was gone, and then we both ran out of energy and I could sense that our first big adventure was coming to a close.

"So when you got up this morning," she said, "could you ever have imagined how the day would end up?"

"No," I said. "I could never have imagined this."

"Most days, most people know exactly where their day is going, unless some bit of bad luck hits them. How much more exciting would life be if every morning when you got up you didn't have a clue what would happen before you got to bed?"

"You've got a good point," I said.

Audrey wrapped her arms around her knees and made a small nod, as if my understanding of her philosophy justified it in her own mind.

"Have you ever done it in a graveyard?" she asked.

So that is how we started our relationship, by doing

impulsive things. Over the years, things moved from impulsive to compulsive. Now we've reached repulsive, and that's why I'm writing this.

Audrey was not crazy like that all the time, but she did everything a little differently. She made large architectural sandwiches. She drank about fifteen cups of tea a day. She liked to watch reality TV shows in her pyjamas, and to pamper herself by buying a pair of expensive socks whenever she had her period.

But then she'd rev up. Something atmospheric or astronomic, or astrologic, would catch her sails, and she'd go nuts, like she had on our first night together, and we'd have some real adventures. Sometimes they were fun, and sometimes they were frightening. One time, she almost got us killed when she persuaded me to shuffle along the outside edge of a bridge over a motorway. These moments became more rare over time, but as our sense of adventure diminished, Audrey's sexual preferences became more and more peculiar.

I didn't call the bum rape game the bum rape game from the start. There was no bum raping involved to begin with. It took about eight months for her to work that in. It started as just a simple bedroom kink.

"Do you ever fancy getting any toys?" she asked.

I said that I really didn't know what kind of toys we could use, picturing us wearing pig masks and handcuffs. I didn't much like the sound of that. One day the postman brought us a big fat vibrator in the post. Audrey couldn't wait to try it out. She insisted that Proud Ernie was for both of us, and I had to admit that it did feel quite good when she rubbed me with it.

Sharing our bed with a vibrator was an intimidating thing.

It was longer and wider than I am. It had nobbles and tongues that were in all the right places. It made Audrey go crazy in ways that were sometimes frightening.

Audrey tried to reassure me. "It's not that you're not good enough," she said. "You've got a wonderful willy."

It was impossible to argue the advantage of one cock in the bed over two. Audrey liked both at once, and so whenever we made love, I felt like a sexual cyborg, part man, part machine. I wondered what other additions could be made to the human body to increase sexual pleasure. I didn't have to wait long to find out.

Audrey didn't like to tie me down — that took all the inter-activity out of it. She liked to tie bits of us together. Her ankle to my ankle. Her wrist to my wrist. A stretchy elastic band around our middles. As we moved, these restraints would inhibit our movements, or give us leverage for pushing in new and exhilarating directions.

The tying up started at about the time we moved into her parents' house. I'd just lost my job after someone at work added "hey fuck nuts" as a title in the magazine I was proofreading, and somehow I managed to miss it.

It took me a few months to get another job, and Audrey said that her parents would be happy for us to stay with them for a while. It sounded like a good idea at first. But then on the nights when the mood would catch her, and she'd want to play what was the progenitor of the bum rape game, I would be terrified that her parents could hear us. There was only a ceiling between their gameshows and our toys and bonds. I think it was my fear that excited Audrey so much. When I'd whisper to her, all sweaty and panicking, "Sssh, they'll hear us," she'd grin and make a booming laugh, pumping the bed until it squeaked.

I eventually got a job at a smaller publishing house, and we could afford to move out. But Audrey was reluctant. She said we could save up for a bit, because her parents weren't charging us any rent, and we could go on a great holiday together. So we stayed for a little longer. But one night Audrey's mum walked in on us. We were trussed up like a couple of dangerous animals, arses in the air, bodies squeezed into great convoluted sausages with medical tape, our hair dripping with olive oil.

The scariest moment wasn't when she poked her old grey head around the door and said, "Are you okay?" It was after she'd gone, when I was no longer in the mood and began to extricate myself from the mess of straps, when my disinclination drove Audrey to a new level of crazy. Spit actually flew from her mouth. She was possessed. And the force with which she ground against me while I struggled to get free knocked two holes in the wall where the headboard beat against it.

"I'm moving out, with or without you," I said. "It's freaky. I can't stay here any longer."

"But if we stay a little longer, we can go on a really amazing holiday," she said. "Alaska, or Australia, anywhere."

"I'd rather never go on holiday than go through an experience like that again."

And then Audrey got really mean, in the way that she can when she doesn't get her way. And she started saying all kinds of hurtful things. I lost my temper, and then we just started yelling at each other in the street outside her parents' house.

"You know what," I said. "I think there's something mentally wrong with you. There's something very weird about a forty-year-old woman who wants to live with her boyfriend in her parents' house."

So we moved out. At first Audrey was quite sulky about it. But then she devised the next layer of the game, and this had an immense effect on her mood. This is when she liked me to pretend that I was no longer complicit in the act. And this is when sex became fearful for me, but it was this fear that she seemed to enjoy so much, and even though it turned our love-making into a traumatic ordeal, she was so kind afterwards that I let her do what she wanted.

She would make my breakfast the following morning, call me from work to say that she was thinking about me. She bought me expensive gifts: a new watch, an iPod, running shoes. But then after a few days, her mood would decline, and after a couple of weeks, she would get angry, picking fights over silly things, complaining about everything I did, or didn't do, and then I'd know that any night soon, she'd want to play the game again.

I now dread these times, and start to drink heavily when I sense another one coming. I even went to the doctor and pretended I suffer from severe migraines to get some weighty painkillers, which I take in advance of the game, because it hurts a lot.

Now, I'm always on edge, waiting for Audrey to lean over and whisper softly, "Do you want to play, *you know?*"

Soon I'm going to have to leave her. But my biggest fear is that if I left, she'd still come after me to play, that my genuine lack of complicity would be the final element to the game, that she might break into my house one night and just do it, and not stop until she'd drilled a few new holes into me. It's because I don't think she'd stop the game, even if we broke up, that I stay with her. Somehow, it's better that I give my consent. That way, I've got a little bit of control. Just a little.

ROBOT WASPS

Hum watched the nest from the window. There were always at least ten wasps around the entrance hole, their metal bodies glinting in the sun. The nest was the size of a baseball, made on the Y-shaped branch of a dead apple tree in the garden. Not a huge nest, but it didn't need to be.

Hum had seen a story on TV about a man who had a basketball-sized nest in his garden. He couldn't afford to pay the exterminators, so decided to deal with it himself. A real epsilon. He took a hammer to the nest, as if that would do anything. He was dead a couple of stings later. But the wasps didn't stop attacking. They continued driving their metal stingers into his dead flesh without relent, injecting their payload of toxins. His family and the paramedics couldn't get anywhere near him until the exterminators came and deactivated the wasps. The photo of his body on the news had made Hum shiver. Even though it was a low-resolution picture, he could see the lumpy texture of the body. It looked like it had been smashed with a tenderising mallet.

"Why'd they make robot wasps?" Hum asked.

He turned from the window when Aud didn't reply. She was

perched on the edge of the sofa, her neon yellow stockings bunched up round her ankles, her white hair full of magna-rollers, making it curly and brown again. She had the remote board on her lap and was stabbing at keys with her fingers, trying to set up a group chat with Stace and Nik on TVs four and six. The bank of screens on the walnut sideboard buzzed back at her.

"I can't remember which is the accept button," Aud said. "The symbols have rubbed off the keys."

Hum got up from the sofa and shuffled across to Aud. His hip was aching again, but he had to wait another eight months to get it reprogrammed. He picked up the remote board from Aud's lap and punched three keys. TVs four and six flashed a picture of the earth, and then both screens said "unavailable." Hum pressed the accept button to retry in five minutes.

"The robot snails and worms I can understand," Hum said. "I couldn't grow my tomatoes without them. But why wasps? They don't serve any purpose."

"I wonder where Stace and Nik are?" Aud said. "They were supposed to be around to chat about the wedding."

"I'm not going to pay three thousand quid to have the exterminators come round. I'm sure it's them that made the wasps. It's the only explanation I can think of. The Governments should do something about it. They could deactivate them all at once. All they'd need to do is tap the right codes into a big enough antenna and they'd all drop out of the sky."

Aud was pressing random buttons again. TVs five and three flashed up a vitamin advert. TV one showed an Icelandic porn movie with robo-horse racing results skimming along the bottom. "That's not what I wanted," Aud said. Hum raised his eyebrows, then turned to look at the nest again.

"My tomatoes are turning purple," he said. "I've not been able to get out there for over a week. If we have another flare, they'll be ruined."

"I told you to put the screen up back in February."

"I can't get up the ladder with my hip."

Aud succeeded in turning over the porn movie, but the grunting continued. She furrowed the skin above her eyes on which her eyebrows were painted. Hum took the remote board from her and held down a green key. The volume on all twelve TVs dropped, until the only sounds they could hear were the hum of cars moving along the tracks outside, the buzz of the wasps in the garden and the grunting noises.

"It's those two next door again," Hum said.

An acid spasm in his stomach knocked him so hard that he dropped to his knees.

"Don't get so worked up," Aud said. "You'll burst."

Hum couldn't reply. The pain went right through him, like an earthquake in his guts. He focused on the tips of his fingers reflected in the floor covering, and when the pain began to subside, he took the air syringe from his shirt pocket. Three squirts in the throat later, the pain began to drop away, but left him feeling weak. He lay on the floor and listened to the next door neighbours groaning and squealing.

"Turn the TVs up, Aud," he said. "I can't stand it."

The new neighbours had moved in six weeks ago and been no problem. They'd just got married, and seemed friendly enough. The kid was called Trey, and the girl Vanni. Trey had just got a job servicing the advertising zeppelins. "That one's scheduled for a fix up in a few weeks," Trey had said when they first met, pointing up at the sky. The zeppelin above Hum and Aud's street had been infiltrated by terrorists, and occasionally stopped broadcasting adverts to show anti-Governments propaganda.

Vanni worked from home. She was a representative for Magna-cosmetics, which excited Aud. They talked about getting together one day to discuss how Aud could make her eyebrows look more realistic, but they'd not met up in the six weeks since Vanni and Trey moved in.

Just a few days ago, the humping had started. "Damn," Hum had said when the groans first came through the wall. "Their licence must have come through."

Aud had been pleased for them. She remembered fondly when she and Hum received their procreation licence. It had been one of the happiest times of her life. They went at it like wild dogs for three years before they conceived and the licence expired.

Hum lay on the floor, his strength returning after the stomach acid attack, and listened to them groaning.

"Come on, Hum," Aud said. "They're young."

"This could go on for years," Hum said. "I might take up drum lessons."

Hum sat in his pyjamas watching the wasp nest from the bed-room window. The small LED on each of the wasps' heads showed that they were all clustered together. A faint glow came from within the nest. The wasps were solar powered. At night they had only enough energy for a few seconds' flight, although that would be all they'd need to launch an attack and deliver a deadly sting.

Aud climbed into bed next to him, wearing her electric blue boxer shorts and some polka-dot knee socks, and nothing else. Hum watched the movement of the dimples and ripples on her body as she shifted her bottom down the bed and placed her hands behind her head.

"What's up with you?" she asked.

"Nothing," he said. "Just looking at the wasp nest. I'm won-dering if I can put some kind of protective gear on and destroy it at night."

"Don't be stupid," Aud said, rolling over to face him, her breasts lying on the bed like half-filled balloons of water. "It's not worth the risk. We're just going to have to pay for an exterminator."

"We can't afford it. Not with Nik and Stace's wedding coming up."

Next door, Vanni let out a high pitched scream that descended in tone to a guttural groan. Trey punctuated this descent with short breathless gasps. Hum's hearing aid could just pick out the electric whirr of some kind of device. He turned the sensitivity up and could hear a chugging sound, like the old lawnmowers — some kind of sex aid. Vanni roared again, nearly blowing Hum's eardrums. He turned his hearing aid off, but was still too restless to sleep.

Hum didn't get to sleep until the middle of the night. Aud let him lie in the next morning. When he came downstairs, his face feeling swollen with sleep, it was mid-morning. He could hear crying and quickened his pace down the stairs.

In the living room, Stace appeared on TV three. Her eyes were red and she was sobbing. Aud stood on the balls of her feet in front of the TV, her hands raised, as if she could reach up and stroke Stace's hair.

"What happened?" Hum said.

"Nik broke up with her," Aud whispered.

"Nik broke up with me, Dadda," Stace wailed, then sobbed harder. Strands of her long blond hair were stuck to her face with tears.

"We've already put a deposit down on the . . ."

"Hummer!" Aud said.

"I mean, what happened, Stace? I'm sure you guys can work it out."

"We can't. It's too late. He's gone."

"I'm sure he'll come back."

"Yes, darla," Aud said. "Just give him a day to cool off and then call him."

"Why'd he leave?" Hum asked.

"He spent our honeymoon money on a new bike."

"He what?"

"When I had a go at him about it, he said he didn't want to get married anyway and took off." Stace broke down into sobs again.

Hum ground his teeth together. He imagined himself chasing Nik and pummelling him. He thought about the tens of thousands he'd already invested in the wedding, and wondered whether he'd be able to get some of the deposits back.

Aud made consoling noises with Stace, but Hum was distracted by another sound. A buzzing in the garden. He moved closer to the window at the back of the house. The wasps were in a frenzy, buzzing madly around the nest. They were congregating around an area of the trunk just down from the nest, but there were so many wasps flitting about in a flurry of gold that he couldn't see what was distressing them.

A squirrel dropped from the swarm onto the earth at the base of the tree. The stings on its body were visible through its fur.

Hum crept up behind Aud and rested his chin on her shoulder. Steam rising from the pan of boiling avocados bathed his face. He touched her stomach, and moved his hands up her body. He turned his face to inhale the sweet smell of menthol and biscuits behind her ear.

"Get off," Aud said, barely looking up.

Hum's blood boiled for a second. He felt foul words rising

in his mouth, but swallowed them back down. He turned away and moved to go out into the garden — a tinker with his tomatoes might make him feel better — but then he remembered the wasps.

"What the hell am I supposed to do?" Hum said.

"I'm not in the mood," Aud said, peeling sweet potatoes.

"I mean the wasps."

"Call the exterminator."

"I won't pay all that money. It's robbery. They've invented those wasps to con money out of people."

"There must be some reason for them," Aud said. "Why don't you give Stace a call. She's so upset about the wedding. I'm sure she'd love to hear from you."

"I can't cope with her crying right now."

"That's a terrible thing to say." Aud looked up at him for the first time. Hum puffed a breath out and stormed into the living room. He picked up the remote and was about to press the phone book button, but stopped himself. He didn't have the energy to speak to Stace. Instead, he moved to the window at the back end of the living room and looked out into the garden. The dead squirrel lay under the tree. The wasps flew in and out of their nest, gleaming gold against the overcast sky. Hum watched one fly high up into the air then disappear over the top of the roof.

Far above the house, the advertising zeppelin screen was bright blue. It was slowly descending. Hum watched it come down, growing larger all the time, until it vanished behind the roof. He moved to the other end of the living room in time to see it land in front of the house. He'd never seen one so close. They were longer than the house and about twice as tall. A group of people were gathered around the zeppelin carrying devices with antennae, which they pointed at it. Hum recognised one of the men as Trey, his next door neighbour.

Trey opened up a panel in the side of the zeppelin and connected it to a laptop computer. He sat on an equipment box, balancing the computer on his knees while he tapped away. The blue screen flickered and went dark, then was replaced by text in a foreign language. Hum watched the people working around the zeppelin until an insurance advert popped onto the screen and they packed up. They sent the zeppelin back to its position above the street and went home. Hum was disappointed. The anti-Governments propaganda that the zeppelin had been displaying was far more entertaining.

Aud called Stace later that day and dragged Hum into the living room. "She wants to talk to you," Aud said.

Hum looked at Stace's face, her eyes swollen from crying, and didn't know what to say.

"Mumma said you wanted to talk to me," she said.

"Yes," Hum said. "I wanted to see if you were okay."

"Oh I'm fine, yes, except for my whole life being over."

"It's not so bad," Hum said. "You'll move on. I know it doesn't seem like it now, but you'll have forgotten all about it in a few weeks. Nik was a bit of a . . ."

"Hummer!" Aud said, then leaned in to whisper, spitting in his ear. "You're supposed to be helping. Why don't you go and play with your tomatoes?"

"How can I? The wasps are still out there."

"Go out there anyway."

Hum rolled his eyes, blew a kiss to Stace and went into the kitchen. He stood by the back door and looked through the window at his garden. The tomatoes were a dark purple now, completely inedible. He should have put up the solar flare screen months ago. He should have called an exterminator as soon as the wasps arrived. But he hated spending money on these kinds of things. He and Aud had always struggled with money, and never had enough to do all the things they'd dreamed of. They used to talk about the exciting journeys they would make when they'd retired, how they'd spend the summer in an orbit liner watching storms roll over the earth below them, their worn joints soothed by the low-gravity rooms. They'd always assumed that money would come to them eventually. They'd win the lottery, or Hum would get a big promotion, but it hadn't happened, and now they were in the same financial situation they'd always been. Dreams of orbit liners seemed fanciful now.

Hum watched the tomatoes rotting on the vine, and the wasps whizzing about his garden. His pulse quickened. The garden was the only thing that kept him sane. Why should he pay three thousand pounds for the exterminators to remove the wasps? There must be something he could do himself.

"You're not going out there like that," Aud said, pointing at the night-filled garden through the glass door.

"It will only take a minute," Hum said. "They won't be able to get through all this." He had on three pairs of trousers tucked into four pairs of socks. Several of the four jumpers he wore were tucked into his trousers. The hood of one jumper was up, and he'd tied tea towels around his head and mouth and neck, so that the only exposed bits of skin were his eyes and hands. He put some safety goggles on, then oven gloves, asking Aud to tape down the open ends so that no wasps could fly in.

"I won't help you with this," Aud said. "It's crazy. You'll be stung to death. What are you going to kill them with anyway?"

"Cavity insulation foam," Hum said. "I'm gonna spray the tree full of this stuff and they'll all be stuck in there. No sunlight can get through this. Then I'll chop the tree down and put it through the shredder at the dump."

"It won't work, Hum. Please don't do it. We can just call in the exterminator and be done with it."

"We can't afford it. If you don't tape my gloves down, I'll just go out like this."

Aud looked at him. Her eyes were red. "Fine," she said. "You kill yourself, and I'll just look after myself then, shall I?"

"I'll be five minutes, and then I'll be back inside, and the wasps will be gone. Can you just check around me to make sure there are no gaps?"

Aud turned Hum around, lifting and tugging at the many layers of clothes until she was certain that he was wasp-tight. "You're okay," she said. "But I think you're crazy. If one of them gets through, you'll be dead before I can call the ambulance. I hope you've kept up to date with the insurance payments."

Hum tried to open the back door, but his hands were not dextrous enough through the oven gloves, so Aud had to do it for him. It felt wonderful to be out in his garden again, even wrapped up like that. The advertising zeppelin threw down a flickering rainbow of light across the garden. It was a cool summer evening, but Hum was hot inside his clothes. He picked up the foam gun and closed the door behind him. Aud stood on the inside of the door with her arms folded. She said something, but he made no effort to listen.

Hum shuffled to the bottom of the garden and stood in front of the dead apple tree, staring at the red LEDs of the wasps grouped together in the nest. It glowed like a heart, like the skin and muscle of the tree had rotted away, and all that was left was the skeleton and this robot-organ, full of deadly insects. Aud tapped on the window behind him and made some kind of gesture, which he couldn't decipher. He showed her the palm-side of his hand and moved closer to the tree.

Grunting noises came from nearby. Hum looked round at Trey and Vanni's house. Their bedroom window was open. Even through the tea towels wrapped round his head, Hum could hear them moaning. He bit his teeth together and moved down the garden.

When he was right in front of the nest, he could discern the individual lights of the wasps glowing through the papery nest material. He guessed there must be over a hundred in there. Hum took a few steps back and fired a test shot of the insulation foam into a patch of weeds that had grown since he'd been kept out of the garden. The liquid shot out of the end of the gun and expanded rapidly, like a mutant cake exploding over the edge of its tin. After a second, the foam expansion slowed, small bubbles popping on the surface. Within three seconds, the foam had cooled into a hard ball, its shiny surface reflecting light from the zeppelin.

The gun fired a thinner jet than Hum remembered, and it travelled less far. He'd have to stand quite close to the nest to get a decent shot. He took a few steps closer and pointed the gun at the tree. He hadn't noticed that the sex noises from next door had stopped until he heard Trey calling to him. He ignored him at first, but there was an angry tone in the kid's voice that he felt compelled to acknowledge.

Trey leaned through the window, bare chested, bare balled. His hands gripped the windowsill. Hum could only just read the expression on his face — the plastic goggles distorted his vision slightly. Trey looked mad.

"What are you doing?" he said. "Those things'll kill you."

Hum tried to reply, but the tea towel muffled his words. Instead he raised his hand as if to say that everything was okay, that he knew what he was doing.

"Hang on," Trey called. He looked around, as if checking to see if anyone was listening, then whisper-shouted into the night, "Just give me a minute."

Trey moved away from the window. Hum stood there staring

at the vacant space, rubbing the trigger of the foam gun. What did the kid want? He looked back at the house, but Aud had gone. The nest glowed in the darkness. Hum sweated in his clothes. It would only take a second to blast the nest. But what if the foam didn't set fast enough to stop the wasps? What if he didn't have on enough layers to protect himself from their stings?

Looking at the nest he felt a sense of equilibrium. He wasn't bothering the wasps, and they were unaware of his presence. He could stand there like this for hours. The second he fired the trigger, however, the balance would be upset, and he would be caught in a life or death struggle with them. Either he or the wasps would die, because one wouldn't stop until the other was dead.

There was a knock on the gate at the side of the garden. If Hum was going to do anything, it had to be now. He squeezed another test shot into the weeds. The foam bubbled and set. It seemed to take longer than the first time. He tried to imagine whether a robot wasp would be strong enough to fly through the half-set foam. Trey knocked again, then called out.

Hum felt itchy under his skin. He chewed at the inside of his cheek. He didn't need the kid's help. He could do it himself. He walked to the front gate and popped the latch.

"Nice outfit," Trey said. "Are you trying to get yourself killed?"

Hum mumbled something as Trey pushed past him and came into the garden. He held a laptop computer and a black box, which he placed on top of a low wall surrounding a flower bed.

The kid's fingers moved fast over the keys, bringing up symbols and lines of computer code that meant nothing to Hum. The old man rubbed the trigger of the foam gun through the oven glove. He was tempted to blast the boy. Seal him there in the garden. That would stop the all–day and night humping.

Trey stabbed the return key. "There you go," he said.

The red glow within the tree faded.

"That's it?" Hum said.

"All done."

Hum lifted the goggles from his eyes. His face was sore where the plastic had dug in.

"Is that what the exterminators do, exactly the same thing?"

"Pretty much, yes. But I won't charge you a few thousand for doing it. Just don't tell anyone about it, okay?"

"No, yes, sure, of course." Hum looked from the tree to the small computer, to Trey's face. "Is there any danger of them coming back to life?"

"None at all. They're fried. Vanni and I had a nest of them in the roof of our old place. It took a bit of tinkering before I worked out how to tap into their signal, but I got them in the end. I'm sure the exterminators invented the wasps themselves."

"I agree," Hum said. "Hey listen, thanks a lot."

"No problem. I'd better get back. Night."

Trey shut the gate behind him. Hum pulled the oven gloves from his hands, struggling because the tape was so firmly stuck. He untied the tea towels from his head and took off two of the jumpers, tossing them onto the lawn. He removed clothes until he felt cooler and comfortable. The air in the garden seemed sweeter, the light from the zeppelin brighter.

Walking towards the nest, he half-feared that the LEDs would ignite, and the wasps would swarm out. His heart quickened as he crouched in front of the nest, his face only a metre away. The papery surface was covered in a design of swirls. He reached his hands towards it, then pulled away twice before he could will himself to touch the nest. He almost expected it to be writhing.

The nest was cool and smooth. It came away from the branches with little effort. It was so light. Hum held it in his hands and felt a flicker of adrenalin. To have something so powerful and deadly in his hands was exhilarating. He watched it while he carried it back into the house, then placed it on the kitchen table. He turned it around under the orange glow of the ceiling light. The swirling pattern was even clearer under artificial illumination. It looked as if two different materials had been used to fashion the nest, one matt, one reflective.

Hum used a carving knife to slice off a section of the nest. The cut started cleanly, but when the blade hit the metal wasps, it pushed them against the papery cells inside, breaking the nest apart. The wasps tumbled out, rattling on the tabletop. They gleamed, perfect and gold. He lined them up on the table and counted them, his warm fingerprints lingering on them for a second before fading. There were fifty-seven. The grunting began again next door. Hum turned the sound down on his hearing aid until all he could hear was a faint buzz.

THE CENTIPEDE'S WIFE

Autumn dripped from the bare branches and clogged up the drains. Just three miles away, three miles of unwalked woods and abandoned farms, autumn dripped through the roof of a hut and splashed into a sink full of dead leaves. The drips ran down the walls, chasing spiders from their webs, and fell on the swollen floorboards. Accompanying the sound of the dripping was another noise. To Grady, it sounded like someone choking, but it was quite the opposite.

Grady watched the centipede eat. It tore meat and bone with its powerful mandibles, and it was this that made the sound — a whiskery noise punctuated by the cracking of bone. Grady looked at his mushroom but could not eat. The sound and smell of the centipede eating had turned his stomach more and more recently. He wasn't building up a tolerance to it, but a hypersensitivity. The centipede shifted around in the corner on its many jointed legs, the hooks on its feet scraping up little channels of mud. It pinned the rabbit to the floor with several of its legs and manipulated it this way and that, exposing pieces that, to its eyes, were more delicious than others. The centipede's segmented back rose and fell, as if breathing — although it breathed through air holes in its skin. This movement was to help food make the long journey from its mouth to its gut. The rabbit looked small in its barbed claws.

Grady wondered how many more meals like this he could stand, how long he could endure the stench, like rotting flowers. He put the mushroom aside and used both hands around his knee to pull his leg closer to him. Pressing his teeth tight together, he lifted the bandage around his lower leg a little. A string of something liquid stretched between bandage and skin, then snapped. Grady squirmed. Beneath the bandage was an unhealthy mess of tissue. His leg was healing slowly in the cold and damp, in the filth of the centipede's hut. The texture of his leg was not unlike the chewed rabbit meat hanging from the centipede's mandibles. It looked darker than it should do, with shiny lumps where the skin was swollen with infection. He remembered seeing an article on the news saying that maggots were a miracle cure for infected wounds such as this. They would eat only dead flesh, leaving the good stuff to heal. But Grady couldn't stomach the thought of maggots nibbling away at him, and so he kept the bandages tight, to stop the flies getting in, and when they landed near, drawn to his own decaying stench, he swatted at them. He wondered grimly whether his leg would ever heal.

The centipede paused for a moment, masticated rabbit flesh making a vibrating tone in its voice. "You-not-eating-that?" it said. Grady shook his head. "If-you-don't-eat, you-won't-heal." The centipede's voice sounded like two dry hands rubbing together, and the words ran into each other, so Grady had to concentrate to make any sense of it.

"I'll eat later," Grady said.

The centipede stared at him, as if about to say something, but then decided not to and returned to scoffing its rabbit. While it chewed pieces of the juicy flesh, it imagined that it was eating the man lying on the bed in the corner. Since the centipede had come across Grady four days ago, he had thought of nothing else. The centipede had been marching through the forest when he heard a scream and went to investigate. A man was caught in a bear trap. The metal jaws had made a mess of his right leg, biting in deep with rusted teeth and dead leaves. The man had forgotten his agony for a second when he saw the centipede, then redoubled his efforts to prize the trap open to escape. The centipede was joyous. This much meat would provide food for a week, but as he leaned in close to paralyse the man with a nip from his toxic pincers, he smelled something familiar. Something in the man's sweat and fear reminded him of his wife. They had been together for years before he lost her. Thinking about her still caused juices in his gut to bubble. Rather than eat the man, he decided to take him back to his hut. The familiar smell might bring back some of what he had lost.

Grady was sometimes able to sleep for minutes at a time. He would slip into dreams about falling down a long staircase, bouncing almost weightless, until he hit the bottom with a painless crack, and woke up in agony. His damaged leg would always pull him back from sleep, that and fear of the centipede. He knew he should be grateful to the centipede for rescuing him, but the creature was so abject that he couldn't stand to look at it. He had a constant sensation in his throat, like a ball was stuck in there, and an acidic prickle in his cheeks, as if he might vomit. He wondered what he would do if his leg never healed. He couldn't bear to stay there. Even if he had to drag himself on his elbows and fingers through the forest for days to reach another human, it would be better than breathing in the stink of the centipede, inhaling shedded scales of exoskeleton.

It wouldn't be difficult to escape. He was not a prisoner. The door was never locked. He would have to wait for the centipede to go out, and then listen closely to make sure he went in the opposite direction. His only difficulty would be his leg, but he felt sure that he could go through the pain by keeping the thought of returning home in his mind.

"Do you want something else to eat? Don't you like mushrooms?"

"I'm not hungry. I just feel sick."

"Do you mind if I eat your mushroom? Those ones dissolve if you don't eat them quick."

"Help yourself."

Grady was about to pick up the mushroom from the bed cover and throw it across the room to the centipede, when the creature scuttled across the floor and snatched it up in its pincers. The bristles and barbs that erupted from its mouth brushed against the back of Grady's hand, leaving a dark residue that burned slightly. He retched and tried to rub the goo off on the side of the bed.

"Sorry," the centipede said. "Winter's coming. Got to stuff myself."

Grady looked at the distance between the bed and the door. Even if he could only make it that far, he would be free.

Grady's opportunity came sooner than he had hoped. Late that night, the centipede announced that he was going to hunt. A nighttime escape wasn't ideal for Grady. It would be hard work to find his way through the forest, but the centipede only hunted at night, when the rabbits were out.

He listened to the centipede scuttling through the dry

leaves to the right of the hut, then leaned forward and tipped himself out of the bed. The pain in his leg as it touched the floor made him gasp, and he wondered how he would cope with such pain over a journey of several miles. He crawled towards the door, covering his palms in mud and shedded exoskeleton, then spotted a broom leaning up in the corner, which he could use as a crutch. That way he would move a lot faster. He rooted the broom firmly on the floor by pushing his weight into it, then climbed up, hand over hand. He could only exert a small force from his good leg. The pain from the damaged leg had telegraphed the good leg, and it had sympathy pain, acting as if it too were injured. His arms had to take most of his weight. He feared he would lose his grip and fall to the floor, so he gripped so tightly his fingernails dug into the heel of his palm. His face and body were damp with sweat when he managed to stand up. A splinter from the broom slipped under his skin, but the pain of this was nothing compared with his leg. It felt like something was gnawing at him, and his leg sung out to lie down again. Gravity had forced blood down into the wound. It filled up the mangled valleys of nerves and sent shockwaves of agony up his body. Fear of being caught escaping by the centipede gave him the fuel to push himself past the pain, and leaning on the broom, he shuffled out into the night.

A half moon threw down a faint mist of light, enough to tell the difference between a tree and the space that surrounded it, but only when he was close. Grady shivered, and his teeth chattered together. His skin erupted with goosebumps, but he sweated as if it were a baking summer day.

He had to get far enough away so that when the centipede came back to the hut, it would not be able to see him. He knew the centipede had some kind of special faculty for seeing in the dark, and this was what allowed it to catch rabbits so effectively. Grady looked behind him and could still make out the dim candlelight shining through the open door. He didn't know what he would say if the centipede caught him. He squeezed the broom handle and wondered if it could be used as a weapon.

The centipede gripped an enormous tree limb that hung out over the rabbit colony. He could smell their peppery faeces on the ground and hear their snuffling. There were tens of them munching on the grass below him. They were nervous little things, panting warm breaths and chlorophyll burps into the cold night air, pausing regularly to look about for predators. If they'd looked up, all they would have seen was the silhouette of the tree limb — the centipede was expert at camouflaging its long, segmented form. He watched the rabbits, tensing his legs, coiling up the energies in his body, preparing to pounce. He would only have one chance. If he missed his prey, they would not come out again for a long while.

There were two particularly juicy-looking rabbits gnawing at the grass beside a molehill. The centipede prepared himself and sprang from the tree limb. This was his favourite moment, flying through the air, when the rabbit hadn't noticed him. It was always frustrating if the rabbit saw him as he leapt, and he would plummet while watching the rabbit escape, and by the time he hit the ground, it would be gone. But not this time. The rabbit hadn't noticed him, and now he was falling towards it, silent, and with his toxic pincers pulled back. He loved the way his pincers almost fired by themselves when he landed on the ground. The last thing he had to get right was the leap from the tree limb. Once he was in the air and unnoticed, his body became automatic. Now that he was almost on the ground, he became excited; the rabbit was already his.

The centipede paused on his return journey to search out some more mushrooms for the man. He hadn't liked the last ones, so the centipede snuffled through the dead leaves for the small brown ones that smelled so rich. Maybe he would prefer those. The centipede wondered if subconsciously he was concerned about what the man ate because he wanted to fatten him up for eating. But he knew that he could never eat the man, not when he smelled like his wife.

With a few claws full of mushrooms and a warm rabbit, the centipede began the journey home to his hut. Well, not his hut. He hadn't built it. He had discovered it shortly after his wife died. There was no one living there, although it looked like it had been recently abandoned. The floor had been swept not long ago, and no damp had crept into the bedclothes. There were all kinds of devices for which he could discern no purpose, but after the incident with his wife, when he was in self-loathing, he found it comforting to be around these things, as if he were of a different species.

When he'd first brought the man back to the hut, he had marvelled when he saw him pick up the wax sticks and splinters of wood, which he'd taken for food, and produce heat and light with them. The centipede was a nocturnal creature, but he found a strange pleasure in living within an illuminated hut with the injured man.

Up ahead, the centipede could see a small window of candlelight through the trees, and it warmed a part of him that most centipedes are never even aware of. The candlelight snuffed out, but he was still capable of seeing the hut. He shuffled onwards, waiting for the man to re-light the candle, which he always did quickly, being so afraid of the dark. When the candle was not re-lit, the centipede began to worry. Was something wrong with the man? If he died, the centipede would blame himself entirely, so he sped up, running over fallen stumps and round mossy trunks to get home.

Grady thought he heard shuffling behind him in the forest, and quickened his pace, biting his teeth together hard against the agony. Each step whacked his body with a raw pain that he felt in every nerve. He wiped the sweat from his face with his sleeve, which was already soaked. The sweat made his shirt stick to his back. It ran into his eyes and stung them, making him blink repeatedly.

He heard the shuffling sound again, but this time it was from the side. He did not look round, but kept going. Every step brought him closer to safety.

Something bright and green flared next to him, like a camera flash, capturing an image of the trees around Grady, then leaving their burning residue on his retinas. Disoriented, he stumbled over a fallen branch, and the green flare came again, twice, so bright that it hurt. Something heavy slammed into him. It knocked him to the ground and pinned him there. Grady's leg roared.

The green light fired again, illuminating an enormous beetle, its abdomen glowing with bioluminescence. With four of its legs it made a cage around Grady, the other two pinned his chest and shoulder to the ground. Its head bore two serrated pincers, which it angled this way and that, looking for a way to Grady's neck. It stank of rotting meat, and its weight squashed all the air from his chest, so that he couldn't breathe. Grady flailed his arms at the beetle legs pinning him down, but he was too weak.

The beetle's abdomen flashed, this time capturing an image of the centipede charging, his legs everywhere, and his pincers wide. He slammed into the beetle and knocked it from Grady's chest. The beetle's luminous abdomen pulsed rapidly, like a strobe. In these flares, lit up like a macabre animation, the centipede and the beetle wrestled. The centipede was twice the size of the beetle and was able to root himself to the ground with his lower half, while using his upper half to push the beetle to the ground and tear at its wing casings with his jaws. But the beetle's mandibles were huge — bigger than the centipede's head, and it snapped at the centipede, trying to scissor his neck. The beetle used its flashing abdomen to distract the centipede, and it worked, because the centipede kept trying to turn his head away from the pulses of light. The beetle saw its opportunity and snapped at the centipede's head, but missed. When it went in for a second time, it caught a jawful of legs and sheared them off. The centipede roared, a high-pitched sound that Grady felt in his bones. The beetle barked back and twisted itself from under the centipede's weight.

Grady could feel shockwaves in the mud beneath him from the two creatures fighting. He thought that he should make his escape while both creatures were distracted, but his leg was howling. With the shock of the beetle attack, he hadn't noticed it stomping his leg, but now he was in agony, and could not even lift his weight from the ground.

The beetle got his weight above the centipede and pushed down on him, snapping his pincers. The centipede's short legs could not hold the beetle far enough away, and its pincers raked at his exoskeleton, tearing the armour. The beetle lunged in, going for a killing bite to the centipede's neck, but he had been waiting for this. As the beetle committed all its weight into the lunge, the centipede twisted from beneath it and used the beetle's momentum to flip it in the air and dump it on its back. While the beetle was dazed, the centipede attacked the soft underparts beneath its head with his mandibles. He knew this might be his only chance to defeat the beetle, so he ignored his exhaustion and his instinct to flee, and instead bit at the beetle's underside, carving valleys of toxic liquid into its chest and neck. The beetle's legs flailed madly for a second, and then it was still.

The centipede crawled off of the beetle and hung his head

for a moment, recovering. Grady's heart thumped. Would the centipede be angry with him?

"Thank you," Grady said. "You've saved my life a second time."

The centipede looked up at him and crawled over. He was still able to move despite losing several legs, but the smooth conveyor belt of movement now had a kink in it, and he jerked as the surrounding legs tried to compensate. "Why-did-you-try-to-leave?" The centipede asked. "Your-leg-is-not-healed-and-now-it's-much-worse."

"I'm sorry. I didn't want to be a burden on you. I didn't want you to have to find food for two."

"If you were a burden, I'd have eaten you a long time ago. Come on, I'll take you back to the hut." The centipede grabbed the back of the man's jacket in his mandibles and lifted him like a puppy. His feet dragged on the floor, causing spikes of pain every time they struck a branch or bump in the ground. It only took a couple of minutes to reach the hut. Despite Grady's frantic struggle to escape, he had covered little distance. The centipede laid him on the bed, and when his nerves were quiet, Grady re-lit the candles beside him. In the soft illumination, he could see a pile of brown fungus on the tea chest beside the bed. They smelled strongly of feet, but he was starving and devoured them. They tasted better than they smelled. He paused half way through to thank the centipede, who was secreting a liquid from his mouthparts and spreading it over the stumps where his legs were missing and the deep grooves cut into his armour. Grady still felt sick watching him, but this time he fought to ignore those feelings. He blinked away the sweat stinging his eyes. "Are you okay?" he asked.

"It will heal," the centipede replied. "My legs will grow back. I'll just have to be careful when I'm out hunting for a while. Injured like this, I'll be easy prey for some of the things that live out there."

The centipede watched the man eating the mushrooms he had collected, and it made him feel good. He wondered about the meaning of the man's escape, and the beetle that attacked him. He'd been given another chance to atone, and he had done it. Even though his instinct had been to leave the beetle to devour the man, and maybe pick over what was left, he'd dived in and fought, risking his own life. Surely his conscience would release him now? But it hadn't. When he thought about his wife, his long insides filled with self-loathing. And then it came to him. The only way he could escape from his crime was to share it with someone, to allow their judgement of him to decide whether or not he had made amends. He watched the man finishing the last of the mushrooms, and wondered whether he would be able to understand, and if he had the power to cure him of his guilt.

The centipede didn't know how to bring the subject up. He didn't want to just blurt it out, so he tried to lead the man into asking him.

"It's not a bad place, this, is it?" the centipede said.

The man looked at the centipede, and then around the room. "It's good," he said.

The centipede waited for him to continue, but Grady just shuffled lower in the bed and grimaced. "Are you married?" the centipede asked.

"I nearly was, once, but it didn't work out."

"What happened?"

Grady looked at the centipede, barely disguising his surprise. "I guess it was my fault really. I walked out on her a few days before our wedding."

"Oh," the centipede said.

"Her friends were a nightmare, always criticising me and talking about her ex-boyfriends, telling her she could do better than me. So in the end I'd just had enough. She seemed to think the same way as her friends eventually. She might even have been relieved when I left."

The centipede waited for a reciprocal question, but when none came, he began talking anyway. "I had a partner once."

"Really," Grady coughed. "What was she like?" He tried to conceal a smile.

"She was beautiful, and so loving. I only found this place after she was gone. We used to live together in a hollow beneath a dead oak miles from here. We'd lie together all day in the damp, dozing and listening for when the birds stopped singing. We even had kids together."

"So what happened?"

This was what the centipede had been waiting for, and now that it was here, he found the words hard to form in his whiskered mouth. "There was an outbreak of myxomatosis round here. It wiped out all the rabbits. We looked around for other things to eat, mice and things like that, but they were much harder to catch, and we couldn't get enough to keep us alive. My partner started getting sick, and our babies. In the end, something inside me just clicked. It was like instinct took over. I ate her, and then I ate the kids too. I wasn't in control of myself. They were so delicious while I was eating them, but afterwards, when I came to my senses, I felt sick. I couldn't stand the guilt, and I still feel sick about it now."

Grady looked at the centipede. He found it comical that the centipede seemed capable of almost human emotions. If his leg were better, he would have killed to take the centipede out of the forest with him. He could make a fortune selling him to a research lab or zoo.

"That's terrible," Grady said. "But isn't it natural for your kind to do that? I know mantises and spiders eat each other. Don't beat yourself up about it."

The centipede looked at Grady, who half-smiled back. The

centipede was incapable of registering emotion on his face, but inside he was raging. How could the man be so flippant? He'd just told him his most awful secret. Now that it was out, he didn't feel any better at all. There was no absolution. Instead, he felt vulnerable. The man knew his secret. The centipede turned away from him to sleep off the rabbit. But he could not sleep. Instead he listened to the man breathing, to the awful noise of his organs producing gas, and him squeezing them out, filling the room with his stink. Vile, he thought.

Grady wrapped his arms around himself for comfort. He was still hungry. He wanted to ask the centipede to go and get some more mushrooms for him, but the centipede ignored his coughing. The pain from his leg was up in his stomach now. He fell asleep wondering how and when he could next try to escape.

When the centipede awoke the next morning, he smelled something familiar in the hut. He uncoiled himself from the corner and flexed his legs, sniffing about the floor. He followed the smell along the floorboards, until it led him to the bed.

The man looked asleep, but a colour like putty had crept under his skin, forced his mouth open and pushed his life out of his mouth, and it was this smell that the centipede had detected: the smell of death. To the centipede it was a sweet smell, like rotting apples and damp earth, but he was not pleased to smell it. It meant he had failed. The weight of his crime was still bearing down on him. He'd not been able to save the man, or even to absolve himself by telling the man about his wife and children. The centipede poked at the dead man with his mandibles and wondered at what an opportunity he'd had, and managed to lose. He couldn't imagine the same thing ever happening again. How was he ever going to achieve peace of mind?

The sweet smell that had escaped from Grady made the

centipede hungry. Here was what he'd wanted since he first saw the man — a feast, and he knew that the man would be delicious, his insides stuffed with truffles. The centipede's mouthparts were secreting digestive fluids just thinking about it. But when he tried to take a bite from the man's cheek, he gagged. He urged himself on. He was starving, and he'd never eaten a meal as exquisite as this, but his conscience stopped him. It made him think about the taste of his children, and the tough parts of his wife's exoskeleton that he couldn't eat and had to bury. The man smelled like his family. He couldn't do it. He couldn't even be near the man, the temptation and revulsion were unbearable.

The centipede left the hut, not caring that it was daytime and that there might be predators around. He had to get far away. Maybe if he began again, found a new life, and a new wife to have children with. Maybe if he didn't eat them this time, he would begin to feel normal once again.

IPODS FOR CATS

The windowsill was too small for George's bum, but still he perched on it, the window open onto the night. The sound of bats clicking by outside never reached George's ears, or that of foxes raiding a bin three doors down or of two drunk teenagers laughing so hard they couldn't speak. Instead, his head was filled with Björk's animated voice, the sounds drawing shapes in his mind. White earphones connected his head to the device in his palm, and he rolled his thumb around degrees of the click wheel to allow Björk's voice to grow louder, penetrate him deeper. He closed his eyes so that even the streetlights and lit windows of his neighbours could not intrude on this moment with his new iPod.

Something soft brushed against his elbow and startled him. He immediately thought of spiders. This jolt back to reality almost sent him tumbling off the sill, and he grabbed the windowframe for support.

On the outside sill of the window was a small black cat. Its coat was glossy with licks, worn almost bare in places. It examined him with pea-green eyes and scrunched its face up, maybe sniffing, or blowing an unpleasant odour from its nostrils.

Björk's voice in his ear was too loud, now that his moment had been broken, and he rolled his thumb back the other way to turn the sound down. With the iPod nestled securely between his stomach and bent leg, he smoothed the cat's head with his palm, then tickled the underside of its chin with his fingers.

"What's your name?" he asked, and felt around the cat's neck for a collar, but it wasn't wearing one. The cat ducked its head beneath George's fingers and nuzzled them with the crown of its head, twisting to the side, showing George how it wanted to be touched, how its ears needed attention. George complied for a few moments, then feeling the air turn chill outside, slid off the sill and rubbed the cramp out of his backside.

He was taking the earphones from his ears, and about to pull the window shut, when the cat leapt through with a desperate noise. It hit the carpet, and after doing a quick survey of the room with its nose, jumped up onto George's bed and looked at him.

"What?" George said. "You're not staying here."

The cat was bony looking, like an old, hard teddy. Its nose was rough and wet, prodding against the back of George's hand. George picked the cat up, holding it at a distance, and opened the window to put it outside, but the cat did something ungraceful with straightened legs and whips of its tail and wrestled out of George's grip, bounced off the sill and leapt back onto the bed.

"Fine," he said. "You can stay here for a moment."

He lay down on his side on the bed, the cat patrolling the triangular space between his chest and bent knees, and clicked through other songs until he came to Pink Floyd's "Wish You Were Here." When the small screen on the iPod illuminated, the cat pressed its nose onto the device, leaving a wet trail. It made a small plaintive purr, then jabbed at the iPod with demanding movements of its head. One of these jabs managed to slide the volume up, and George pushed the cat away, swearing at it. The cat followed the white wires up to the earphones and began prodding George's ears with its wet teddy nose. George picked up the skinny cat, took it over to the window and put it outside.

The cat meowed and paced back and forth with quick balletic skips of its feet. As George closed the curtains, it narrowed the band of its pacing until it was peering through the last open slice, somehow doing something forlorn with its face.

George got back onto the bed. He'd had the window open for long enough to allow the sharp night air to tug goosepimples out of his arms. He put on a hooded top for warmth, pulling the hood over his head, and over the earphones, and he curled on his side and resumed his Pink Floyd reverie.

The bed was freshly made — a state rare enough for George to take unusual pleasure in lying upon it. Jess had been over earlier that day, so he'd spent four hours beforehand finding homes for the orphaned clothes, magazines and crockery that loitered on every surface. He'd taken the vacuum cleaner for a walk around the house and washed all the stale towels.

Jess had stayed for a late lunch. She'd already eaten, but George had gone to such trouble, making pancake tagliatelle, that she couldn't leave without trying it. He'd even managed to get her to stay for a piece of pecan pie, even though she said she was fit to burst. Eventually though, despite George's questions about any crazy patients she had at the moment, Jess had to go, and George had been left standing at the closed door, his nose close to the decorative glass, watching her fractured image walk down the path and away.

Jess was an occupational therapist. She went into people's homes when they returned from hospital, usually recovering from strokes, and helped them to adjust to life with impaired functions. George had met her one baking afternoon when she'd quietly explained to him and a group of other onlookers that the man scooping up the dead fox from the gutter was really a very sweet man. They'd all stopped to watch him shovelling the orange creature into a black bin liner, and wondered what use he would have for such a thing. Jess whispered that he took them home and buried them. He had a roadkill graveyard in his back garden, with lolly stick crosses marking the graves of frogs, birds and even a badger.

"Does he name them?" George had asked, leaning close to the petite woman. He admired her short sharp hair, which whipped around her head and curved down the side of her elfin face.

"No," she replied. "He doesn't think of them as pets. Hill just doesn't want them to rot alone in the gutter."

George had been eager not to let her walk away, and even when the other onlookers, and even the roadkill man himself, had gone, he clung to her with polite questions, and she seemed happy to stay and talk. He'd not had the courage to ask for her number on that occasion, but she was often around the area visiting patients, and the third time he ran into her, it seemed like the right time to ask if she wanted coffee.

Conversation with Jess was easy. She talked with great enthusiasm about her work and interests. She could lay out her thoughts in an impressive coherent way while holding his eye contact. George wanted to know all about her, and she was happy to share.

They had lots in common. They were both big fans of *The Hitchhiker's Guide to the Galaxy*, and they both loathed beetroot. Bizarrely, they both had uncles named Robert that had died in motorcycle accidents.

These details formed the bonds of a quick-set friendship — a friendship set so fast that they moved straight past the window of opportunity for kissing and went directly to a platonic comfort zone, where Jess was happy to fart in front of him, and even pick her nose. But these things did not make her any less attractive. They were just a little spice in the pudding of his infatuation.

The next night, George put a pillow on the windowsill. It was not wide enough for him to get comfortable, but he was enjoying watching raindrops rolling down the pane, making fireworks of the lights in his neighbours' windows.

He rolled through his list of music, which had increased, as he'd spent a couple of hours late that afternoon downloading the songs he'd most longed for. There were songs that he'd heard on car journeys with his parents, songs he'd listened to on a giant eighties Walkman, trudging through leaves on the way home from school. There were songs used on adverts, which he'd never been able to find in record shops, songs he'd listened to, drunk and morose, at seventeen, feeling sorry for himself because he was too ugly and self-conscious to date someone like Stacy Kellegan. All these songs, touchstones to transport him to moments from his past, he'd harvested from the Internet in just a couple of hours, and now they were preserved in a playlist. A musical history of George in forty-seven minutes.

The light from the iPod made a crisp blue shape in the window. He gazed into it, letting his eyes drift out of focus, thinking about—

The cat leapt at the window, wet and wide-eyed, and George leapt off the sill, heart thumping, his hands shaking and unable to catch the iPod as it fell and tugged the headphones from his ears.

While he retrieved his iPod from the floor, he struggled to control his breath. Inside him, the blood pumped hard against the underside of his skin. "Bloody cat," he said. "Piss off."

The cat opened its mouth, showing teeth and a pink tongue,

but the rain drowned the sound of its meow. George made shooing gestures with his hands.

"Go home," George said. "You're not coming in here soaking wet."

He thought to himself that he would let the cat in if it stayed there another fifteen seconds. But the cat jumped down onto the flat roof of his kitchen below and scampered away.

George put on brushed cotton pyjamas and climbed under his duvet. It was late, and he had work in the morning, but he was still feeling unsettled. He put on his earphones and listened to the music he had downloaded earlier. With his head, he made a tent beneath the duvet, illuminated by the screen of his iPod. The music made him feel solid, like he'd made a connection with something inside himself that had remained constant throughout his life, unchanging despite age, fashions and shifts of geographical location. The tent grew warm with his breath and his memories.

His arm escaped from beneath the duvet and rooted, trunk-like, through his bag for his mobile phone. When he located it, he pulled it into the tent and dialled Jess's number.

"Hi, George," she said as she picked up the phone.

"How, oh have you got—"

"I've got your number on my list."

"I was just wondering if you want to come round again tomorrow night?"

"Tomorrow? I, er, hang on a minute, I'm—"

"There's that new show on that—"

"Oh yeah, the—"

"And I'll make you some cannelloni."

"Okay, sure, yeah. That would be great," she said. "Are you okay? You sound like you're . . . I don't know, you sound—"

"Oh I'm just freaked out because this cat just scared the shit out of me and I was feeling paranoid."

"O-kay," Jess said in two big syllables. "Was it a very big cat?"

"It was a monster. No, it was just a regular cat. I guess I've just been feeling a bit delicate for the last week."

"How come?"

"I don't know. It'll sound weird, but I got this new iPod last weekend, and I love it, and I've got all this great music on it that I've always wanted, but since I've had it, there's been this uneasy feeling in the house. I just feel . . . unbalanced."

"Then get rid of it."

"I couldn't do that. Maybe it's something else. I don't know. It's not the iPod. It's just a coincidence. Maybe something astrological. I'll feel better when you're here tomorrow. I just feel like I don't want to be alone at the moment."

They made polite goodbyes, and when Jess's line was disconnected, he pushed the phone and the iPod out from his tent and curled up, trapping the echoes of their conversation under the duvet, holding them tight until morning.

The cat was at the kitchen windowsill again, watching George stuff steaming bolognese sauce into cannelloni shells. George wanted to let it in — he could do with the companionship, but once he'd let the cat in, he might never be able to get rid of it. It might bring all kinds of crap into his life — dead birds, fleas, muddy footprints.

The cat was making a broken purring sound, pulling its whiskered upper lip back from its teeth. "I'm sorry," George said. "I can't let you in right now."

The cat persevered, despite George ignoring it and then flicking a tea towel in its direction. George grew tired of feeling guilty, so he went to straighten things up in the dining room.

Jess arrived on time with red wine and chocolate mints.

"I like your hairclip," George said. "Is it new?"

Jess's fingers went to it. "I bought it a couple of weeks ago," she said. "I've just not had an opportunity to wear it yet."

George poured them both a big glass of wine and put some Japanese seaweed crackers in a bowl for them to nibble on. They hovered in the kitchen while George grated yellow and orange cheese over the tray of cannelloni.

"Where did you learn to cook?" Jess asked.

"I didn't know I *could* cook," George said. "My grandad was the cook of the family. He used to make these massive roast dinners for everyone on a Sunday, with a joint of beef and Yorkshires and roast potatoes and parsnips and cauliflower cheese. And he made this amazing gravy with little pasta bits in it because he used dried minestrone soup as a base. I used to hate those dinners. He'd scowl at me across the table until I'd finished, but thinking back to it now, they were the best meals I ever had. I think if I could go back in time, I'd go back to one of those Sunday roasts at Grandma and Grandad's house, and this time I'd enjoy it."

"That's so sweet."

"I like cooking — I'm just no good at getting the quantities right. Whenever I cook for myself, I always make way too much."

Jess smiled at him over the top of her wine glass. "I wish I could cook," she said. "The only thing I can do well is cheese on toast."

"O-kay," George said.

"I know anyone can make cheese on toast, but no one can make it taste the way I do. I bet that even if you bought the same ingredients and cooked it on my grill, it would taste different to my cheese on toast. I've got some kind of cheese on toast magic powers in my fingers. Next time you come round, we'll do a taste challenge."

"It's a deal," George said.

Two glasses of wine later, they both squatted on the kitchen floor in front of the oven to watch the cheese on top of the cannelloni rising in volcanic bubbles. "This is almost as good as an open fire," George said.

Squatting like this, the oven throwing warmth and orange light over their faces, they started to giggle, and then Jess fell back, and through a miracle of balance managed not to spill a drop of her wine.

After dinner, they moved into the living room, carrying their glasses and the almost-empty second bottle of wine. "It's a bit dark in here," Jess said.

"Sorry, I'll turn it up a bit," George said.

"Don't worry, it's fine."

George watched her black shirt ride up her back, revealing a band of flawless white flesh and the smooth ripple of her spine, as she sat down. He plugged his iPod into the speakers on the windowsill. "What do you fancy listening to?" he asked.

"What have you got?"

"I've got a bit of almost everything on here."

"So you've made friends with your iPod now?"

"Oh right, yeah. I was in a weird mood the other night. Do you ever get those nights when you feel like you're the only candle burning on the whole planet?"

Jess smiled. "I think I do, yes."

"Is Suzanne Vega okay?"

"Suzanne Vega's great."

"I saw her at Glastonbury a few years ago," George said. "She was so laid back. She even forgot some of the words to one of her songs, and she just brushed it off like, whatever. I was—"

The cat banged against the window, making George jump.

"What was that?" Jess moved to a perch on the edge of the sofa and put her glass down on the floor.

"It's that bloody cat again. It keeps jumping up at the windows. I think it's trying to give me a heart attack."

"It's probably soaking out there, poor thing."

Jess came over to the window, and together they looked at the cat on the windowsill. It made a sorrowful shape with its green eyes. Its fur was soaked and tight against its scrawny body.

"Aww, George let it in. It must be freezing."

"Once I've let it in, I'll never get rid of it."

Jess pulled a face, and George sighed, opening the window enough for the cat to leap in.

It hit the floor and shook itself, spraying water over their feet, then made a tiny purr of pleasure, circling George's legs and coiling its rat tail around him.

"See how happy you made it," Jess said. She squatted down and smoothed its fur along the length of its back. It lifted its head up and closed its eyes with an expression of delight. "Hey, I think this is Hill's cat, Rabbit."

"Hill the mad guy?"

"He's not mad. He just has his own way of doing things."

"Rabbit's a pretty mad name for a cat. Well, I guess he keeps the streets clean of roadkill."

"Rabbit never leaves Hill's garden though. Hill found her abandoned by the river when Rabbit was just a kitten — she's a bit sensitive."

"Well, she's treading mud all over my carpet. Should we take her back to Hill's?"

"Would you mind? It's not like Rabbit. Something might be wrong."

They put their coats on. The rain, which had been a fine drizzle when Jess arrived, was now thundering against the rooftops, bouncing spray off cars, and hanging in curtains from the streetlights. Jess borrowed George's wellingtons to wade through the river of water running along the path. The boots were way too big for her and made her unsteady on her feet, so she held onto George's arm for support. They had their hoods up, and George nestled the damp cat inside his coat.

They knocked at Hill's door three times, but he did not answer. While they waited, Rabbit struggled inside George's coat, poking her claws into his stomach. Despite wanting to let the cat go, and maybe cuff her over the back of the head for hurting him, George held onto her. He wouldn't want to have to explain to Hill, whose faculty for understanding was thread-bare, that he'd found his cat but didn't have her anymore.

"Let's have a look round the back," Jess suggested.

They moved round the side of the house, stepping over stacked flowerpots and sodden plastic bags filled with stolen cuttings from the local parks. Round the back, they saw a light inside, through the kitchen window. The light was dim, maybe thrown from a table lamp, but it was enough to indicate that Hill was in. Jess said he was paranoid about leaving anything electrical plugged in while he was out. They tapped on the window, while Rabbit grew more violent inside George's coat. He was sure that she must be drawing blood from his stomach.

Hill did not answer.

They threw pebbles at the upstairs window, while rain spattered on their upturned faces. "Something's definitely wrong," Jess said. "Shall we break in?"

"We can't do that," George said.

"He might be hurt."

"Does being an occupational therapist give you any special licence for breaking into patient's houses?"

"No," Jess said. "But he might be lying in there right now. He might even be able to hear us but can't respond. What if he's fallen down the stairs or something? We have to see if he's okay. Do you want me to break the glass?"

"No, don't worry. You take this cat and I'll do it."

They transferred the cat between their coats. She thrashed about when exposed to the rain, but calmed when curled inside Jess's coat. George picked up a hefty flint from the rockery, noticing as he did all the lollystick graves arranged on the lawn. He tapped the glass with the rock. He'd never broken a window before and wasn't sure how much force it took.

"You need to do it a bit harder than that," Jess said.

George tapped the glass three more times, increasing the force until it cracked.

"We need to get through it. Give it a good whack," Jess said.

George wrapped the wet sleeve of his coat over his knuckles and took the glass out of the panel with four solid smashes of the flint. He pulled his fingers close together and moved his hand through the empty pane, reaching inside to pull across the deadbolt. It was a thrilling sensation, twisting the handle and opening the door into someone else's house. He could see himself volunteering to do it again if the situation arose.

Inside the house, Jess called out for Hill, but there was still no answer. They wiped their feet on the mat and turned the light on, closing the door behind them. Jess called out again as she walked through into the living room. George heard Hill's name die in her throat and the cat's feet hit the floor as she dropped her.

George followed her into the living room, tripping over Rabbit as she scooted under his feet. Hill, a man in his fifties fed on pork pies and crumpets, sat in the floral armchair his wife had picked over thirty years before she died. His trousers and pants were round his ankles, his hands in his lap, the right curled loosely around his large floppy penis. His shirt was open. He wore a black plastic bag over his head, with a belt tied around his neck. Over the top of the bag was a pair of hefty earphones. George could hear the tinny rattle of music playing from them. He followed the wire down to the side of the couch, where an iPod dangled, connected to the mains by a white lead.

"Sweet old man," George said.

"Jesus, George, don't," Jess said.

George wanted to know what the man was listening to, but didn't want to get close enough to see. "His iPod is still playing," George said. "He must have it on shuffle."

"What was he doing?" Jess asked. Her hands were on her forehead, her fingers pulling apart her crafted fringe.

They both looked around the room, as if there were more clues to this bizarre tableau to be found. The room stank of animals and rubbish, a smell that made George sweat in his coat. Jess moved to turn on the main light, as the table lamp beside Hill only illuminated the objects close to him, but then changed her mind, letting her hand fall to her side.

"Is it still 999 from a mobile?" George asked, pulling his phone from his jeans pocket.

Jess nodded, and her mouth curled under in an expression of genuine sorrow, as if George's question had marked the last full stop in Hill's story.

George stepped back from Hill's body while he gave the address to the police. He imagined for a horrible moment that Hill's eyes were open beneath the plastic bag.

From the room adjoining the kitchen, they heard frantic meowing and scratching. Relieved to be out of the living room, they following the sound back through the kitchen to the front hallway, where they found Rabbit on her hind legs, pawing at the door to the cupboard beneath the stairs.

Jess knelt down and stroked Rabbit, and the cat acknowledged her attention only briefly before returning to her assault on the door. "What is it?" Jess asked. She pulled across the latch and opened the triangular door. Rabbit gave an appreciative meep and skipped round Jess to get into the cupboard. Jess opened the door further, and George turned on the hallway light so they could see better.

Rabbit was deep inside the cupboard, so deep that Jess and George could only just make out the shape of the kittens' heads, the sound of their lapping lost amongst the rain. "Oh my God," Jess said. "How cute is that?"

"Jesus," George said, "this cat's been at my window for days. Do you think those kittens have been locked in there for that long?"

"Oh don't," Jess said. "I don't want to know."

"Should we, like, check they're all okay?"

"I can see them moving," Jess said.

The signs of life were minute, but present, a tiny difference in the density of darkness separating the kittens from their surroundings. Jess and George perched in the open doorway, straining their ears and eyes for these motes of new life. The inertia holding George's hand on the edge of the door broke, and his fingers slipped down until they collided with Jess's. Their fingers tumbled down the door together for a second until they gripped the paintwork, a weave of digits, and they stayed like this for long enough to change the atmosphere in the house.

THE THORN

Wellie Page was the kind of kid that would always be getting into scrapes of one kind or another. If he wasn't falling out of trees or carving his name in something he'd be wrestling with the other children from his neighbourhood. "Stop flicking dog shit at my boy!" was a commonly heard complaint.

His dad had mysteriously vanished when he was four and his mum was always working, so most of the time Wellie was looked after by his grandparents. Most people attributed his unruly behaviour to them.

Wellie's maternal grandparents poured boundless love into him. His absent father had left a big hole in Wellie's life and they wanted to make sure he never felt it. Their hearts were huge. Literally. It had caused them circulatory problems throughout their lives. Most people would agree that the probability of two unrelated people having the same organ deformity was pretty phenomenal. For this reason most people thought that Wellie's gran and grandad were probably related.

So it wasn't really Wellie's fault that he was always getting into scrapes. Inbreeding would explain all his rambunctiousness.

Wellie was round at his grandparents' one overcast Sunday

afternoon. His gran had just come out of hospital in London where she'd had a polyp removed from the inside of her nose. Wellie was convinced that she had a plant growing out of her nose. He ran around telling everyone how his gran had to have this thing cut out before it grew too big and split her head right open. He was terrified that a seed would blow up his nose and grow there and so had taken to stuffing rolled lumps of tissue paper up his nostrils.

Wellie was helping Grandad dig dandelions out of the crazy paving. Gran brought them out a cup of her sweet tea, and it was while he was dunking fat cookies that he noticed a pain in his big toe.

"You got a thorn," Grandad stated.

"Told you ya should have worn shoes, Wellie. Would you like me to get it out for you?" Grandma asked.

"It's ok I can do it."

The thorn looked as if it was wedged in deep. He pincered it between his long, muddy fingernails and pulled. Wellie expected it to come out easily because the bit sticking out was pretty big and he had a good grip, but to his frustration it sprang out of his nails, remaining firmly lodged in his toe.

"Do you want some tweezers?" Grandma asked.

He nodded.

While Grandma was off getting tweezers Wellie continued to pull at the thorn with no success. When she got back with them he felt good having the extra weaponry with which to battle the splinter. He clamped the metal tips around the end of the thorn and gently pulled. His skin lifted up in a small volcano shape. The thorn slipped out a little, but was then snapped out of the tweezers it was wedged in so deeply.

Wellie squealed. His toe was red and sore from fussing. He'd managed to lift the thorn out a few millimetres. He realised that it must be bigger than he first thought. He was starting to feel a bit sick. He'd eaten about twelve cookies and for some reason he imagined that the only way he wasn't going to vomit was if he could get this thorn out of his toe. That's the kind of crazy thing that Wellie was always thinking.

Once one of the neighbours found him by the side of the road holding his breath. He asked him what he was doing and after Wellie finally exhaled he said that if he breathed when a car was going past he'd be poisoned. The neighbour had looked at him with pity and thought that it was such a shame what inbreeding could do to a boy.

"Do you want me to try?" Grandma asked.

Wellie didn't really want to let her. From his experience it was far more painful if someone else pulled a splinter out, but Grandma looked as if she really wanted to help and so he agreed to let her have a go.

Grandma wielded the tweezers with expert fingers. She was well practised with these babies. Her eyebrows had given up hope of ever growing back. Her sight wasn't too good so she leaned in close, inches away from his foot and with her free hand used her thick glasses like a magnifying glass, sliding them back and forth for optimum magnification.

"She's a biggun," she announced.

"Would you look at that," Grandad said.

"What?" Grandma asked.

"This robin."

A robin was on the crazy paving, right beside Grandad's hand. He could have grabbed it if he wanted to. The robin was cocking its head left and right, watching Wellie's toe, as if it expected Grandma to pull a worm out.

"I'm trying to concentrate," Grandma said.

Grandad smiled at the robin and continued weeding gently, so as not to scare the bird away. Grandma refocused her attention on the thorn, slurping air through her false teeth as she breathed. She pushed the two ends of the tweezers into the skin on either side of the thorn until Wellie yelped, then pinched them in, getting a good grip on it. She paused and flexed her free fingers. Her tongue licked her lips, as if this were an Olympic sport.

When she was ready she pulled, increasing the pressure at a steady rate. The thorn lifted the volcano of skin around it again and once more the skin let the thorn slip a little, but then the tweezers' grasp gave out.

"Jeezus!" Wellie yelled.

They both stared at his swollen red toe. It had easily a centimetre of thorn sticking out.

"She's a beast," said Grandma.

"It really hurts," said Wellie.

"Here let me have a look at her," said Grandad in a "man to do a man's job" kind of voice. He knelt down and picked up Wellie's foot, small and white in his red callused hands. He twisted the foot this way and that, examining it with a professional's eye.

"That's no thorn" was his conclusion.

"Are you sure?" said Grandma leaning in closer.

They were both slurping their air now. Wellie could feel their warm breath on his foot. His whole body felt hot and infected. His foot felt like it wasn't his own.

"I'm not sure what it is," said Grandad.

"Can we get it out? It hurts like mad," Wellie pleaded.

"Of course," said Grandad, coming out of his trance. He seemed to suddenly realise that the thorn was stuck in a human and not a piece of furniture. "I'll get some pliers."

"What?" Wellie said. "I don't want him to hurt me." What if he couldn't ever get the thorn out? What if it had roots, just like the dandelions, burrowed into his foot, enmeshed with his veins? Just like Grandma's polyp. Maybe he'd have to go to hospital too.

Grandad came back from the shed with a pair of heavy pliers, the kind that an evil dentist might use in a cartoon. He squatted down, steadied himself with one hand on Wellie's shin and shakily lowered the pliers onto the thorn.

"Hold still now."

Grandad clamped the thing, then quickly yanked at it. Wellie screamed.

"What are you doing!" Grandma scolded him. "Did you think you could trick it by pulling it out fast! You have to go slow or you might break the end off and then we'll never get the whole thing out!"

Grandad looked angry that his skills had been challenged.

"Right. This time you hold him, I'll pull and you stop him from squirming," said Grandad.

Wellie got the impression they were talking about some rodent stuck in a trap. Grandma sat behind him, her legs splayed either side of him. She held him around the waist. Grandad knelt in front of him and held his leg a little too tightly. He re-clamped the thorn, catching a piece of skin with it. Wellie yelled stop, but Grandad seemed to think that he was onto something and so pulled anyway. Wellie howled. Tears were leaking out of his eyes. Grandma squeezed him tighter. He wasn't sure whether it was to comfort or restrain him.

"It's coming! The little bugger's coming!" Grandad grinned maniacally.

Grandma pulled harder in the other direction. Wellie bit into his lip to relocate the pain, but it was no good. The torture had to end soon or he'd go mad. It didn't feel like Grandad had a thorn clamped in his pliers, it felt like he had the whole toe and he was trying to wrench it off his foot.

"It's coming!" Grandad reiterated.

Wellie felt something shift in his foot. Not by the toe, but towards the ankle.

"You're pulling my tendons out!" he bawled.

All three pairs of their eyes opened wide in astonishment as the thorn began to come out, but as it did, three more dark thorn shapes pierced through the toe, from the inside. Wellie tasted copper as he chomped a lump out of the inside of his mouth.

"What on earth is it?" Grandma exclaimed.

Grandad looked like a fisherman reeling in a vast pike after not catching even a minnow for years. The four thorns were coming out simultaneously, as if they were joined. They were over two centimetres long now. Wellie felt like he was going to vomit. The pain was bolting up his body, from his toe to the top of his head. He wanted Grandad to let go, for it to be over, but he wanted the thorns out too. He stared at the robin, which was still staring at his foot. He tried to focus on just the robin, his orange-red breast, his shiny black eyes, but the pain was too much.

"I need a break," Wellie said.

Suddenly his toe resisted, and the thorns wouldn't come out any further. His bum slid along the floor as Grandma's grip loosened and Grandad pulled him towards him.

"Hold him tight!" Grandad spat.

Grandma squeezed him hard. Grandad let go of Wellie's shin and used both hands to grip the pliers. The thorn was stuck again. Grandad wedged one of his feet into Wellie's stomach and straightened his leg for leverage.

"Ow! Watch my hands!" Grandma snapped.

Wellie howled and tried to push Grandad's foot away, but he couldn't budge it.

Grandad's teeth were gritted, and it was onto these yellow tombstones that blood spurted as the thorn gave way once more.

Grandad gave a grunt of satisfaction, then surprise, as he realised that it wasn't all out.

"Don't let it get away!" Grandma squealed with excitement.

Grandad eased his foot up on Wellie's stomach; he could sense that the tough bit was over now and pulled out the final section with crowd-pleasing slowness. Wellie opened his tear-misted eyes. His foot was spurting blood. The toe was open at the end like a poisonous flower. Protruding from it were the four spikes, joined at the base about two inches down.

"What is it?" Grandma sounded twenty years younger with excitement.

"I don't know, but it's big!" said Grandad, still pulling. The base from which the four spikes protruded curved slightly then narrowed suddenly. Inches and inches of it were coming out.

The pain filled Wellie's leg up to the hip, like someone was sawing at his insides with a cheese grater.

"It's a fork!" said Grandma.

"You're right, it bloody is!" said Grandad.

"Get it out!" Wellie screamed.

Finally, the end of the thing slipped out of Wellie's toe, bloody and warm. They all sat there staring at it, Grandma with excitement, Grandad with pride, and Wellie with horror. After a minute or two Grandma remembered herself and went into the kitchen to get nursing items. Grandad followed behind her, still in a trance, to the sink. He washed the fork carefully while Grandma bandaged up Wellie's gored toe, first with butterfly plasters, then regular ones, then bandages. It hurt like hell.

"A fork. Incredible," said Grandad as he came out of the kitchen.

The fork was quite a large fork and rather ornate. Grandad sat down next to Grandma and Wellie turning it over, examining it closer. "It's got a hallmark," he said.

"How could it have gotten in there?" Grandma asked.

"Might be worth a few bob," said Grandad.

"Can I have a look?" Wellie asked.

"Yeah in a minute," said Grandad not looking away from the fork.

"You know I think I've heard of this before," said Grandma.

"You have not. When?" Grandad scoffed.

"When I was a nurse. Foreign bodies in the body they're called. I heard of one chap who stepped on a nail and the end broke off in his foot. It came out of his hand a few years later. The body moves these things around until it can get rid of them."

"But a fork!"

"How did I get a fork in my foot, Grandad?"

"I'm blowed if I know, Wellie."

"Can I have it?"

"Of course! It's your fork." Grandad handed it over then dabbed at the blood on his face with a handkerchief. It was dried on, so he spat on the handkerchief.

Wellie held the warm fork, stupefied.

"Maybe you've got a whole silver service inside you," Grandad laughed. "Knives, spoons, fish knives, soup spoons, lobster shell crackers, fondue forks, sweet corn holders, who knows what you've got swimming around in there, Wellie. We should get you a full body x-ray."

Wellie did not sleep at all that night. He lay there holding the fork, his toe still throbbing, wondering grimly if there were more where that came from.

For years Wellie was too scared to put cutlery anywhere near his mouth in case it should leap in and travel around his insides. Instead he ate with his fingers, behaviour which further fuelled the rumours about his heritage.

A GILBERT AND GEORGE
TALIBANIMATION

Luke's whole world became focused around his throat, and the piece of raw tuna stuck within it. Every muscle in his body galvanised with the task of saving his life. Pressure rushed up into his head and pushed his eyeballs from behind. He reached out his hand to Gemma. Why had it taken her so long to notice?

He slipped from the stool and dropped to his knees on the floor. A dramatic plummet for a public place, but he was beyond feelings of embarrassment. He might die. The lights of the bar became violent. The sushi conveyor belt rolled on, with its coloured bowls and polished gleam. Why hadn't the belt stopped? he wondered. Why hadn't everything stopped? He tried to will a lungfull of air into himself by tensing all the wires in his throat.

And then he was lifted up from behind, a sensation he'd not felt since he was a child. His feet came clear off the floor as strong arms squeezed him and tipped him back. He saw the ceiling for the first time, and its tiny portholes of light. His head flopped forward and the floor spun, a dizzying blur, before another contraction came and he went limp in the arms of his rescuer. He felt the pressure behind the blockage in his throat just before it popped out. The tuna flew threw the air and slapped the ground with an audible schlopping sound.

He doubled over, his hands on his knees, sucking in great bellyfuls of delicious air. The sound of chopsticks on bowls was like the sweet tinkling of windchimes. A heavy hand slapped his back.

"You okay?"

Luke looked up at the waiter and nodded. He wiped spittle from his mouth with the back of his hand and took a couple more breaths before being able to say thank you.

He gripped the stool, steadying himself, as the walls and furniture and lights came to a rest. A petite waitress knelt down beside the expelled tuna and picked it up with a serviette. She sprayed a green solution onto the floor, then wiped it up. All the evidence was gone.

Luke looked up at Gemma, and then at the other customers in the St. Paul's branch of Yo! Sushi. He smiled. *Yes, everything is okay.*

"Jesus, Luke," Gemma said, little creases appearing at the corners of her eyes. "Chew your food for God's sake."

Luke couldn't face putting anything else in his mouth, and Gemma had lost her appetite, so he paid the bill and they left. On the way to the Tate Modern, they stopped on the Millennium Bridge to absorb the view. Little spits of rain flew at their faces. They rested their arms on the metal vertebrae. Gulls chased boats down the Thames, landing on the stony shore and picking at invisible pieces of crap.

"It's an amazing view, isn't it?" Luke said. "It reminds me of that Maurice Sendak book *In the Night Kitchen*. You know, the one where the city is made out of food boxes and kitchen implements?"

Gemma smiled and gave a knowing blink, but nothing more.

"I wish you'd tell me what's wrong," he said.

"Nothing's wrong," she said. "Just ignore me."

A great grey rhino of cloud rolled over, and a heavy shower of rain spilled from it. Luke and Gemma ran to the gallery, their hands held over their heads. Outside the entrance of the Tate Modern, a man was searching for something on the floor. He was so intent on finding whatever he had lost, that he ignored the rain soaking up through the knees of his suit trousers. His fingers explored the dimples of the ramp that led down to the sliding glass doors. His face was close to the ground, so close that his dripping fringe dragged across it.

Luke and Gemma stepped around him to get inside. Luke shook the rain from his fingers and kept light on his toes, imagining that the man might do something sudden and unpredictable. Maybe he would turn onto his back and show the soles of his feet and palms to the clouds, or maybe he would leap up full of piss and venom, hurling handfuls of his own shit at the tourists.

"Do you think he's okay?" Gemma said, looking back through the glass door.

"He doesn't look okay," Luke said. "I'm sure one of the staff will come and sort him out."

Gemma rolled her eyes. "We should do something." She pulled her phone from her coat pocket and looked at the screen, as if the answer could be found there.

"Maybe he's got a very good reason for being there," Luke said. "Maybe he's a piece of art."

Gemma paused for a second, and scrunched her eyebrows, before replying. "He can't be."

"How embarrassed would you be if he was though?" Luke

ran his fingers through his hair to pull his fringe out of his eyes and smiled.

They watched other people coming into the museum to see their reactions to the man. Most looked straight ahead, but some looked down with a confused glance before continuing on inside.

"Go and ask him if he's okay," Gemma said.

"No way," Luke said. "I'll tell you what, we'll go and tell someone at the desk. They'll sort him out, and if he is a piece of art, we won't look like total arses."

They walked down the great concrete tongue of the Turbine Hall. The iron girders, like linked arms, held inside the echoes of footsteps and chatter. Enormous silver slides sprouted from three of the gallery floors. These connective tubes carried a regulated stream of visitors from great heights down to the cushioned crash mats on the ground level. Through the windows of the gallery floors, Gemma and Luke could see people queuing for this well-ordered evacuation.

"I heard about these," Gemma said.

"Can you really class that as art?" Luke said.

"Of course you can. It's about the experience you get sliding down one, that's the art. I think they're beautiful."

Luke agreed that they were impressive. There were five of these winding snakes carrying people safely through the air. They threw enormous convoluted shadows against the wall. At the end of the slides, a group of visitors were gathered to watch people emerge, to see the strange expression of delight, fear and embarrassment on their faces.

"It looks like you go pretty fast on the big ones," Luke said.

"Why don't you get us tickets to have a go."

"Er, sure, okay," Luke said. "You start queuing. I need a pee."

Luke headed for the bathrooms. A little girl in a sailor suit was staring up at the slides. Luke followed her gaze. From below, the slides looked like frozen alien appendages. His attention was so fixed on what was going on overhead that he almost tripped over the woman on the floor.

He apologised and skipped round her, but she didn't acknowledge him. Instead, she kept her attention focused on her boots — calf length leather boots with one big strap across the instep. She held the strap and the buckle in each hand and stared at them with a look of distress on her face.

"Are you okay?" he asked.

"Yes. Yes, fine," she said, but did not look up at him.

Back at the queue for the slides, Luke easily found Gemma. She was wearing her new red coat, a beautiful, well-tailored thing that pulled in tight at her waist. She looked firm and sculptural in it. When she'd brought it home, and after they'd argued about how much it cost, Luke had asked if she would leave it on in bed, but she'd baulked at the idea of getting his spunk splashed up the silk lining.

The coat was the latest in a series of pleasure purchases for Gemma. Luke had noticed how her mood seemed to rise out of its ditch for a few days after she'd bought herself gifts like this, before it sank again. Each new item that she bought grew more and more expensive. It was an unsustainable habit. He kept asking what was wrong, but she always said the same thing, that nothing was wrong. He'd started to think of these depressions as weather fronts that he had no power over. The best he could do was shelter and wait for them to pass.

He put his arm round Gemma to show the rest of the queue that he was with her and not just pushing in.

"Are you sure you want to go on these things?" he asked.

"Why, don't you?"

"No, I want to, but . . ."

Gemma took in a dramatic breath. "You can always wait for me at the bottom."

"No, I'll come on."

They shuffled forward another step towards the ticket booths. A sign at the front of the roped-off queuing area said that tickets were now available for the three o'clock slot. It was almost two o'clock. Luke took a packet of crisps from his bag.

"Are you allowed to eat in here?" Gemma looked at the bag like it might set off an alarm.

Luke tried to reply through a mouthful of crisps, then just pointed to a family sitting on the floor of the hall. They had sandwiches and plastic pots of chopped fruit and vegetables arranged on top of a child's blue jumper.

Luke offered the bag to Gemma, but she shook her head. Someone in the hall shrieked, and she turned her small, fierce ears in that direction. Her tight ponytail flicked over her shoulder. The shriek turned into laughter. A mother was trying to stop her son running about by holding the hem of his coat, but he was spinning around, screwing his coat into a tight knot that locked his arms in position. His face was red with laughter.

"Do you think we'll ever have kids?" Luke asked.

Gemma looked at him, pinching her features in. "You want to talk about that *now*? *Here*?" she said. She turned the volume down on her voice to a whisper. "I can't believe you can bring that up so flippantly."

"What?" Luke said. Her reaction was disproportionate, surely? "We've never talked about it. I was only asking." He picked crisp crumbs from the bottom of the packet, tilted back his head and dropped them in.

Gemma turned her back to him. He screwed up the crisp

packet and put it back in his bag. "What do you want to do while we're waiting to go on the slides?" He asked.

"Well, we're in an art gallery. We could look at some art."

"Genius," he said.

They were close to the front of the queue. Luke looked back to the entrance. "The guy on the floor is gone," he said. "I guess we don't need to mention it to the guys on the desk."

Gemma looked at the entrance. She had her arms folded across her chest. "*I* don't need to mention it, you mean," she said.

Luke and Gemma checked their bags into the cloakroom. Gemma hung onto her coat, insisting that she needed it. But it was hot in the galleries, and she carried it over her arm, often adjusting the way it was folded so that it didn't crease.

They walked quickly through the galleries, only pausing when they saw something they liked. They'd been together long enough now, and had been to enough galleries, not to have any pretensions about standing in front of each work for the five seconds of assessment most people seemed to give them. Instead, they swept through, scanning the works, rejecting most, lingering on maybe one piece per room.

On the fifth floor was a piece of video art, shown in a darkened room with a single long bench running through the middle. A wide screen was divided into four sections, each showing clips from movies of people playing instruments, and the sound from each was audible. Sometimes the sounds would clang against each other, and it was a dizzying mess, but then there were moments when all four tracks found harmony, and it would make Luke smile. Jimmy Stewart playing the harmonica, Michael J. Fox playing the guitar in *Back to the Future*, Marilyn Monroe singing. Somehow they complemented each other. Luke and Gemma sat down on one of the benches. In the darkness he felt for her hand, and squeezed it when he found it.

Gemma turned her head to him for a second, and gave a single, small squeeze in reply.

In the queue for the slide, they stood behind a huge man who was having trouble with his breathing. His inhalations and exhalations made a wheezing noise in his throat. The man let out streams of inaudible farts, whose potency caused Luke and Gemma to tug as far from the queue as they could get without losing their place.

Luke leaned in close to Gemma, breathing in the comforting smell of her wool collar. "Maybe he's nervous," he whispered.

"Maybe he needs the loo," Gemma whispered back.

"I hope he doesn't go on the way down. We'd be the first to know about it."

"You go down first then," Gemma said, and then, "I mean it."

They were queuing for one of the slides on the fifth floor, the longest ones. Luke looked at the steep decline and wondered how fast he was going to shoot down this thing. At the mouth of the slide sat a Tate girl with a video monitor, checking that each person was out safely before sending down the next one. Beside this girl was a pile of white cloth sacks, which people were sitting on to slide. As they went down, many people let out exclamations of surprise, or delight, or terror. The slide trembled, making a metallic clanging sound, as the support structures struggled to maintain the integrity of this robot oesophagus.

"Are you sure this thing's safe?" Luke said.

"They wouldn't let people on if it wasn't," Gemma replied.

"Maybe the artist's cruel joke is that the real art is the news reports that come when the slides collapse and kill dozens of people."

"You're right. That's probably what he had in mind."

They were only a few people away from the yawning metal maw. Luke looked about him. A woman with two kids clinging to her pockets was behind them in the queue.

"I've been on this one once, and the small one three times," the elder girl counted to her mother, who patted her on the head.

"You've been down this one already?" Luke asked the girl, but looked at the mother and smiled, indicating that he wasn't a paedo.

"Yeah," the girl said. "And next I'm going on the other one."

"They've been up and down the slides all day," the girls' mother sighed. "We've not seen anything else yet, have we?"

The big man in front of Luke and Gemma was about to slide when a terrific shouting came from ground level. A woman was shrieking in a foreign language. The Tate girl held up her hand to indicate that the big man should wait.

On the video monitor, Luke could see a woman in her thirties pointing at her mouth and her throat as she spat out words that must have been curses. Two security guards approached the woman, at first using calming body language to placate her, and then when that didn't work, grasping each of her arms and guiding her out towards the exit. But her yelling was still audible, finding its way up the long slide, which gave it a metallic ring, as if it wasn't the sound of a person at all.

The Tate girl made a few soft words into a walkie-talkie, and then nodded that it was okay for the big man to slide. He laid down the white cloth in the tube and stood on it, then sat down and tucked his feet into the pocket at the end. The top of his trousers pulled down, revealing the hairy valley of his butt crack to the queue. He held onto the upper rim of the slide and used it to swing his bulk into the tube.

Luke leaned forward to watch him hurtle down. He counted. The slide rattled, and Luke hoped that he hadn't loosened all the bolts. The big man came out at the bottom, twisting sideways and rolling onto the crash mat. Luke had counted ten seconds.

"Are you sure you want me to go first?" Luke asked.

Gemma nodded, her irritation obvious in her shrinking lips.

The Tate girl pointed at Gemma and indicated that she'd have to wear her coat to slide.

"I don't want it to get damaged," Gemma said.

"You can't carry anything on the slide," the Tate girl said. "For your own safety."

"What's the worst that can happen?" she asked the girl.

"Shall we give it a miss?" Luke said.

The Tate girl, flustered that the queue had stopped again, gestured at the slide, a signal which somehow meant both "slide down" to Luke and "put your coat on" to Gemma. Luke put his white sack down on the tube and pulled up his jeans as he sat down. He tucked in his feet, then held onto the upper rim of the slide.

Thin echoes of sound drifted up towards him. He felt precarious, like the slide might drop away at any moment and just let him freefall five floors. The Tate girl said again that he should go. Luke swung himself gently forward. He didn't want to start off too fast in case he accelerated to terrifying speed. But he didn't give himself enough of a push and didn't move anywhere. He had to place his hands on either side of the tube and shuffle forward until his inertia broke.

The first section of the slide was straight, and he accelerated quickly. He pushed his feet against the floor of the slide, but the cloth sack removed almost all friction, and he couldn't slow himself down. When he hit the first bend, he sped up, and the slide squeezed a little gasp from his mouth. He moved up and down the curved sides as gravity and centrifugal forces fought for control of his body. The metal bands that circled the glass top of the slide made the light in the Turbine Hall strobe.

Halfway down the slide, he imagined for a second that the tube was gently pulsing, and that he was being carried down by some peristaltic action. In that second, the tube felt soft beneath him, no longer cold metal, but a soft organic surface. He felt something tugging at his insides, a sensation wholly different to the forces pulling him down. And then something came loose inside him. He couldn't locate the sensation in his body. He just felt the vacuum created by a tiny thing disappearing inside him, before everything rushed in to fill the space.

He came out of the last bend onto the straight section, and then he was moving over the crash mat, slowing down, and the slide was over. He felt a sense of peace and belonging. He had now joined the ranks of sliders and embraced his fear.

He waited at the side for Gemma, and saw her red shape moving through the tube. It looked like she was travelling slower than he had done. At first, as she came out of the metallic tunnel, Luke thought she had hated the experience. Her expression was taut and fearful, but when she came to a stop, a big smile broke across her face.

"That was great," she said. "Let's go and get some tea."

On the escalator up to the third floor, Gemma reached out for his hand and rested her head against his shoulder. He squeezed his palm against hers and kissed the top of her head, breathing in the electric tang of her hairspray.

A Gilbert and George exhibition filled the fourth floor. Although there was an entry fee for the main exhibition, there were works up on the walls around the double helix of escalators that ran through the gallery. There were enormous panels of red, black and white, with newspaper headlines about the July 7th terrorist bombings in London. And in every work, like avenging angels, the two suited artists glared out, sometimes with their eyes on fire.

The café was also filled with their stained glass panels,

transforming it into a church of poo, penises and good tailoring. Gemma searched for a table while Luke bought large paper cups of tea and mean slices of plastic-wrapped carrot cake. As he searched for Gemma, he heard a cracking sound, like he'd stepped on the surface of a frozen pond. And he looked around, fearful that he'd broken something by accident. But he could not see where the sound had come from.

Gemma had found a table beneath an enormous stained glass crucifix made out of turds. She grinned while she unwrapped her cake.

"What?" Luke said.

"Nothing," she said.

"What are you grinning about?"

"I don't know."

Luke rubbed his temples with his fingertips, then massaged the back of his neck with his hand. "Look," he said. "I know things have been a bit, you know, between us recently, and I just want to say I'm sorry for my part in that."

Gemma stared at him. At first, he thought she was trying to calculate in her mind how best to assemble her argument against him, piling up the layers of complaint into a cohesive tower of dissatisfaction. But then he saw a blankness in her eyes.

"This cake is delicious," she said.

Luke sipped his tea and unwrapped his own cake. "I think I know what you're pissed off about," he said, not looking up at her. "I think it's about how I don't appreciate you enough, that you maybe think I've started to take you for granted." He paused, waiting for a response, and when none came, he carried on. "I know I've been a bit preoccupied lately. Things have been crazy at work, and I've been getting these awful stomach pains. I think I've got an ulcer or IBS or something. It's just all so distracting, and I'm sorry if I haven't been making you feel special enough. I'm just . . ." He looked up to see Gemma's expression.

Her attention was focused on the piece of cake in her hand. She smiled as she chewed. Was she mocking him? "But I don't think it's just me," he said, turning the card cup around in his hands. "You've been pretty cold recently. I don't remember the last time you asked me what kind of day I had, and you say we don't go out together anymore, that we just stay in, but you've not suggested anywhere we could go. It's not my job to arrange everything. You could make things a bit easier for me if you told me what you're actually thinking rather than telling me off about something unrelated."

Gemma took a sip of her tea, then reached a warm hand across the table and wrapped her palm around Luke's hand. "It's okay," she said. "Let's just start again." And then she smiled and broke off a piece of Luke's cake and ate it in one mouthful.

"What do you mean, start again?" Luke asked. He felt sure she was building him up for something awful. Her expression of delight couldn't be genuine. She only looked this way after a long soak in the bath with a spliff.

A cracking sound came again, and Luke looked at his feet, even though the sound had come from above. He imagined that at any second the floor might give way and they'd all tumble through three ceilings.

He watched a man in a suit carrying a Tate carrier bag and a cup of tea walk straight into a wall, bouncing off it and falling on his arse and spilling tea all over himself. Several people sitting much closer jumped up to help him, so Luke stayed where he was. "What's up with everyone today?" he said.

"We should do this more often," Gemma said. Her smile was wide and her eyes were dreamy. "I'm having the best time with you."

On the other side of the café, two young men talked with animated hand gestures over a pile of books and papers. The Gilbert and George stained glass above them rippled for a second, as if an electric current were passing through it. And then, with a sound like a waterfall, the glass cracked, and the turd crucifix fell straight out of the painting and smashed on the table between them, no longer a glass turd, but a real one, a leviathan movement that filled the whole café with a sharp stench.

The two men leapt back out of the way, sending their chairs flying behind them. The people in the café got up from their tables and backed away from the turd, as if it might do something else. Explode, or maybe say something.

"What the fuck?" Luke said as he got up and reached out for Gemma's hand.

Gemma just giggled, a fluttering child-like chuckle. A sound he'd never heard her make before. "Now, those guys are funny," she said.

"Who?"

"Gilbert and George."

"I don't think that was supposed to happen."

Security guards were there within a few seconds and began creating a circle of safety around the shit with their arms and their voices. They ushered people out of the café into the area around the escalators.

Luke and Gemma shuffled out with everyone else, looking back at the turd as they went. "Maybe that was trapped in there the whole time," Gemma said.

"Have you taken something?" Luke asked. "Have you given me some of it too? I'm totally losing it."

Gemma laughed and stroked his arm with her hands. "Don't be silly, Lukey," she said. "Don't complain now that I'm happy."

The sound of cracking glass came again, louder than before, and then the security guards themselves began to back out of the café. But in the entrance hall of the fourth floor they were not safe either. A humming sound began to emanate from the huge Gilbert and George stained glass called *Bombs*. The red panels glowed as a supernatural light burned through them. It shone through Gilbert and George's eyes, and they blinked against it, thrusting their hands through the glass barrier that held them against the wall. Glass crashed down around the nine-foot-tall artists as they stepped out of the work.

The visitors on the fourth floor shouted and screamed as they barged against each other, desperate to get out. Hands clawed the air, and arms and feet pushed through the fray, struggling to rise to the front of the human tide. Some pushed onto the escalators, but others, in their desperation, ran for the slide. The queue broke down as people pushed against the metal mouths of the slide, diving in headfirst, feet first, any way they could get in.

A Tate girl at the slide lifted her hands, showing the crowd her palms, a gesture meant to instil peace and harmony, but behind her more artworks were cracking, and dreadful things were dropping out of them onto the gallery floor.

"One at a time please!" the Tate girl said. "Fold your arms across your chest and tuck your head in!"

But the people didn't listen, and from inside the tube their screams could be heard as gravity smashed them against each other, turned them every way and spat them out of the tubes at the end, bruised and bloody.

"STOP!" an enormous booming voice came from above. Gilbert and George, nine feet tall, impeccably dressed, with blazing eyes, strode through the crowd. "Get away from the slide. DANGER," they said. But the two demons lurching forwards only forced the people to hurl themselves into the slide with even greater abandon.

"Keep close to me," Luke said, grasping Gemma's hand.

Gemma squeezed his hand back, her head darting this way

and that as people fell beneath the feet of other people and glass smashed all around.

Gilbert and George split up. George stood on the black rubber handrails of the escalator, riding them down like skis. Gilbert stretched out his hands in front of him, like a conjuror, and a fierce light glowed between them. From this light grew a three-dimensional stained glass cock, diamond-like sparkles flashing on its veined underside. Gilbert muttered secret words, and the light between his hands and around the cock intensified, making it grow, until it was a huge member, and he had to wrap his whole arms around its girth to control it. Pushing people out of the way with this phallus, he advanced on the slide. "MOVE ASIDE," he boomed. And when people saw what he was going to do, they dived out of the way, clearing a path for the artist.

Gilbert jammed the cock into the slide, filling up the entrance, and he pushed his weight against the balls at the base to wedge it firmly inside.

Driven along by the crowd, Luke and Gemma fell onto the escalator down to the third floor. While descending, bodies crushing him, Luke watched George grab the mouth of the third-floor slide and twist it back and forth. It made awful metallic squealing noises as rivets buckled and popped, and the tense suspension wires twanged like guitar strings, filling the Turbine Hall with discordant notes.

Luke and Gemma ran round to the next escalator down, tumbling against each other. Gemma's nails were deep in Luke's palms. Other visitors pushed against them. They teetered on the narrow steps like gulls on a cliff face. Luke stood on the foot of a vicious little woman, and she squawked at him, showing her teeth. Gemma pulled him forwards, and he lost his grip on the steps, but the crowd was squeezed so tightly together that it held him aloft, and he drifted down, only the edge of one heel on the escalator.

They spilled out at the bottom of the escalator on the ground floor. Through the whole gallery, Tate guardians in luminous jackets ran, shouting into their walkie-talkies. Sounds of violence and destruction fell from the upper floors, and shards of stained glass rained down the escalators, getting caught in people's hair and drawing out little threads of blood.

On the ground level, Luke and Gemma pushed through the people to get to the glass doors leading into the Turbine Hall, when Gemma suddenly shouted, "My bag!"

Luke looked back at the cloakroom, as if he expected to see an attendant still handing out bags and tags amongst the chaos. And the strange thing was that an attendant was there, and he was working like a maniac.

The crowd was completely disregarding the queuing barriers and had trampled them. They leaned over the counter thrusting their metal number counters at the man. He took two at a time, running along the corridor of coats and bags, pulling them off the shelf and handing them back to the right people. Sweat was dripping off his hair, but he had an aura of happiness, as if this was the moment he had trained for, his moment to shine, when he could apply his skills to this awesome event. And he was glowing with power, as if the spirit of the building, of London itself, was flowing through him. And when a man dared to jump onto the counter, attempting to retrieve something himself, the cloakroom worker had only to hold up his big hand and say no, and that was enough to stop him and push him back onto the right side of the counter.

"You're not serious," Luke said.

"I have to get it," she said. "It was the first birthday present you bought for me."

Luke stopped.

In the middle of the frenzy he paused for a second of reverie. He hadn't even noticed which bag Gemma was carrying. He had bought it for her when they'd been going out for six months. It cost two weeks' salary — the most expensive gift he had ever bought. That she had brought it out with her today had not been an accident. It was a sign that beneath the bitterness of the last few months, the people they had been in that first passionate year were still inside them.

"I'll get it," he said.

He pushed and stumbled his way into the crowd at the cloakroom, holding his tags out to the attendant, as did everyone else, their arms making an anemone that caught bags and coats in the air. And just when Luke thought he was going to be passed over again, the attendant plucked the metal tags from his fingers and returned seconds later with his and Gemma's bags.

From the Turbine Hall came a terrific sound like gunfire. As Luke fought his way back through the people at the cloakroom, he saw one of the slides rip out the bolts that held it to the floor. Each bolt exploded from the concrete sending up a cloud of powder. The slide snaked around, as if sniffing the air, then darted forwards, smashing through the glass wall. Its mouth flared as it surged towards Gemma and grabbed her, plucking her from the ground and pulling her back into the hall. Her thin legs kicked at the corner of its shiny steel lips, and her shoes flew off.

Luke ran out into the main hall, jumping through the hole in the shattered window and slipping on the glass under his feet as he landed. The Turbine Hall echoed with screams. People ran up the ramp to the exits, clutching children and rolled up posters at their chests. The slide on the third floor, the one that had Gemma in its mouth, was twisting and coiling in the air, fully animated. Its top end was still attached to the glass wall on the third floor, but the enormous George was kicking it away, ripping it from the wall.

The fourth floor slide, the one that Gilbert had jammed a

huge cock into, hung limply, giving an occasional twitch. The other four slides, as if sensing that the first two were in trouble, began to creak and groan, pulling against their taut suspension wires.

Luke stood at the base of these great metal snakes, helpless, watching Gemma's legs flying around the hall. She was still kicking. One of the smallest slides on the second floor pulled itself free of its bonds and crawled, caterpillar-like, up the side of the Turbine Hall. It smashed one end of itself through the glass and disappeared inside. Through the broken glass, Luke could see flashes of light flying off the slide as it went into a frenzy, tossing people out into the Hall. Bodies fell through the air in their tens, no longer guided down gently by the slides, but dropping, a straight and ugly descent, and gravity ruined them against the ground.

From the fourth floor came a guttural groan, a men's choir of deep voices, and a glow shone out, like sunlight through stained glass. Gilberts and Georges leapt out of the broken fourth floor like paratroopers. They slid down the outside of the slides, dozens of them, some naked, some suited, all different sizes, from knee-high Gilbert and Georges to the nine-foot giants that had first broken free of their works.

Sensing this increased danger, all of the slides ripped free of their bonds, gripping the walls with one end, the floor ends darting about, plucking Gilberts and Georges from the backs of each other. The slide holding Gemma dragged her feet across the ground a way before opening its mouth and letting her spill out onto the floor. Luke ran to her.

"Gemma!" he called into her unconscious face. "Gemma, wake up!"

But she didn't move. He wrapped his arms around her back and lifted her up onto his shoulder. She was light, but he was not strong and his back and knees strained beneath her. Luke ran up the ramp, Gemma's weight driving him forwards. Behind him, the sound came again, the cry of the Gilberts and Georges, a Gregorian chant, resonating in the walls of the Turbine Hall. Luke turned in time to see the two nine-foot Georges, their faces creased up with concentration, begin to shine. And with a sound like air filling a vacuum, they grew.

Gilbert and George swelled to twenty feet, and light, like fire, burned from their enormous eyes. They each took a slide, wrapped their arms around it and tugged it down from the wall, forcing it squirming to the floor, then drove their knees and fists into it, buckling the metal and breaking the glass.

The other slides wrapped around Gilbert and George like silver prehistoric snakes, and the titanic artists fell against each other, and against the walls of the Hall, as they wrestled the metal monsters.

Luke ran on towards the exit, struggling to keep on his feet as fleeing people bumped into him. At his side, a man's body sailed through the air and burst against the iron-ribbed walls. George gurgled behind him as one of the slides wound itself around his neck and constricted.

Outside the Tate, as if the glass doors offered them protection, people had stopped running and were standing on the ramp in the rain watching the leviathan artworks going at it. Some had even begun to cheer for Gilbert and George, because it was somehow clear that they were the ones to root for.

At the top of the ramp, Luke strained his back as he set Gemma down on the wall. The cold brick against her bum had a restorative effect, and she awoke. She looked at him and held his gaze, as if his eyes were the point around which she could orient her confused mind. Her fingers moved to the torn arm of her red coat, and she explored the wounded fabric.

"Are you hurt?" Luke asked. "Is anything broken?"

Gemma gazed up into the overhanging ridge of her eyebrows. "I'm fine," she said. "I'm really fine."

Luke wrapped his arms around her, pushing his face into her neck and kissing it with such force that he could feel the architecture beneath her skin with his lips. "Can you walk?" he spoke into her hair.

She stood up and wiggled her feet in the same way she might explore new shoes in a shoe shop. "I feel good," she said.

Luke put his arm around her back, and they walked around the front of the gallery, where the magnetic flow of the building had changed and was now drawing people to it. They were running in their hundreds along the riverfront, their mouths and eyes open, because news of the colossal battle had spread fast. From the rings of people around the building came the playground cheer, "Gilbert and George! Gilbert and George!"

Luke and Gemma stopped on the Millennium Bridge and looked back. From here, the great chaos inside was invisible and silent. The old factory, its windpipe stretching up into the sky, kept hidden all the destruction, and let none of it spill out into London.

Luke picked a piece of broken glass from Gemma's hair, then stroked her ear. She smiled at him, and it was a reflex smile, not a manufactured one. A boat full of tourists passed below the bridge, and Luke thought how strange it was that none of them was aware of the incredible events happening within the Tate. None of them was aware that he and Gemma were different people from the couple who crossed the bridge just a few hours ago. They were lighter, more handsome and deeper in love.

CUCKOO

We only ever see one side of the moon. The moon takes the same time to circle the Earth as it does to turn on its own axis, which means that the same point on the moon always faces the Earth. A strange coincidence, but then everything about the universe is miraculous. Miracles are the milk on which all life flourishes.

The moon's rotation and orbit are so perfectly synchronised that from the moon's surface, the earth is frozen in the sky. There is no Earth-rise or Earth-set, just the Earth rotating in the sky, a great rolling ball that never reaches its destination.

This was one of the first things Alice told me. She was always coming out with facts like that. She had an amazing power to make me see familiar things in a new way, as if for the first time. After she'd told me one of her facts, she would flick her head to the side to get her long hair out of her eyes, then tuck her hair behind her left ear. It was always like that, as if the movement were the full stop at the end of her story.

Alice was half my age, but twice as intelligent. She knew what was going on in the world. She could explain the Israel/ Palestine conflict in neat little sentences. She knew the names of everything, of trees, of birds, of cars. She was modest. She always credited her knowledge as coming from someone else, as if she had just happened across it accidentally.

"Oh, my dad spent three years rebuilding a Volkswagen Beetle from scratch, so I got to learn a bit about engines," she would say, or, "My uncle's a real nature nut and he told me how to tell all the seabirds apart when we were on holiday in Scotland one year."

She met informed people all the time and absorbed whatever knowledge they had to impart. I have no such ability. I could spend a week with someone smart and not learn a single thing from them. I've managed to live my first thirty-two years without accumulating any kind of knowledge.

I first spoke to Alice a couple of years ago at a climate change rally in Trafalgar Square. She was standing on the fountain wall, just above me, wearing a T-shirt that said, "Jesus is coming, look busy." She'd looked down at me a couple of times during KT Tunstall's set, and I smiled back. And when the rally finished, she jumped down next to me and said, "That was a bloody waste of time."

"Sorry?" I said, grabbing her arm to help her up.

"Couldn't you feel it? There was all this anticipation in the air before and during, but then when they said goodbye, you could actually feel the inertia setting back in."

Her friends jumped down beside her. They looked younger than she did. They gave me suspicious looks. "These people really cared about the planet for a couple of hours, and now they're back to their old ways of thinking," she said. "They've just been hearing about how consumerism is eating away at the planet, and now they're all taking advantage of being in London to go shopping for clothes and DVDs."

"Maybe they're not," I said. "Maybe they're going home to write to their MPs."

"I don't think so," she said, smoothing her whole face with her palms.

"And how do you know that?"

"I just know these things. My instincts are good. I've got intuition. Like I saw you watching me, and I knew you were going to be important in my life somehow."

I couldn't help but be excited to hear her say that.

"Really?" I said.

Her friends tried to get her to leave with them, but she said she'd call on her mobile later to catch up with them.

"I'm starving," she said. "I've not had any lunch yet. Buy me something and we can chat, and maybe I'll work out why we met."

I offered to take her to Gili Gulu, a sushi bar in Covent Garden, but she wanted to eat at McDonald's. She didn't look like the kind of person that eats regularly at McDonald's, but the way she reeled out her order without looking at the menu suggested that she did.

"Isn't this place one of the worst consumerist, anti-environmental places you could eat?" I asked.

"Probably, yes. But I don't care," she said, her mouth full of Big Mac. She wiped a blob of something from the corner of her mouth with the back of her wrist.

"So doesn't that make you as bad as everyone you said was going out to buy clothes and DVDs after the rally?"

"Yes," she said. "I'm just as bad as everyone else. I don't believe in climate change, but I want to."

"You don't believe in it?"

"No," she spoke in short sentences punctuated by chewing. "I was hoping the rally would change my mind. And it almost did for a second. But I just can't bring myself to care."

"That's scary."

"I just think that in the grand scheme of things it doesn't really matter. In the history of the universe, humans have only been around for a fraction of a fraction of a nothing. Species come, species go. Planets bloom and die. If you watched the universe on fast forward, the planets would be coming and going so fast they'd look like the bubbles fizzing at the top of your Coke."

"But doesn't that make the planet even more precious, that it's here for such a short time?"

I popped a couple of chips into my mouth and folded my arms across the table, leaning in and breathing in the smell of Alice's sticky sweet perfume. She had thick make-up around her eyes, inexpertly applied.

Alice took a sip of Coke and rubbed her plucked eyebrow. "I'd like to believe that. But I can't. We're only getting so worked up about climate change because we want to feel like we count. We think we're more important than anything else. Environmentalism is just our way of asserting our dominance over the planet again. It's just the latest incarnation of whale hunting or mining. We're robbing the earth, and this time we're stealing its authority. If we have the power to create and destroy the world, we're its masters. It's just another ego trip for the human race."

"Wow, how did you get to be so cynical?"

"Not cynical. I just see the big picture. The BIG picture."

While Alice ate, she asked me questions. She seemed determined that she had met me for a reason. That I had something important to impart, or influence to have on her. She wanted to know all about me so she could work out what it was.

"You ask a lot of questions," I said.

"That's how I find out stuff."

When Alice had finished her food, she said she had to go

and meet her friends, and I felt a hiccup of emptiness at the thought of never seeing her again. But I was relieved when she took out a pen from her handbag and wrote her mobile number on a napkin and then handed it to me.

"I'm afraid we'll have to meet again," she said. "I'm still not sure why we met. Give me a call."

I sent a text message to Alice that night. "Great to meet you today. Want to get together and ask some more questions?"

I only had to wait two minutes for her reply, but it seemed like longer. I could not keep my feet still. Her message read, "Yes meet outside golders green station next sat at 4."

Alice was all I could think about that week. Things at home weren't going so well, and my new friend was the only source of pleasure in my mind.

Beth and I were arguing a lot. Our baby, Isobel, was six months old and had terrible colic. She was screaming all the time and we couldn't stand it. Neither of us was getting any sleep, and I was wondering why we'd decided to have a baby in the first place. When Saturday came around, I was panicking about how to get out of the house for a few hours without raising suspicion. Isobel had woken up seven times during the night, and Beth and I had barely slept. We were fractious enough for a violent argument to break out over a tea bag, which I'd left on the draining board. It soon escalated until we were screaming the most poisonous things we could think of, and then with a final, "You've ruined my life," I left the house and slammed the door behind me.

I arrived at Golders Green Station half an hour early, so I got a gingerbread latte from Starbucks. It was one of their Christmas specials. Drinking that hot, sweet coffee outside the station in the cold, watching bus lights flare in the gloom, was a delicious moment. I wondered whether Alice would come.

And when she hadn't arrived at 4:20, I began to worry. I couldn't go home straight after that argument. It would take Beth a while to calm down. I sent a text message to Alice, "are you coming?" and then a few seconds later, my phone rang.

"Can you see me?" she said.

I held the phone to my ear and looked around. There were people moving everywhere. And then I saw her on the other side of the road waving at me. She was wearing a pink ski jacket, hat and gloves. I know if Beth could see me like this, she would assume that something terrible was going on, but when Alice was in front of me, I felt like there was some magic left in the universe, and I wouldn't let go of my tiny sliver of it for anything.

"Where shall we go?" she said.

"Straight in with the questions," I said. "Do you want to go into town?"

"Can we get one of those first?" She pointed at the cup in my hand. "It smells lovely."

Alice grabbed a table while I queued for coffees. I wondered then whether anyone I knew might see us. I would have trouble explaining what I was doing. No one would believe me. While I waited for the staff to froth up our coffees, I thought of excuses I would give if anyone asked.

Back at the table, Alice took a sip of her gingerbread latte and closed her eyes. "Wow, that's good," she said.

"I'm not going to be able to sleep tonight after two cups."

Around us, people rattled spoons and warmed their noses in steaming cups.

"Are you married?" Alice asked.

"Yes," I said. "I have a baby too."

"What's your baby's name?"

"Isobel. She's six months old. She has colic at the moment, so she screams all the time."

"Poor thing."

This will sound awful, and maybe I am a terrible person, but until Alice said that, I'd only thought of Isobel's colic as something that affected Beth and me. The broken sleep, the screaming, the winding and the vomiting after her milk. It was all dominating my life. I couldn't believe I'd not considered that Isobel was doing this because she was in pain. I had no natural empathy with her. All I could see was how it was affecting me. I was so ashamed I couldn't look up for a second.

"I bet your wife is gorgeous," Alice said, smiling to herself and flicking her hair back.

"She used to have long hair like yours, but she cut it all off a couple of months ago. It's a practical haircut. Short hair doesn't get full of baby sick all the time."

"Yuck, gross. I don't think I'm ever going to have kids."

"How come?"

"I just can't see myself with a kid. It's not an image I can make in my head."

"One of your intuitions?"

"I guess. I can see myself standing on a boat out at sea doing research on octopuses, or in a jungle in Borneo taking samples of bat droppings, but not pushing a pram around."

"It's difficult to imagine what you're going to do when you're older," I said. "And you never end up where you thought you were going to be. Sometimes, it's like discovering you're wearing someone else's clothes, but they fit you perfectly."

"So you're not happy with how your life ended up?"

"Don't say it like it's over," I smiled. "I'm only thirty-two. I'm still considered young by everyone thirty-three and over."

"I guess you are young, relative to everyone else on the planet," she said. "But if you were the last person on the earth, would you still be young?"

"I think my self image would be the last thing I'd think about in that situation."

We finished our coffees and walked outside where the air was cold. I asked where she wanted to go next. She said surprise her. She had to be home by nine, so we still had a few hours. I took her on a bus ride into town, the 13, which goes down Baker Street and then Oxford Street. I wanted to show her the Christmas lights.

We got off at Oxford Circus and walked down the length of Regent Street. The shop windows were full of sparkling beads, and great gleaming baubles hung above the street. Shoppers jostled against each other, clashing bags. Sometimes I put my arm around Alice to protect her from the crowds. Wherever there was an impressive window display, we would stop in front of it and point things out to each other.

We walked all the way down to Trafalgar Square. Sometimes I would look at Alice and smile to make sure she was okay, and sometimes she would take a tissue from her pocket to blow her nose.

"This is the first time I've worn this coat this winter," she said. "It's weird when you put on an old coat and you find things in your pockets. They're like little time capsules."

"So what did you find in your pocket?"

She took out each of the items in her pocket and identified them one by one. "A throat sweet from when I had a cold last year. A cinema ticket with a boy's phone number on it. He was a real dick. Some beads from my favourite necklace that broke. An almond? The left-overs of a dried flower from my sister's wedding."

"You have a sister?" I said.

"Clare. She's five years older than me. She got married last

November. There were gale-force winds. It was so funny. The photos are all hilarious. Everyone's holding their hats on, and their dresses and hair are flapping about."

We stood at the bus stop and listened to a Japanese busker playing Beatles songs on an acoustic guitar.

"So what have you got in your pocket?" she asked.

"Nothing exciting. A bus ticket, my phone, one of Isobel's socks, and a stone from the beach."

"Which beach?"

"A place in Dorset. I can't remember the name of it. We were there a couple of months ago."

"Why did you keep that particular stone?"

"Do you think my choice of stone reveals something about my personality?"

"Maybe," she smiled. "I'm not an expert, but there has to be a reason you chose that stone to take home, over all the others on the beach."

"This one just stood out, I suppose."

She frowned, dissatisfied.

When we got back in the bus, we were warm, sitting close together. Our hot breath steamed up the window, and Alice frequently wiped it away with the sleeve of her jacket. The bus took us back down Oxford Street.

"Did your parents ever bring you here to see the Christmas lights?" I asked.

"Maybe once," she said. "Well, my mum and step dad."

"Your parents are divorced?"

"Since I was four."

"Why did they break up?"

"I don't know. I think they just hated each other."

"Do you think it was for the best?"

"I guess so. If they'd stayed together, they might have killed each other. And my step dad wouldn't have been my step dad, and it's weird to think of him living somewhere else and not knowing him."

"So you think it was fate that they split up?"

"I thought I was supposed to be the question asker."

"Sorry," I said.

Alice asked me all about my work. She'd never met anyone that worked in the film industry before. I could see her clever interview style working round, building up a mental image of my day, and then tracing back to fill in gaps where she hadn't understood something. And then just as we got to Swiss Cottage she smiled and nodded to herself, as if she'd reached saturation point for that subject. She stared out of the window, resting the side of her forehead on the glass. Little strands of her hair stuck to the condensation and made patterns like roots.

I couldn't get over how pretty she was. I could have just stared at her smooth skin and bright eyes forever. Her mouth was perfectly formed, maybe from her sixteen years of question asking, toned from constant exercise.

"Would you like to meet up again?" I asked when we were back outside the station. Buses groaned and belched behind us.

"Sure," she said. "You're not letting your secret out easily. It's going to take me a bit longer to get it out of you."

I smiled and thrust my hands into my pockets, shrugging my shoulders up around my neck for warmth. I hadn't decided then whether I would tell her my secret. I couldn't bear to frighten her off. "Shall I send you a text message?" I said.

"Okay." And then she blew me a kiss and ran away.

"Hey," I called after her. "I should walk you back."

"I'm just round the corner. Don't worry. I've got pepper spray."

I watched her feet beating against the pavement. The soles of her Converse boots made slapping sounds as they hit the path. It was almost nine. I called Beth and told her I was sorry about losing my temper. I felt awful, I said. I picked up her favourite Iraqi-style falafel and a pack of dark chocolate and went home.

I saw Alice three more times over the Christmas season. Each time, the level of her questions dropped, as if her inquisitive mechanism were growing weary of me.

"My instincts have never been wrong before," she said one night as we sat on the sofa in her parents' house. They'd gone away for the weekend. Alice rested her head on my chest and I put my arm around her. "I have to assume that you're holding something back from me. And that isn't fair."

"Everyone keeps something back," I said. "Do you think anyone on the planet fully reveals themselves to other people? I think we just show one side of ourselves, and we keep the other side hidden from view, like the moon."

"But that's probably what's wrong with the world," she said. "If everyone just pretends to be what they think other people will like, then we'll never really feel accepted or understood. Maybe that's our basic flaw."

"I think our pretences are the things that hold society together. The thing that makes us human is the way we restrain ourselves so that others will accept us. If we all acted the way we felt like, there'd be chaos. There'd be sex and fighting in the streets. We're like molecules holding hands to form a solid. A block of ice say. If we all ran around living out our instincts, free of restraint, the structure would collapse. We'd be water."

"But water can go places that a block of ice never could."

"Okay, maybe that's a bad analogy," I said.

"It's not," Alice said. "I think if we really were free, there would be some of the chaos that you talk about, but we wouldn't all be like that. I'm never tempted to just kill someone on the street or to rip off my clothes and screw someone I fancy on the tube. And in the end, it doesn't really matter what we do. Like you say, we're all just molecules. It's not the individual parts that are important, but the shape of the whole."

"This is your, 'the human race is only around for the blink of a cosmic eye' thing again."

"I still haven't made my mind up about that," Alice said. "I say that, but then I enjoy being alive, and I want to learn things and to experience things, but I don't really know what it's all for."

"Well, that's the big question, isn't it. And I definitely don't have an answer for that one."

"You disappoint me."

"You know," I said. "I can't tell if you're really smart, or really naïve."

Alice laughed and tucked her hair behind her ear. "I can't tell if that's a compliment or an insult."

While Alice made tea for us, I looked at the family photos pinned to the walls. There were only pictures of Alice, her sister and her parents, no friends or relatives, as if they were a genealogical island floating in a sea without time. This gave further evidence towards my theory about her, but I still couldn't entirely grasp it. Maybe I would never fully understand why I had been compelled to follow Alice. I kept asking her questions, as she did to me, and sometimes she'd say something that would make me put together another link, but still it was a mystery. I was now convinced that the universe was playing some kind of game with me, and I just hoped that I would solve it before it tore my family to pieces.

I'd been seeing Alice as often as I could for three months when Beth found the birthday card from her. Beth seldom had reason to go into my work bag, but one day she was looking for the nail scissors and had exhausted every other hiding place in the house.

"What's this?" she said.

"Oh that," I said, and knew instantly that my pause held in it all the gravity of what I'd been doing. "It's a card from someone at work."

Beth ran her fingers along the side of her head — a habit left over from when she had long hair. Her face was red and blotchy, with some barely controlled emotion, and just looking at her made my face feel the same way. We continued an implied conversation, one that had no words, just a heavy silence, like a hot fog filling the room. And then Beth tossed the card onto the table and stormed upstairs.

I gave her a few minutes, thinking about what I would say, and decided that the only way I was going to make things okay would be to tell her the truth, no matter how bizarre it sounded.

I found her upstairs folding sheets on the bed. She was snapping the fabric into neat folds and slamming them down in a pile. She did not look up at me.

"It's not what you think," I said. "I know that sounds stupid, and that's what people always say when they're having an affair, but I promise you I'm not. I'm absolutely not having an affair. Alice is only sixteen. She's . . ."

Beth looked up at me with such horror that I began to doubt myself.

"Sixteen?" she said.

"She's a friend, that's all. I promise."

Beth pushed past me and went back downstairs.

"Please give me a chance to explain," I said, following her.

"Shut up," she snapped from the stairs. "You'll wake Isobel up."

She dropped herself onto the sofa downstairs and I squatted

in front of her. A vulnerable position. She could easily have kicked me in the face from there, and she looked like she wanted to.

"Okay, listen," I began. "A few months ago I was sitting on the bus when I saw this girl a few seats in front, and I could just tell instantly that there was something strange about her."

Beth's eyes were bulging in her head. I had to get to the point quickly, or she really might have done something terrible to me.

"It's hard to explain, but I knew she was Isobel."

Beth's angry eyebrows twitched with confusion.

"Our Isobel," I said. "Our baby, but grown up."

"What?" She screwed up her face and shook her head.

"I can barely make sense of it myself."

Beth started to stand up but I put my hands on her legs to stop her. She smacked my hands away and then sat down and folded her arms. "Go on then," she said. "You explain to me why you're sleeping with a child."

"I promise you, it's nothing like that," I said. I sat on the opposite end of the sofa to her. "I saw this girl on the bus, and I just knew it was her. Our Isobel. But she was grown up. I don't know what it was about her, but it was a parental instinct. It's the only parental instinct I've had."

Beth snorted at this. "Tell me about it," she said.

"She just seemed to glow. Imagine if you met yourself out on the street. That was what it felt like. I don't know how the universe works, and how it's possible, but it was her. When she got off the bus, I knew I couldn't lose her, so I followed her home."

Beth rolled her eyes again and refolded her arms.

"I came home then, but I couldn't stop thinking about her. I've had a pretty ordinary life really, but now something bizarre was happening, something supernatural. I just couldn't let it go. So I went back to her house a few days later, and I sat in the car for hours until I saw her come out with her parents."

"And did her parents look exactly like us?" She raised her eyebrows.

"No, they . . ."

"You're really scaring me," she said. "I think you should go now."

"Please just let me finish. Her parents weren't us, but their daughter was our daughter, only grown up. I can't explain what it was about her. I just felt it so deeply. So I followed her parents' car until they dropped her off at a friend's, and then I followed her and her friend into town. I know it sounds weird, but there was a reason I had seen her, and I had to find out what it was. I followed her a few more times until she noticed me for the first time in Trafalgar Square. When we started talking, I knew there was something special about her. I knew I hadn't been wrong. She's so smart. She knows twice as much as me, but she's half my age."

Beth huffed air out of her nose.

"It's not an affair," I said. "It's our daughter. Can't you see how exciting it was to see her grown up? She's going to be amazing. She's this incredible kid. The thoughts she has in her head, they just sparkle."

"I wish you could hear yourself. You sound absolutely nuts. Do you know what, I think maybe you're not having an affair. Maybe you have just lost it. I'm going to stay with my parents for a few weeks. You can go crazy here by yourself. I don't want you near our daughter, either of them. I can't trust you."

So Beth left, but I had to see Alice again, just one last time.

I sent her a text message and asked her to meet me outside the station, and then I took her to the Natural History Museum. It was my favourite place as a kid, and I'd always thought that if ever I had kids, I would take them there as often as possible.

"Did you know," she said, as we walked through the stuffed birds exhibit, "that young cuckoos find their way to Africa in the winter without any help from their real parents? They hatch in another bird's nest, but somehow they still know that they're cuckoos and they know where to go."

"I did know that," I said. "There are still more mysteries in the world than explanations. And wouldn't it be awful to live in a world where everything had a reason?"

"I guess so, but then, why do we work so hard to explain everything?"

"Maybe the human race is just hard wired to shoot itself in the foot, to do something even though we know it will bring us misery eventually."

"I thought I was supposed to be the pessimist," she said.

I held her hand and smiled. "Can I show you the blue whale?" I asked.

"I've seen it before."

"Can I show it to you anyway?"

"Sure."

We stood in front of the blue whale and looked up at the massive creature, flanked by two skeletal companions. It looked more real when I was a kid. There were only a few people in the gallery with us, but lots of dolphins and whales swimming through the air.

"What would it be like to swim with a blue whale?" Alice asked.

"I think I'd be terrified," I said.

"But they don't eat people."

"I'd still be terrified. Something that big, moving. I'd be like a caveman seeing a dinosaur for the first time."

"Cavemen and dinosaurs weren't around at the same time."

"I knew that. Bad analogy."

"It looks so lonely," Alice said.

We walked along the length of the blue whale and I wondered whether you could swim around inside one.

"Listen," I said, stopping and putting my hand on Alice's shoulder. "I've got to tell you something." Alice looked up at me, and she was so lovely. I felt awful. "This is crazy, but my wife thinks I'm having an affair with you."

Alice's cheeks flushed red, and she looked like she was about to say something and stopped.

"She's really gone nuts about it," I said. "And I can't explain to her the relationship we have. I . . . this is the last thing I want to do, believe me, I would love to spend every day with you like this. You're all I think about. But I don't think it's such a good . . . we can't get together like this anymore."

When I stopped, the only sound in the gallery was the slow heartbeat of the blue whale. The walls reverberated with it. While I watched red estuaries fill up the space beneath Alice's cheeks, my vision wavered, as if the room were full of water. Tiny organisms darted between us.

We stood like that for four of the blue whale's ponderous heartbeats, and then saltwater began to leak out of her eyes and she ran away from me. I called after her, and followed her, but lost her in the maze of corridors. I ran right out to the main entrance and looked down the path from the museum, but she wasn't there. She couldn't have got away so quickly. I walked the galleries for the next few hours, imagining her crying, crouched in a primate exhibit, their cold glass eyes consoling her. But I didn't find her.

When I left, I felt like I'd been stuffed and my bones replaced with mechanical armatures. The thought of going back to a life without Alice was unbearable.

On the tube on the way home, I thought about baby Isobel. If I didn't screw things up with Beth, I would get to see Isobel grow up into Alice, and it wouldn't be long before I'd be able to take her to the Natural History Museum, or into town to see the Christmas lights.

I got a text message from Alice a week later, just when I was getting used to the idea of life without her. She said, "Now I know why I met you." That was all. And I could only imagine what awful lesson about the betrayal of trust or friendship she had learned from me.

I never saw Alice again. I resisted the urge to go to her house. To do so would just restart the whole process of my marriage dissolving. But I did look out for her wherever I went, hoping to catch a fragment of her smile across a crowd, or to see her push her hair behind her ear one more time, and imagine that somehow I was important to her.

INSTRUCTION MANUAL
FOR SWALLOWING

I was driving to work this morning and became aware that I'd travelled two-thirds of the way — a journey of more than ten miles — without being conscious of it. I remember getting into the car and pulling out of the drive and waving to the guy who walks his kids to school at the same time every day. The next thing I remember after that was seeing the speed camera outside the glass pyramid building and pressing the brakes. I'd been driving for over ten minutes and had no memory of it. My subconscious had been driving the car.

Should I be worried about it? My autopilot managed to get me that far safely. Maybe if I hadn't seen the speed camera and been forced to take control of the car I would have remained unaware the whole way. My subconscious might have carried on in the driving seat even after I'd stepped out of the car. My day always tends to follow the same kind of routine. What if I went about my whole day unconsciously? Maybe one day I'd see a speed camera and hit the brakes and realise thirty years had passed. I might get to be an old man without experiencing anything consciously.

So the rest of the journey I started thinking about my

subconscious, imagining it as another person within me. In this daydream he looked like Busta Rhymes (because a Busta Rhymes track was on the radio at the time) wearing a waxed trench coat, sou'wester and wellingtons. I imagined that Busta moves around my subconscious turning stopcocks, pulling levers and scraping leaves from the floor with an oversized spade. In my subconscious, time moves slowly, so slowly that Busta might spend a whole day just making the necessary moves to allow me to swallow a piece of muffin.

Time is so different in Busta's world, that those lost ten minutes were a fortnight.

I got to thinking about all the other things Busta takes care of. He makes sure I blink enough. He keeps my blood moving through my body. He processes the food I eat and excretes what I don't need. He makes my toenails grow and slowly feeds hairs through my scalp (why?). Some of these things can be placed under my control. Busta winds the lung machine thousands of times in one of my days, but I can take control. Does this piss Busta off? If I go from Busta's regular slow breaths, which release a precise stream of oxygen into my blood, to a frenetic burst of panting, or even holding my breath, does Buster wonder what I am doing? Maybe he thinks his boss is a madman. What if I blink my eyes as fast as I can, trying to make them flutter like butterfly wings — for what possible reason can he think I am doing this?

I wondered whether I could communicate with Busta by interrupting his work. I've seen documentaries about monks who can control their body through meditation. They can slow their heart rate, or galvanise their white blood cells to fight off infections faster than the average person. The monks might have reached, through meditation, some kind of accord with their own Bustas. I could see the benefit of having this kind of relationship with one's internal operator. I'd like to be able to persuade Busta to give me confidence boosts when I am nervous about making a presentation, or make my skin exude powerful pheromones when I'm trying to chat up a woman. Or maybe I could persuade him to put unnecessary stuff on the back burner (hair growing for example) to put double time into more impressive things — like helping me leap over cars or break wooden boards with my bare hands.

The more I thought about it, the more I became convinced that if I could make contact with Busta, I could transform myself. It might be that Busta has no idea what the modern person requires of an internal operator. His instruction manual might have been written forty thousand years ago, and he's been running my body to fit the environment of that time. How great would it be to go through this instruction manual with Busta and tell him exactly how I'd like my body run? Bring him up to speed on some modern management techniques?

I didn't much fancy spending forty years on a mountain somewhere, eating rice and groaning to the accompaniment of drums and handclaps. I preferred the idea of engaging with the autopilot by usurping the controls. And so that's what I did.

I picked a night when there was nothing amazing on television, and when Elkie, my ex-wife, would be at pilates and was unlikely to pop round. I unplugged the phone and climbed up to the top of the house — a converted attic. Its sloped ceiling was reminiscent of a pyramid and seemed fitting for what I was about to do. I didn't light any candles, because I was afraid that I might burn the house down in my altered state, so I threw one of Elkie's old scarves over the top of a lamp to create the right mood.

All the heat the house had stored up during the day had floated up to the attic, so that even in my underpants I was sweating. I planned to attempt contact with Busta in complete silence, but I live in a terraced house, and my neighbour on one side always has her TV on full blast, so I brought up a Walkman and put on a didgeridoo tape from my student days. These sounds would put me in a state of altered consciousness, even if it were only one of profound irritation.

First I tried to make myself hyperventilate. Then I took the deepest breath I could and held it until my whole body started twitching with panic. Next I tried the eyelid fluttering thing. I wasn't getting anywhere. I felt too conscious. I needed to transport myself deep into my own guts. My head was hanging too tightly to the real world.

I hadn't owned any drugs for over twenty years and didn't know where I could buy some. It's ironic that it was so easy to get hold of dope at school, when all I had was pocket money, yet now I wouldn't have a clue how to get some, and I could afford to buy as much as I liked.

I had a bottle of Jack Daniel's and an almost full pack of codeine pills in the cupboard. I did half the pack of pills with half the bottle of whiskey. If it sounds like I was trying to kill myself, I can assure you that I wasn't. Quite the opposite in fact. I was trying to shake myself alive, from the inside.

I changed the didgeridoo tape to one called *Om*. It's a load of blokes chanting "om" over and over. That, plus the pills and booze, made me feel quite otherworldly. I tried the breathing thing again, puffing and panting in short breaths, making it look like I was laughing.

I had this glorious moment when the whisky and codeine and breathing all kicked in together, and I felt weightless then heavy, weightless then heavy, as if I were bobbing up and down on a vast ocean whose peaks licked the stars and whose troughs scraped the earth's crust. I felt like these waves were carrying me somewhere, taking me to Busta. But then I slammed back into my body as it leaned over and gushed half-digested pills and booze and falafel all over the floor. My guts contracted again and again, trying to eject everything, and when there was nothing left to come, I hovered on the edge of one of these retches, unable to breathe, my eyes bulging.

This was when I met Busta.

He looked exactly like he did in my imagination. Just like Busta Rhymes, but wearing an ancient sou'wester and macintosh and long wellingtons. He was carrying a plunger. Something like ectoplasm was dripping from his waterproofs and the end of his nose. He wiped at it with the back of his sleeve and looked at me the way you might look at an old dog that's just shat all over the kitchen while you've got friends round for dinner.

I started to speak, but Busta waved his hand in front of his mouth, silencing me. He gestured around the room with his eyes, and I translated this to mean that talking might interrupt the machinery. And the room was full of machinery. And when I say room, I'm not conveying the size of this place at all. It was like being in the engine room of an enormous ship. There were metal pipes and steam and rivets everywhere. Levers stuck out of consoles, and arrays of dials clustered around pipes like colonies of industrial fungus. The air rang with the puff and wheeze of hot steam flying through valves and water dripping from great heights. The air smelled salty. It was all so mechanical, so turn-of-the-last-century.

I opened my mouth again, about to ask where the computers were, to ask why Busta had to negotiate a gargantuan engine room to keep me going, when he could probably do the whole thing from a laptop in a café, but Busta put his hand in front of my mouth. He wore a fingerless glove, and it smelled of old pennies. He used this hand to point to the floor, where there was a trapdoor. He leaned down to open it. The trapdoor looked like it should weigh a tonne, but Busta lifted it with ease.

If I'd been shocked to see that my inner workings hadn't been updated since 1900, this was nothing compared to when I saw that through the trapdoor, there was a mountain range of clouds, and a ladder that disappeared into the slowly churning surface.

Busta climbed down this ladder and gestured that I should follow.

The air outside the engine room was icy and pure. The perspiration in my palms froze to the rungs of the ladder. The air was so crisp that it hurt my lungs to breathe. White clouds whirled below us, curled into creamy eddies by the wind. I kept my eyes on Busta, wondering how far we would climb down. I was sweating, despite the cold, because I had the worst vertigo I've ever had in my life. I didn't know how far above land we were, even if there was land below us.

I looked up and saw the underside of the engine room. It was a copper-gold colour, made of panels riveted together, and it gleamed in the white light. It curved away from me, like the belly of a whale. Above me, the trapdoor we had come through was a gloomy hole, but I longed to climb up, terrified that at any moment the clouds would part and I would see that I was far enough above the earth to discern continents.

And then Busta stopped. The upper wisps of cloud were licking around his grimy boots. He looked up at me, his face weathered with centuries of rust and oil. "What the hell were you thinking, you moron?" he said. His voice was throaty, like he was recovering from a phlegmy cold. "Screw you and screw your job, you can stick it up your arse!" And with that, he let go of the ladder and leapt from it, spreading his arms wide.

He looked up at me as he plummeted towards the clouds, then pierced through them, a small, dark T shape.

My hand was outstretched towards him, and my heart was thumping in my chest. The blood was gushing round my body so fast it was making me weak, and I barely had the strength to grip the ladder.

"Hello!" I called down.

I hung there in the icy wind for a few minutes, until my eyeballs began to creak in their sockets they were so cold. I looked up. I looked down. Which way should I go? Maybe Busta was playing a trick on me and was sitting on a cloud just out of my range of sight? I took twenty steps down, counting them as I went. The ladder went down forever into the clouds. I was so cold I was losing my grip. If I didn't turn back then, I may never have had the strength to get back up. I climbed, moving faster each rung, desperate to get into the sweaty warmth of the engine room.

I panicked when I put my hands onto the floor. If my arms didn't have the strength to lift me up through the trapdoor, I might fall and fall forever. I took time over the simple procedure of climbing through the trapdoor, because I didn't want to get it wrong. Once inside, I rolled onto my back and stared up into the great machine room.

The ceiling was so far above me that it was lost in darkness. The machines ground on, bashing and clonking life through my body. Busta was gone, and Busta had kept things running. What did that mean?

I wondered whether there was anyone else there. Maybe a whole race of Bustas worked the machines that kept me going, and the loss of one would make no difference. I took in breath to call out, then held it because Busta seemed to think making any noise was a bad idea, which didn't make sense, as the machines were making more sound than I could ever produce.

I got up and started walking through the engine room, kicking piles of decaying leaves as I went, wondering how they came to be there. I could see no light sources, but there was light for me to see the machines. I passed a row of what looked like boilers, thirty long and hundreds high, each sprouting four pipes and making a low churring noise, the needles in their readouts flicking from one side to the other in unison.

I passed an enormous tank, big enough to hold several swimming pools of water. Through a glass panel in the side I could see a green liquid, bubbling. I touched the surface and it was hot. There were structures like these everywhere, many far above me with ladders that stretched up to meet them. If you can imagine a boiler room designed by Escher, this is where I was.

And then I came to a great metal wall, which stretched up and to both sides further than I could see. Its surface was made of plates the size of cinema screens bolted together with rivets I could just fit inside my cupped hand. In this metal edifice was a small door. It was copper, with a window that was opaque with grime, like an ancient oven door with decades of fat burned on. The handle turned easily.

The space inside took my breath away. On the other side of the door I found a dome-shaped hall, in which planes could perform landing circles. It was white and clean, and filled with thousands of windows and doors. At the apex was a white circle of light, so pure and dazzling that it made my eyes sore to look at it, and I had to look back through into the dark engine room to soothe them. Ladders ran up and down the surface of the dome, but I couldn't imagine anything other than spiders being able to ascend these ladders.

The floor of the dome was covered in concave pits, which were just the right size to lie within, and this is what I did. I lay down in one of these great dimples and stared up into the dome of light, contemplating the windows and doors and wondering what they would lead to. It would take several lifetimes to explore all of these entrances.

And then I grew afraid, because there was no sign of anyone else, and Busta was gone. What would happen if there were no one to operate the machines? How could I get out again? Would I be trapped here until the machines that made my body work chugged to a halt and I died? How long would that take? I looked at my watch. The second hand wasn't moving.

"What am I supposed to do?" I asked quietly.

As if in response, the vast dome erupted into life, the windows and doors revolving on thousands of horizontal planes, hurling round in one direction, then clicking into place and slowly turning back a few clicks. It felt like I was watching the tumblers of a great lock. The rows stopped one by one, until only a few were spinning as if searching for their correct place. When the final one stopped, a bright white spike of light erupted from the side furthest away from me, stretching up to the central white light at the top.

I clambered out of the convex dip in the ground and ran towards this light, seeing as I got closer that it was an opening in the surface of the dome.

I don't know what I hoped I'd find on the other side, the answer to the great mysteries of life, a room full of machinery operators, all the people I'd ever known. Least of all did I expect to find a library.

The library was tall and thin. If I'd lain down on the floor, my head and feet would be close to touching either side, but it was tall enough for there to be hundreds of rows of books. Several ladders on wheels were placed around the sides so that any book could be reached. I read the spines of the books, and occasionally saw ones that I recognised but had not read. There were books by Dickens, Nabokov, William Burroughs, in no particular order, not organised by date or genre or even fiction and non-fiction. I moved to take a book down from the shelf and found it stuck. At first I thought that maybe this was because they were packed in so tightly, but when I applied more force, the whole row shifted slightly. They were fakes, like the rows of plastic books you get in furniture stores. What did that mean? I moved from row to row, tugging at the books, and every time it was the same. Fakes.

I climbed back down to the ground, and for the first time noticed a wooden chest. Within it were real books that I could pick up and flick through. They were instruction manuals, filled with diagrams of machines, all the components labelled with letters and numbers. The titles were plain: *the throat, gaseous exchange, bile production, perspiration, the tongue.* These books did not have authors. There were hundreds of them.

I've been reading through the books in the chest now for what seems like weeks. It could take forever to learn how to operate my body, and I guess this is what I have to do if I am to stay alive. My life depends on my ability to work this machinery, but the crazy thing is that I just can't seem to retain any information from the manuals. They're really dull.

I wonder what made Busta do the work? There seems to be no incentive at all. A big part of me just feels like chucking it in. Even if I did manage to get everything going, if my body is just stretched out unconscious in the attic, I won't live for long anyway without food and water.

I keep thinking back to the image of Busta leaping from the ladder and falling through the clouds. And I try to remember what expression he had on his face as he fell. Was it happiness, or a grim acceptance that all was at an end? I wonder whether I too should leap from the ladder, but I think that would be too big a leap of faith.

MEATY'S BOYS

Meaty's boys came back, their bags bulging. Their eyes were wide with coke, and the hair on their forearms was plastered to their skin with blood. They strode through the kitchen with their chins high, arms swinging. Dan, the great ape of the pack, pointed his finger, gun-like, at Reed and winked. Reed gave a little upwards nod in reply, then set the pile of clean plates by the serving hatch.

There was always a feeling of elation when the boys came back, of abundance. Even though their foraging expeditions took them out daily, you could never be sure when or even if they would return. Meaty would greet them with wide wobbly arms and a prickly grin. "Boys! My boys!" He would smile, drooling over the bags. If the bags were light in their hands, Meaty's smile would soon fade, and everyone at the café would keep their heads down for the rest of the night. But on days like this, when the bags were bulging, things poking out from inside, Meaty's mood was high.

"Wash up boys, then get out on the gate," Meaty said, taking the bags from them and dragging them across to his block.

"Wait up," Dan said rubbing his bicep with a bloody hand. "Troy's got some more."

Troy dragged another bag into the kitchen, this one too big to lift. At first, Meaty made a wide grin that showed his teeth, and even his tongue, but then his brow dropped over his eyes, and his lips came together, flabby and fish-like.

"Where'd you get all this?" he asked. His hands were on his hips, his great belly pushing against his apron.

"At the turners' camp," Dan said.

"How many'd you get?"

"Ten."

"Ten?" Meaty played with the flesh on his face. "Okay boys, okay. Good haul."

The boys, Dan, Troy, Wes and Albie, crowded round the sink. They stuck their arms into it and lathered up with soap. Reed blasted away the blood and pink froth with the pressure hose, paying special attention to a string of meat caught under Dan's watch.

The boys dried their hands on Reed's hair and T-shirt, laughing. "Thanks, guys," Reed said. "Can I get any of you some moisturizer?"

Dan stuck his fingers up at Reed as he opened the metal cupboard and got out the credit card reader.

"You got a lot tonight," Reed said.

"Yup," Dan said. "It was a good hunt. You should come with us sometime."

Reed smiled and nodded, not meeting Dan's gaze. Dan slammed the metal door, and the boys marched out behind him, rubbing their shoulders and groaning from their afternoon of exertions.

At the chopping block, Meaty began laying into the boys' catch, slamming a cleaver into the meat, breaking it into portions. Layla pushed the kitchen door open with her hip. "They're coming, Meaty," she said. "Are you ready to plate up?" Most of her hair had escaped from her ponytail, and was hanging about her face, strands sticking to her forehead. She winked at Reed and warmth rushed through him.

"Yeah yeah yeah," Meaty said, "almost there." He arranged chopped up medallions of an arm on plates. "The rest'll be a couple of minutes." He wiped his nose with the back of his fist. His body wobbled each time he slammed the cleaver into the board. Breaking up the arms and legs was the grunt work of his job, the bit where he worked up a sweat. When he turned to the head, that was where he became an artist. Reed doubted that the preparation meant anything to Meaty's customers, but Meaty still put in the extra effort, slicing up the brain up into neat cutlets, drizzling them with the juices he scraped from the board, and then arranging around them the internal tangle of tubes and cubed organs.

Meaty insisted that this level of detail was important, and it was his source of self respect. But Reed wondered what difference it really made. Layla said she had once seen one of the customers leave the brains till the end, maybe saving the best till last. It was unnerving when they displayed familiar human characteristics. Much easier just to think of them like animals. And Reed needed coping mechanisms to survive at Meaty's.

"I'm opening the doors," Layla called through from the café.

"Alright, alright," Meaty called through, "it's coming."

Reed could hear the customers begin to groan as they shuffled towards the café, a deep and rattling sound that always made him shiver. He'd worked at Meaty's place for six months, but he could never get used to that sound.

Layla came back into the kitchen and wiped her forehead with the back of her arm.

"Are there many tonight?" Reed asked.

"A lot, yeah."

As the door to the café swung closed, Reed saw a flash of activity through the gap, and his heart knocked against the inside of his chest. He thought for a second one of them was about to come through to the kitchen.

A drip of sweat fell from Reed's nose and splashed onto a plate as he lined them up alongside Meaty's chopping block. He wiped it away with a cloth, which was tucked into his back pocket. It wasn't that he thought the customers would care about, or even notice, a drip of sweat beneath their meat. He didn't want them tasting even a tiny part of him, for fear they would become excited by it, excited enough to throw themselves over the serving counter and come for him.

Meaty arranged neat slices of leg on the next set of plates, with a curved rib lying on top, ragged and pink. Layla picked up two plates. "Come on," she said. "it's filling up out there." Reed followed behind Layla, taking a deep breath before he stepped into the café, the food shaking on his plates.

Reed's favourite part of the day was the journey home. Moving back into normality. Every minute of the drive once he was through the old world perimeter, the layers of decrepitude peeled away, revealing an ordinary city. And how sweet the lights were after a night at Meaty's place, and the sounds of reality, away from the moan and dragged footsteps of the customers.

Reed stopped at a red light, watching the line of cars shoot by in front of him. The tail-lights left vapour trails on his tired eyes. He blinked. He had come close to falling asleep on this same journey home several times. A night at Meaty's was enough to suck all the vigour from his limbs. The journey home was when his mind released its protective layer of fog, covering up the sights and sounds and smells of the night's work, numbing him enough to be able to face another day tomorrow.

The car behind Reed honked its horn, and he pulled away through the green light. He switched on the radio and an old Police track came on — "Walking on the Moon." A group of drunk teenagers ran into the road in front of the car and beat their hands on the bonnet, before sticking their fingers up at Reed, then running back to the pavement. Six months ago, Reed's heart would have been thumping with fear after that kind of thing, but working at Meaty's place had changed him. Real people weren't threatening at all anymore. Nothing in the real world could evoke the fear he felt every time he went into the old world.

Reed lay in bed watching light from the advertising screen outside the window flicker across the wall. He sprayed himself with more water and enjoyed the chill as it evaporated from his skin. There was no breeze tonight, but that was a mercy, because in the summer, the old world oozed a funky smell that could carry fifty miles if the wind was right.

He'd woken up after a nightmare in which the world beneath the floor had dropped away, and he was walking on a thin veneer that cracked with every footstep. And under the floor, the fingers and teeth of the old world were waiting for him.

He got up and made himself some tea. The sounds of the spoon against the cup and of the water rumbling inside the kettle helped to pull him out of the bleak reverie left in the wake of his dream.

He wanted to phone someone, but he didn't know anyone that would appreciate a call at 3 a.m. He tried to picture what Layla was doing at that moment. He imagined her asleep, a thin sheet tucked between her legs and clutched against her chest. And he clung to this image for safety as his thoughts turned again to the weight of the old worlders pushing against the perimeter fence, their mouths no longer capable of forming words, spilling thick strands of dribble down their fronts and splashing in the grime at their feet.

Reed showed his pass at the gate to the old world, and then at the inner gate. Once this place had been a thriving commuter belt — hundreds of thousands of families living in medium-sized towns. American-style coffee bars and Waterstones bookshops were evidence of the lifestyles of the people who used to live here. But now these places were rotten teeth erupting from the ground. Along the A1, the towns of Stevenage, Hitchin and Letchworth, all the way up to Biggleswade and Sandy, had become joined into one great city of the dead, the old world.

Reed drove the truck down the access road along the side of the inner perimeter, past the turners' camp. Eerily, this place used to be a village called Gravely, as if it knew its destiny. The only people that ever used this road were research scientists and those that worked at Meaty's, and the occasional die-hard office workers who came hunting as a team building exercise — completely illegal, but popular.

It was early afternoon when Reed began his shift, and most of the old worlders were hidden away within the buildings, resting their rusty faces against each other, curled up on carpets and sofas and tucked in, four to a bed. The old worlders didn't maintain the family groups they'd belonged to when they were alive, but they appeared to enjoy each other's company. They had their own comfort places. The same groups would go back to the same houses at dawn, exhausted after a hard night of eating and fucking, and they would rest together, even though they had never known each other in the new world or exchanged more than a leaking accidental smile since they turned.

As Reed arrived, Meaty's boys were on their way out, loading machetes and plastic sacks into the back of the jeep. The jeep was dented on all sides, with scrapes along its body where the boys had only just escaped with their lives. Or maybe they'd used the jeep as a hunting tool itself. They would occasionally turn up with damaged meat, which Meaty would reject — always a perfectionist. Meaty tossed these bruised fruits over the perimeter fence to the waiting crowd of shufflers. This bloody manna was always gratefully received, the old worlders dropping to the ground to tear it apart with their teeth and lick the juice from each other's faces. Without this meat, they'd have to survive on the slurry of roadkill and hospital waste that local councils piled into the dumps around the edges of the old world.

"Want to come with us?" Dan said. He brushed dirt from his hands onto his jeans and scratched his stomach.

Reed shielded his eyes from the sun as he stepped out of his car. "Not today, thanks. Meaty'll throw a shit-fit if I'm not here to help him with the preparation."

"We'll only be a couple of hours," Dan said. "We'll get you back in plenty of time for opening." He made a thick knot of his arms across his chest.

Troy and the other two boys climbed up into the jeep, and it sank lower to the ground under their weight.

"No, don't worry," Reed said. "There's not really room for me in the jeep anyway."

"You're only small. We could squeeze you in."

"It's okay," Reed showed Dan his palm, looking round at the back entrance to Meaty's as it opened.

Meaty stuck his muzzle out of the door. "You still 'ere?" he barked.

Dan lifted both his hands in a surrender gesture and

climbed up into the jeep. Reed closed his eyes against the cloud of dust kicked up as the boys moved out along the perimeter fence, towards the turners' camp.

In the kitchen, flies were gathered at the plughole in the sink, flying up into clouds whenever anyone walked past. The air was thick and stinky, tiring to breathe. It left an oily taste on the back of Reed's tongue.

Layla lifted a box of tools up onto the counter, creasing up her face with the weight of it. Sweat stained her cropped top and ran in a glistening trail down her smooth, bare back. "The air con's out again," she said.

"Do you need a hand?" he asked.

"Sure, you can pass me stuff while I've got my head in the ceiling."

Layla dragged the table from the middle of the room until it was underneath the air conditioning unit. She tucked a screwdriver into the back pocket of her shorts, then climbed up onto the table. She pushed up the ceiling tile alongside the unit and stuck her head through the hole.

"Torch," she said, reaching her hand out.

Reed opened up the toolbox and rummaged through, nicking the back of his hand on an old wrench. He passed the torch up to Layla and couldn't help taking the opportunity to admire her legs. Even in the new world they were perfect, but here, in the old world, they were divine. They were underwear model legs. These columns of perfect flesh, between the top of her dusty leather boots and the frayed denim edge of her shorts made Reed's blood quicken.

"Pliers," she said, her hand down again.

Reed felt an ache in his stomach as he longed to touch the creamy skin on her thigh. In the ceiling, Layla hit metal on metal. "Damn," she said. "Get up here and help me. I need a third hand."

Reed stood up on the table. "Where do you want me?"

"I need you to clamp this bit with the pliers, while I unscrew this bit."

Reed put his head up into the ceiling alongside Layla's. The hole was small. As soon as the side of his body touched hers, sweat began to pour out of him.

"Grab these," Layla said, handing him the pliers. "And hold that bolt still while I . . ." The edge of the ceiling hole dug into Reed's back, and as Layla struggled for purchase on the screwdriver, she pushed against him. A sweet perfume evaporated from her hot skin and filled the space between them with an intoxicating dew.

She cursed again as her hand slipped.

"What's up?" He asked.

"I just need to . . ." She moved one of her arms between his arms, her elbow pushing onto the side of his head.

With the better angle, Layla grunted at the screw, blowing her sticky hair from her eyes, until the screw slipped in its threading and came undone.

"Hah," she said. "Thank you."

Reed loosened his grip on the pliers, but held them there. "Do you need some more help?"

"It's okay, I've got it." She moved her hand around his, taking his grip on the pliers. Reed twisted to move out of the hole, but lingered when their faces were close together, and in this moment of desperation, he felt the urge to kiss her so strongly that it hurt to resist.

Meaty's boys were late. The old worlders were groaning at the fences, shaking the mesh against the posts in their impatience.

Reed, Layla and Meaty could hear the metallic clashing from the kitchen. Meaty perched his corpulent form on the corner of his chopping board, arms folded, cleaver in hand.

"If they're not back soon, I'm serving them up," he said.

Reed leaned back on his chair, one knee up against the table. Layla sat on the edge of the table, one hand so close to his knee that he could have sensed it if his eyes were closed.

Meaty opened the door between the kitchen and the café and looked out. From here, the big windows gave a full view of the perimeter. "They're gonna break that fence down," he said.

"They can't do that, can they?" Reed asked.

Layla put her hand on his knee. "They make a lot of noise, but they're feeble," she said.

While Meaty was ranting about the acts of violence he was going to commit on Dan, they all heard the jeep pull up outside. It arrived with a sharp skid, its tyres crunching the ground. And then the doors were thrown open, the mechanism making a pained click against the force. Dan's words were full of panic, his footsteps urgent. Reed stood up alongside Layla, his hand on the table just behind her back.

Meaty was at his block, his hands on his hips, when the boys tumbled into the kitchen. Dan, Troy and Wes were carrying Albie between then, a shoulder or leg each. Meaty rushed towards them, dropping his coarse demeanour in a moment of genuine concern. But then he saw the blood splashed all over Albie, and he backed away.

"You can't bring him in here," he said.

"What happened?" Layla said.

Albie was screwing his face up and grinding his teeth together. Little sputters of pain were slipping through his lips along with his short stuttering breaths.

"You can't put him on there." Meaty took a step back as the boys laid Albie on the kitchen table.

"He's not infected," Dan said.

Reed dragged a wooden bench to the side of the kitchen and went into a top cupboard, where Meaty kept candles, grenades and the first aid kit. He tossed the kit across the room to Troy.

"He can't stay here," Meaty's cleaver had come to his hands.

"Where did this happen?" Layla said.

"There's nothing in here," Troy said, emptying the first aid kit onto the table, pushing the plasters and sterilising wipes around with his fingers.

"Get the fuck away from him," Dan said, holding out his hand to Meaty, a brave gesture, as Meaty's cleaver was now pointed at the boys.

Albie gasped, and a fresh spurt of blood soaked through the side of his t-shirt.

From outside, the groans of the old worlders shifted up a gear as their only sense heightened by zombification picked up the delicious odour of fresh blood, the freshest they'd smelled in a long time. And the chain-link fence rattled against its supports as they heaved and salivated against it.

"Will that fence hold?" Reed said.

"Did you get any food that Meaty can start on?" Layla asked, moving round to the café door to check what was happening outside.

"I want him out of here," Meaty said. "We're all fucked if he stays."

"Back off," Dan said, getting right up in Meaty's face. "It wasn't one of them."

Dan told Wes to go to the jeep, and he returned a moment later with a full sack.

The gate outside made a shrill metallic squeak as its bolts struggled beneath the pressure.

"Jesus," Reed said. "They're gonna break it down."

Meaty looked over Troy's shoulder at Albie on the table, then back, in the direction of the café. He didn't move, and a blank expression of detachment smoothed away the anger and fear that had creased it moments before.

"Reed," Layla said. "Give me a hand with the bag." Reed and Layla picked up the plastic sack and dumped it on Meaty's chopping block. Wes went back outside. "Meaty, get chopping this lot up," Layla said.

Meaty came back to himself and pointed his cleaver at Dan, "And then you're gonna tell me what the fuck happened."

Layla washed her hands in the sink. "You'll have to take him to hospital," she said. "There's nothing you can do here."

Dan and Troy looked at each other, and Dan rubbed his face with his palms, running his fingers through his hair, then linked them behind his head.

Reed helped Wes pull in another sack of body bits. Albie rolled onto his side and groaned, his face bunched up with pain. Reed looked through the kitchen door. The fence was bulging where old worlders were clambering over each other to push against it.

Meaty's cleaver was a metronome on the chopping block, slamming out a rapid beat. He slid the chopped pieces across to Layla and she put them onto serving platters, not bothering with the pleasing arrangements Meaty would usually make.

On the table, Albie passed out. "Dan, you've got to get him to hospital," Layla said.

Meaty, now sweaty and red in the face from his ferocious chopping, spat as he spoke, "You lot start letting them in before they take the fence down. Reed, you take 'im to the 'ospital."

Reed looked at the unconscious man on the table, then at Dan, who was already taking out guns and the credit card reader. "Did you say it wasn't one of them?"

"He's not infected," Dan said. "I'll help you lift him into the jeep." Dan grabbed one of Albie's arms, and Reed grabbed the other, trying to keep the blood off himself. They dragged Albie through the kitchen and outside, where the moans of the old worlders filled the air with a sharp stink.

They stretched Albie out on the back seat, still unconscious, and then Dan ran back towards the café. Wes and Troy were waiting for him at the door, guns in hand, machetes tucked into their belts. They passed him two jackets — one of leather, one of chainmail, the same as they were wearing.

Reed got into the car and watched the boys walking towards the perimeter gate, where the old worlders were heaving against the fence, pressing their faces against the wire, turning their birch-bark flesh into swirling marble.

The boys pointed their machine guns at the old worlders in front of the gate, and when they didn't move back, they let out a few bursts of fire. The dead things shook as the bullets went through them, then gazed down at the place the bullets had entered, absently fingering these little orifices.

The boys raised their guns again, and the zombies under-stood this time. They shuffled back from the gate enough to allow Troy to push it open. Dan then stood in front of the open perimeter with the credit card reader. Troy and Wes gestured with their guns for the old worlders to come forward. One by one they lurched through, flaps of skin and fingernails raining on the ground as they rummaged in their pockets. Old worlders were only capable of the most basic human functions, eating, fucking and sleeping, but nearly all retained the ability to get out their credit cards. Dan took each card in turn and swiped it, before handing the card back. He nodded at the first old worlder, and the second, and they continued on towards Meaty's place. When Dan scanned the third old worlder, he shook his head. Wes stepped in, pushed the machine gun against the zombie's head, and disintegrated it with one squeeze of the trigger.

The force of the blast knocked the old worlder backwards. Troy dragged the body to the side, and Dan gestured for the next old worlder to come forwards.

Reed switched on the engine and pulled away, driving around the edge of the outer perimeter. He turned the radio up as the sound of gunfire came again.

Reed exhaled slowly, realising he'd been holding his breath. He looked at his passenger in the rear-view mirror. Blood was coming out of Albie and making blotting paper of the back seat. His eyes were squeezed shut, his teeth gritted.

"Are you okay?" Reed asked.

Albie made a strained noise but no words.

As Reed came to the boundary of the old world, he felt a change in the atmosphere around the car, as if a heavy cloud had moved away overhead. It was as if the earth's magnetism shifted polarity when he entered the new world, or gravity weakened, releasing weight from his limbs.

The hospital was close to the boundary of the turners' camp — convenient for those poor bastards diagnosed and then expelled from the new world, the real world. Reed pulled up in front of A&E and switched off the engine.

"We're here," he said, as if he was a taxi and expected Albie to get up and check himself in. Albie didn't reply. Reed wouldn't have a hope of lifting him by himself. "I'm gonna go in and get some help," he said.

Albie's face had changed. It was a look Reed had never seen before, but he knew what it meant. Reed could tell that Albie was no longer animated. And yet he went into the hospital, and said he had someone in his car who'd been injured. Somehow he thought things would go better if he checked Albie in while he thought he was still alive.

It took eight hours to process Albie's body. Reed filled in the forms, answered questions, was moved into different rooms with different forms, different posters on the wall, different marks on the floor, different fingerprints on the windows.

Night came. Staff finished their shift, and new staff came in, and he told the story to them too. A fake story of course. If he told them he'd brought Albie out of the old world, they'd stick him in quarantine for two weeks. Instead, he pretended that he didn't know Albie, that he'd found him a few blocks away, apparently the victim of an attack.

Even though he'd given a fake name and address, he felt obliged to stay at the hospital until they'd dismissed him, or maybe he was grateful of the excuse to stay away from Meaty's. While he sat in the waiting room, he imagined what would be going on there. He imagined the boys leaning back on their chairs, clutching cigarettes in their lips, Meaty wiping his hands on his bloody apron, Layla blowing her hair out of her eyes.

Reed got back to Meaty's place just after midnight. There were only a few old worlders outside, on their hands and knees, eating scraps of their comrades who'd not had enough cash in their accounts to get into the café. Old worlders would turn to cannibalism if they couldn't get anything else.

On the dirt outside the café was a square of bright light which shone through the huge front windows, projecting the shadows of the old worlders. Some were still civilised enough to sit on stools, backs arched, driving their faces into their plates of meat. When Reed got out of the jeep, he could hear them eating, a sickening sound, like hundreds of dogs lapping at bowls of water.

Heavy cloud cover kept in the heat of the day, and there was no breeze. A sour smell moved in the air. Reed wondered whether if he worked at Meaty's long enough, that smell would become a part of him, something that couldn't be washed out, and he shivered.

At the kitchen table, Layla, Dan and the boys were slumped over, exhausted. Meaty worked at his chopping block with a pink rag.

"How's Albie?" Dan said. He had been resting his forehead on the top of a bottle of beer, and there was a red circle pressed into his skin.

Reed shook his head and made a sorrowful shape with his mouth. Dan exhaled loudly across the table and rubbed his face with his hands. "He was dead before I got to the hospital."

Layla pushed herself up from the table with her hands, her hair hanging about her face, and went to the fridge. She pulled out a beer and tossed it through the air to Reed, before sitting down again. Dan looked at Layla, and then at Reed, and there was an expression somewhere on his face, but it was too subtle, and Reed was too tired to interpret it. He sat down with them at the table and realised for the first time how exhausted he was.

Meaty washed his hands at the sink. "Do any of you know his family?" he asked. "Someone should tell them."

They were all silent, and then Wes spoke up. "I met his brother once." And the others took this as acceptance that Wes would be the one to tell them.

"All the paperwork's in the jeep," Reed said. "From the hospital, I mean."

From the café came the sound of stools scraping on the ground and falling over. The old worlders were finished eating for the night.

"Let's spray the place down then get out of here," Layla said.

Reed always found spraying down an oddly soothing procedure. It was repeated every night, when all of the old worlders were sated and had left. There was nothing more to fear. Everything just needed to be reset so it could start again the next day.

He unwound the old firehose from the wall. It was greasy from use, the metal mouth heavy in his hands. Meaty turned on the water for him, and it made the hose swell and tighten as it flowed down into Reed's hands.

The café was all white, with tiled walls and floors, and waterproof stools. The tables were bolted to the floor. There was no art on the walls, nothing that could be damaged by water. There were five drains around the room, and Reed used the fierce jet of water to push matter left by the old worlders into them. He opened up the mouth of the hose and let the spray undo the blood and handprints up the walls. He blasted the torn clothing and bits of rotten flesh from the stools, knocking them over, the force of the jet pushing them across the floor. He'd done this enough times now to be able to spin a fallen stool around all angles to remove every trace of old worlder.

When every stain and scab was gone, he switched off the hose. Layla stepped in, a surgical mask over her mouth and safety goggles over her eyes, and an old yellow canister strapped to her back. A tube came from the canister and fed into the spray gun in her hand. She gave the gun a couple of squirts until the high-strength disinfectant came freely, and then she slid through the café in her little pink flipflops, destroying any lingering organic life on the surfaces. No human had ever picked up the contagion via sharing surfaces, the germs had to be introduced directly into freshly broken skin, but Meaty wanted to be safe. He had a clean health and safety record for his café — except for Albie dying of course, but he'd not had to send one employee to the turners' camp since he opened three years ago.

Once Layla had filled the café with foam, Reed switched the hose back on again, sending up clouds of bubbles, driving a tide of froth into the drains.

In the background, he heard the door slam and then the jeep fire up as Meaty's boys left for the night. When all of the bubbles were gone, he wound the hose back, washed his hands and face in the sink and put on his jacket. In the pockets were his keys and the stub of a pencil. He'd not held these things since he arrived that afternoon. It was now three in the morning, and he was tired, and these innocuous touchstones brought him back to safety, back to his real life. He didn't belong to the old world. His keys and his tissues, his socks and shoes and the gel in his hair were all from the new world, and now he could go back there, sleep on the bed that smelled of his body, watch light from the advertising screen filter through the curtains. Put a movie on, something comforting. And he wouldn't have to come back here again until the sun had rolled a couple of hours over its zenith.

Layla zipped up her leather jacket and put on her helmet. She waved, her keys in her hand, and left.

Meaty was drying the space between his fingers with a white cloth. "Hey, Reed," he said. "I want you to go out with Dan and the boys tomorrow. Stand in for Albie."

Reed looked at him and couldn't make a reply. But Meaty didn't wait for one. He just moved into the back room and left Reed standing in the empty kitchen, the air pressing down on him, squeezing sweat from his skin.

On the drive home, Reed's mind was so tangled up with fear that twice he almost crashed his car. The first time when he didn't notice that two lanes had shrunk to one, and he swerved at the last minute to avoid the concrete island. The second time when he entered a roundabout, forgetting to check whether there were any cars on it. He was brought back to awareness by the harsh honk of a truck's horn, and pushed the accelerator pedal, twisting the steering wheel and just getting clear of the truck's path. Maybe subconciously it felt like it would be easier to get wiped out on the road than to go out with Meaty's boys.

He'd never asked the boys about what they did, but it was pretty obvious. They went out to the turners' camp with guns and machetes to get food for Meaty's place. And they came back with arms and legs and torsos and heads. Heads were the prize most enjoyed by the old worlders. Meaty had a way of splitting heads with his machete as easily as opening an oyster. The brains were the super-food of the old worlders.

The turners' camp was a limbo between the old world and the new world, and people infected with the contagion only got to go one way. From the new world, to the camp, to the old world. No one ever got better. It was illegal to go in there, unless you were one of the researchers, so Reed assumed that Meaty must be bribing the guards.

Reed imagined Meaty's boys hacking up old worlders, blood flying everywhere. How could Meaty expect him to do that? He couldn't even kill mice. He'd once left a nest of mice in his flat because he couldn't bare to do anything about it. He ignored the problem until there were so many he'd fall asleep to the sound of their feet on the floor. If he couldn't kill mice, how could he hunt and kill turners?

He hardly slept at all that night. He rolled over in the heat, his sheet detaching from the bed and becoming tangled around his legs. The few wisps of dreams he had were sweaty little descents into wells filled with clutching fingers. He woke much earlier than usual, stared at his uneaten breakfast, and stood in the shower for an hour.

The boys were waiting by the jeep when Reed arrived. Dan gave a big grin and slapped him on the shoulder. "Don't worry, kid," he said. "We'll look after ya."

Layla's bike was parked outside. Reed had hoped she would be there to see him off, because it felt like he was going to war. Even more so when Dan handed him a leather jacket, chainmail and a long machete.

"We'll get armoured up when we get there," Dan said. "It's too hot for this shit right now."

And it was hot. Ripples of distorted air rose from the road and the surrounding fields of baked mud. Rills of sweat ran down the boys' faces, breaking up on their stubbly chins. The sun bouncing off the top of the car made a high pitched shriek, as if from some eyeless summer insect.

Reed climbed into the back of the jeep with Wes. Dan and Troy sat up front. In a cloud of dust they pulled away from Meaty's and towards the turners' camp. Wes gave him an upwards nod. "You ever used one of those before?" he asked, gesturing at the machete in Reed's hands. They bounced up and down in the back of the jeep as its wheels dipped into pot holes and rolled over rocks.

Reed shook his head. "Not yet."

"Well, be careful where you go swinging it around. We come apart just as easy as turners."

From the front seat, Troy looked round at him and winked. He wore a red patterned bandana round his forehead, which was wet with sweat. "Reed can go up front," Troy laughed. "Lead the way, ya know, and then we'll keep back so he doesn't whack any of us by accident."

A wasp flew in through the open window and bounced around the back of the jeep, buzzing angrily. Reed shifted in his seat, ducking left and right, as it hovered around him. Wes chewed on the inside of his cheek and grinned as he watched Reed. "What's the worst that's going to happen, chipmunk?" he asked.

Reed ducked again. "Oh we're way past worst case scenario," he said. "This is the last place on Earth I want to be right now. And I hate fucking wasps."

The wasp landed on Reed's jeans, and he slapped it with the flat of his machete. The dead insect dropped from his leg.

The boys made big, deep laughs.

"Don't worry, kid," Dan said, turning his face slightly towards Reed as he drove. "You'll have fun. I shat my pants the first couple of times I did this, but once you get in there, something takes over, like a primal instinct, ya know. It's just like a computer game. You don't really think about what you're doing. You just get on with it. We wouldn't do it if we didn't enjoy it."

"Do they usually, you know, come out and attack," Reed said, "or do you go in and chase them down?"

Wes and Troy both looked over at Dan. Dan lifted his chin as he spoke to help carry his voice into the back of the jeep. "Depends whereabouts we are," he said. "You'll see. All you gotta think about is that meat equals money. Meat equals money, that's it. Nothing you'll see today will be scarier than going back to Meaty with empty sacks."

The turners' camp had its own perimeter within the old world. At the gate, Dan handed an envelope to the guard, and he waved them on with the barrel of his gun. In the centre of the turners' camp was a derelict school building, and it was towards this that Dan drove.

"Where are they?" Reed asked.

"There aren't so many here any more," Dan said. "We have to find them. We'll start in the school."

Outside the jeep, the air was thick with sunshine and a smell like sour milk. The boys pulled on their chainmail and leathers, and Reed did the same. The armour was heavy, and greasy, and the sweat began to leak out of him as soon as it was on, but he felt a little safer inside it.

A breeze picked up the dust in the empty playground, and from somewhere inside the building came a bark, a hoarse hacking noise like something choking.

The boys pulled out iPods from the pockets of their jackets and put in the earphones. Reed felt in his pocket and found that he had one too, a little square player with a clip on the back. "What's this for?" he asked.

"Atmosphere," Dan said. "You ever watch a movie with the sound turned down?"

"No."

"You don't wanna do this without a background track either."

Reed put in the earphones and pressed play. At first, the soft sound of violins came through, but then underneath rose pounding bass drums, and then the guitars kicked in, a crunching grungy throb of energetic metal. Dan handed him his machete, the blade as wide as his palm and as long as his arm. With this weapon in his hand, the armour on his body, and the music filling his mind, Reed felt invincible. And when the boys all high-fived each other and clapped hands with him, the sense of belonging was awesome. And when the boys started running, he ran with them.

The sounds of internal conversation that usually rattled at the back of his mind, questioning everything and whispering doubt into him were gone. He only had the roar of the music and of blood in his veins and the thump of his comrades' foot-steps on the playground tarmac.

They charged into the entranceway, swinging their blades at the doors, at the noticeboards, at the curtains, chipping out chunks of wood and drawing long slashes in the fabric. There were gashes at the same height all down the corridor, like giant cat scratches.

Dan led the way. Down the corridor, through the broken glass doors, up the stairs to the first floor. Beams of sunlight pasted bright squares onto the floor, and they ran through them to an auditorium at the end of the corridor. The boys jumped up the terraces of slashed chairs like kids hopping on stepping stones. They flashed their machetes into the fake leather coverings and foam spilled out.

At the top of the auditorium they ran into the projection room, and then through a side door, down a small flight of stairs and into the changing rooms. Their blades made harsh rattling sounds as they scraped them along the lockers. Reed drew his blade along the metal doors too, and felt a sense of exhilaration at the sound. He'd spent his whole life being as quiet as possible, dampening his sounds, not wanting to upset people. He whacked an open locker door with his elbow and felt no pain.

In the gym their shouts echoed, and the whole room seemed to revolve around them as they ran across the court, leaping and whooping. Reed was so caught up in the moment that he barely noticed the turner sitting on the floor.

The turner's legs were splayed out, head drooping on his shoulders. Dan, Troy and Wes ran towards him in a V-formation, blades raised high in the air.

The turner lifted his head to look at them as Dan's machete went into his forehead. The top of the turner's head span through the air like a hairy frisbee. Dan's momentum carried him past the turner. Troy was next, and he pulled his blade back, ready to take another slice, but then he stopped. They all stopped. The turner's eyes rolled back, as if looking up into the empty vault of his skull to see the sky through it for the first time. His hands went up to his head, and his fingers explored the sharp bone at the edges of the wound. His jaw hung down, tongue crawling over his lower lip. And then he made a sound like "huh," rolled back and was still.

The boys gathered around the body and pulled their earphones out. "Jesus," Wes said. "I've never seen one of them do that before."

They looked for a second like they were holding their breath, and then Troy laughed, a high-pitched cackle. This laughter was infectious, and Dan and Wes joined in. And the more they laughed, the deeper and more uncontrollable it became, breathless laughter from the pit of their bellies. Reed pushed a smirk into his features, showing his teeth and then retracting them. Once the boys' laughter had settled, the only sound in the hall was the tinny music leaking out of their earphones.

Wes pulled a thick plastic sack from his back pack. Troy grabbed the turner's hand and stretched his arm out. Dan slammed the machete into the shoulder. After three chops, the arm was linked to the shoulder by only a thin band of skin. Troy tugged at the arm, and the body broke its inertia and dragged across the floor before the skin broke and the torso dropped back to the ground.

They did the other arm in the same way. Wes held the bag open. "Reed," Troy said. "Start filling the sacks."

Reed bent down and willed his hands to grasp the arm, but inside he recoiled from the familiar yellow-pink flesh of the old worlders. He'd helped unload the sacks at Meaty's dozens of times, but having seen the arm attached to its owner, and animated, put it in a different context.

"There's hardly any blood," Reed said. "I thought it would be gushing out."

"The blood congeals as they turn," Troy said. "By this stage, they're mud inside."

"How close was he, you know, to turning completely?"

Troy wiped sweat from his cheek with his forearm. "He was almost there. It's easier when they're almost turned. By that stage, they've not eaten for a while. They haven't got into brain munching yet, so they're weak and stupid. It's when they've only just got into the camp that they're sometimes a handful."

Reed started to tie off the sack, but Troy stopped him. "Not yet, wait till it's full," he said.

"So, how turned are people when they first come into the turners' camp?"

"Sometimes they only found out an hour ago that they were infected," Wes said.

The boys put their earphones back in and ran through the rest of the school. Reed had been a good runner as a kid, and was able to keep position ahead of Wes. He didn't want to be at the back. The person at the back was always the first to be taken in the movies.

They didn't find another turner in the whole school, and went back outside, where the sun was loud on the playground.

"What happens now?" Reed asked.

"It's been like this for the last couple of weeks," Troy said. "It's like old worlding's going out of fashion."

"Meaty's place is going outta business, fast," Dan said.

"A year ago, this building would have been crawling with them," Wes said. "We used to go into classrooms and they'd all be crashed out on the floor, their rotten dicks still sticking in each other where they'd been fucking and fallen asleep. We sometimes had to kill more than we could carry just to get out."

"So, what's going to happen then?" Reed asked. A warm nugget had lit up inside him. A hope that they would turn around and head back.

The boys both looked to Dan. "There's another place we can try," he said.

They went back to the jeep and put the sack with the turner's body in the back. Dan revved up the engine and pulled away, driving deeper into the turners' camp. None of them spoke, and Reed watched their faces for clues.

Above them, cumulus clouds were swelling up towards space, tall and fluffy like soft thrones drifting far above the dirt and decay of the old world. Reed wished he could be sitting on one of those thrones, nestled amongst its billowing cushions, pristine and beyond the reach of everything earthbound. A cloud never comes so low to the ground that it gets stained by the earth.

They drove right across the turners' camp, through abandoned lanes of houses, many of which were blackened by fire, some so badly that they had collapsed. "Why don't we check in any of these houses?" Reed asked.

"You don't find many in houses," Wes said. "Once they start turning, they head for the bigger places, places where they can be together. It's weird. It's like they need to be part of a community. We could waste hours looking through these houses and find maybe one turner. Once they've fully turned, this kinda magnet switches on in them, and they gather at the gate to the old world. They want to be together."

"So how do they get from the camp to the old world?" Reed asked.

"When they're ready, they want to go there. They're drawn to it. Security comes along and just lets them through."

They came right up to the perimeter fence. Dan stopped the car, and Troy jumped out. "Where are we going?" Reed asked. Troy ran round the front of the jeep, to the fence, and undid a padlock in the wide gate. Dan drove through, and then Troy locked the gate behind them.

"Where is this?" Reed asked.

Troy ran alongside the jeep, until they came to the outer

perimeter, the fence around the whole of the old world. Troy undid another padlock and Dan drove through.

"This is . . . aren't we in the new world now?"

Wes looked up at him but didn't say anything. His features were loose on his face, like he'd retreated from them.

"Just don't think, don't say anything," Dan said from the front. "We're just shopping for Meaty."

Panic bubbled up inside Reed. Troy locked the perimeter behind them and then jumped back into the jeep. They drove along a rough dirt track with woods on one side and a tall hedge on the other. The jeep pitched from side to side.

About a mile down the dirt track, it turned into a small tarmac road, and there was a guard station with a barrier blocking the way. The guard walked out of his hut and over to the jeep as it slowed. Dan and the guard exchanged a few whispered words, and then Dan handed him an envelope. The guard put the envelope inside his jacket, walked back to the hut and lifted up the barrier.

"Where are we going?" Reed asked.

Wes leaned over and patted him on the leg. "Just switch it off man," he said. "Whatever you're thinking, just switch it off. You have to, like, go into like a Zen place. Be nothing. Dan's the man. Dan's in charge. Just follow and don't think. We'll be out of here in half an hour, loaded with meat, and we'll get a couple of tonne each for our trouble."

The areas around the old world perimeter were worth nothing to the housing market. No one wanted to live within sight of the walking graveyard. But these areas still carried great commercial value. And so once all the people had moved out of the villages around the old world, the houses were bulldozed, and now a great industrial estate, a ring of corrugated metal warehouses, surrounded the land of the undead. Just a short walk away from fornicating corpses, one could buy a widescreen television at bargain prices, or get a great deal on a carpet.

These shops were the airlock between the old world and the new, the limbo in which it was difficult to discern between what was living and what was dead.

This collar of commercialism around the old world was also filled with food packing plants. And it was in front of one of these that Reed stopped the jeep. The sign on the front said *Freezy-Line*. It was a meat-packing plant. And outside there were refrigerator trucks parked in bays waiting to be loaded.

Dan leaned round his seat to address everyone. "We've got two minutes," he said. "Reed, this is like supermarket sweep. When you get inside, there are big trolleys that they use to lug the meat round in. You push one behind us. We'll charge through gathering up the meat and chucking it in the trolley. Just keep up with us."

"Wait," Reed said. "If you've been here before, won't they realise what's happening as soon as we walk in and call the cops or attack us?"

"That's why we've only got two minutes."

They jumped out of the jeep, chainmail rattling. Dan pointed to the main entrance. The door was open already. Reed didn't even have time to contemplate what was about to happen. The boys left the jeep doors wide open and ran for the building. He felt a sense of relief that he wouldn't have to kill anyone. He'd just be pushing the trolley, and the boys would be stealing frozen meat. As they ran into the building he wondered whether the old worlders would even eat frozen meat.

The boys burst onto the packing floor, their panting breaths condensed into clouds by the cold. There were rows of workers in white plastic coats wearing gloves, and no one looked up as they came in. Dan pointed to the row of carts along the wall, and then the boys began to charge down one of the aisles.

Reed grabbed a red plastic trolley and ran to keep up with them. The wheels were locked and steered the trolley off to the side, but he spun the trolley round, grabbing the other side, and the wheels twisted and then the cart followed his direction. The boys were already a distance ahead of him. And now the workers had seen them.

Shouts broke out, but they were muffled by the surgical masks that the workers wore. Everywhere in the room was white, the work surfaces, the high ceiling, the strip lighting, the clothes of the workers, the floor, even the skin of the frozen meat, which lay on every surface in neatly counted piles. But the boys were running straight past the meat. Through this snowy expanse, they cut a dark swathe, their chainmail and blades flashing.

And then up came the first plume of red. It shot high as Dan slammed his machete into the neck of a female worker. Her ponytail stopped the full impact of the blade. Dan ran on, but Troy followed up behind, slicing a neat curve up through her throat. Her head flew off and rolled across the top of the counter. Troy ran on in Dan's wake. The female worker's knees buckled, but before she hit the floor, Wes caught the girl under her arms and lifted her up into the air. His face filled with panic when he saw that Reed was not right behind him.

Convulsions of fear and adrenalin ran through Reed. He could see Wes shouting at him, but the blood was rushing so loudly in his ears that he could barely hear. Reed ran to catch up, and Wes hurled the body over the edge of the trolley, and charged after the other two, not pausing as he picked up the girl's head by her ponytail and tossed it into the trolley. The head bounced off the inside a couple of times, them came to rest face down on the girl's stomach.

They went through the workers in this same way, again and again. Dan sticking in the first shocking strike, Troy, with his impressive strength, delivering the killing blow, and then Wes using the momentum of these falling workers to toss them into the cart.

Reed's jaw was clenched and he chewed at the inside of his cheeks. He chewed so hard on his own flesh that he drew out blood. And he was making little nonsense words with his mouth. They spilled out of him with every panting breath.

The fourth body fell awkwardly into the trolley, leaning over the side, and he grabbed beneath the beautiful knee of the girl and pulled her in, pushing her down to make room for the next one.

Wes was about to turn away from the trolley when he opened his eyes wide and pointed behind Reed, "Look out!" he called. Reed spun round the trolley, using it to cover himself. A big man in a suit, maybe a supervisor, was chasing after them, his face bright red, his jowls swinging on his skull. The man hit the side of the trolley, and when Reed pushed it into him, his momentum pitched him forwards into the bodies. His legs tangled in the air as his head went deep into the mess of workers.

And then Wes and Troy were there with him. They raised their machetes and plunged them into the trolley. The man kicked and thrashed, his screams muffled by the bodies. Wes and Troy laughed as blood sprayed up over their faces. They smashed their blades up and down, and their laughter was the only thing Reed could hear. Reed was laughing too. Something like rocket fuel was shooting through him, lighting him up inside. He felt eight-feet tall, superhuman. The laughter came from deep down inside him. And as he drove his machete down into the bodies with the others, his laughter took over him, hurting his throat it came out so hard.

"Jesus," Dan said. "Don't fuck up the meat. Let's get going."

All four pushed the trolley towards the exit. The workers stared at them from the corners of the room where they had fled, too afraid to move. The boys had a clear path along the bloody aisle. One of them was singing something. A Black Sabbath track, "War Pigs," at the top of his voice. Reed was flying down the aisle with everyone else. They were laughing and a strong arm was round his shoulders.

They broke out of the door, down the ramp to the jeep, and began tossing the bodies into the back. Wes ruffled Reed's hair, wrapped his thick arm round his face and kissed the top of his head.

"You're fucking crazy man!" Wes shouted. "That's the fucking funniest thing I've ever seen! That guy practically fucking jumped in there!"

They leapt back into the van and Dan was screeching away before the doors were even closed, pushing every gear until it screamed, back towards the turners' camp.

Reed's heart was thumping against his ribs, and he was shaking from the excitement. Wes hit him on the leg and laughed out loud again, doing impressions of the supervisor diving into the trolley.

The guard at the station nodded at them as they drove through, and Dan gave him the thumbs up. They drove back along the bumpy track between the hedge and the wood. Some of the cumulus clouds had evolved into vast mountains, miles high, their upper reaches spraying out into an anvil shape. The base of the clouds were black and bubbling, and Reed could hear the grumbling of thunder inside. The setting sun made the trees in front of the cloud bright gold, and this contrast of sunlit orange against the purple-bruise of the clouds transfixed Reed. There was something huge in that moment. He felt it boiling in his stomach.

Once back through the perimeter fence of the turners' camp, Dan pulled the jeep over and the boys all jumped out.

"What are we doing?" Reed asked.

"We can't take the bodies to Meaty like this," Dan said. "He'll get suspicious. They'll look more like turners when they're chopped up."

Beneath the trees the air was cool and still. The cloud mountain overhead rumbled again, and the first fat drops of rain began to spatter through the leaves.

As the rain grew heavier and the sky darker, they unloaded all five bodies, laying them out on the ground, their faces to the sky, their arms and legs stretched out. Dan turned the jeep around and switched the headlights on the bodies, casting long shadows across the forest floor. Before he got out of the jeep, he switched on the CD player and turned the volume up loud. Thumping grunge metal pumped out of the jeep, rusty bass cords and rolling drums, echoing the thunder overhead.

Dan and Troy began undressing one of the female workers. There were three guys and two girls on the ground. Wes knelt down beside the body of the supervisor and looked up at Reed. "He ain't jumpin' now!" he laughed. Reed helped Wes undress the body. At first he tried to rip the clothes off, thinking this would be quicker, and it didn't matter if the clothes were torn, but the fabric was hard to tear. Instead, he had to undo the buttons of the shirt, and the buckle of the belt, and untie the shoe laces.

He'd never undressed another person like this. And beneath the music and the raindrops, feelings began to bubble through, and he pushed them back, clamping his lips tightly together so they couldn't escape. He couldn't be conscious of what he was doing.

When all five bodies were naked and splayed out like pink starfish in the headlights, Troy passed round the machetes. The boys stood alongside one body each. Reed took the supervisor.

The sky overhead was thick black and purple now, and pouring rain through the trees. The boys raised their machetes in the air. The track on the CD changed, a thumping bass heartbeat pulsing through the wood. Troy, Wes and Dan slammed their machetes down on the bodies, then raised them up and drove them down again. Each time stretching up high into the sky, then dropping all their weight, making final impact on the bodies' joints crouched low to the ground.

Reed raised up his own blade and felt that flavour of cognisance coming through, and he swallowed against it to keep it back. He pushed everything of himself down his neck and into his stomach. He let the music and the rain fill his mind. He raised up his machete and smashed it down into the supervisor's shoulder. It cut a deep gouge, but was far from taking the arm off. The boys were already working on their second arms. He would have to hit harder.

He raised the blade again, and dropped it down with all his weight behind it. This time striking a deeper cut into the arm, a little too low. He tried again and again, each time pushing himself, teaching his body how to deliver this chop with maximum force, and after seven cuts, the arm flew up into the air as it came free of the body.

Warm rain trickled down his face, and he spat it out as it ran into his mouth. The boys were already on the legs. He had to catch up. He didn't want to be the last to finish. He didn't want to be standing alone in the forest wreaking havoc upon the body by himself when the lights and the music switched off.

His mouth was working by itself again, chewing the inside of his cheeks, and he was blinking rapidly, making the whole grisly scene strobe. A weakness crept through his limbs but he pushed it away, working himself up into a frothy boil, smashing the machete down again and again, as fast and as hard as he could, and it seemed like only seconds before the next arm came off, and then he went at the legs. He was dropping the blade down in time with the beat of the music, and as the music sped up, he kept pace.

Lightning crackled overhead, and thunder rocked the whole forest. Reed's clothes were saturated, heavy and hanging from him, and slapping against his body as he chopped. The heat in his muscles was unbearable, a fiery pain that coursed through his arms and back and legs. But he kept chopping, as if his life depended on it, and soon realised that all the limbs were off, and he was just sinking the blade down into the wet mud.

He stood up and the machete dropped from his hands. His fingers were frozen in the shape of the handle. Turning his face towards the sky, the lightning was bright through his closed eyes. The rain fell so heavy on his face that he could barely inhale through it. He breathed out the air inside him, and it hurt so much he thought he was breathing out fire. He looked across at the boys, and they were all staring at him.

"Jesus, Reed," Wes said. "I seen a whole new side of you tonight."

Troy ran up behind him and wrapped his arms around his back, lifting him, then dropping him to the ground and rubbing his fingers through his hair. Reed felt the wet mud seeping through his shirt. And then Dan and Wes piled on top of him too. Digging little punches into the side of him, laughing so hard he could feel their breath against him through the rain. And he punched back too, feeling his fists hit backs and ribs and legs, and feeling fists hitting him, fingers tugging at his hair, but he was made of iron, and nothing could hurt him any more.

They rolled off each other and lay on their backs next to the bodies, and let the rain fall down on them. Reed opened his mouth and let the rain pour down the back of his throat. His belly was full of embers, and he ached all over, and it felt so good. Warm tears welled up in his face, but the rain washed them away as soon as they formed.

Dan was the first to stand up, and the rest followed. A track came on the CD that they all knew the words to, "Black Hole

Sun" by Soundgarden, and they sang as they put the wet limbs into the bags.

Each of the boys dragged a heavy sack from the car into Meaty's place. The rain prickled as it bounced off the plastic bags. Through this sound, Reed could just hear the groans of the old worlders already assembling at the perimeter for their dinner.

Dan was first through the door, and then Reed. Meaty was leaning against his block with his arms folded across his chest smoking a fag.

"Holy shit," Meaty said, "have you been mud wrestling?" He looked straight from their muddy dripping clothes to the plastic bags. Wes and Troy came in behind them with more bags. "Don't come in here dripping that shit all over the floor. Hang on, I'll get you something."

Meaty stubbed out his cigarette in the sink and went into a cupboard. He pulled out a couple of decorating sheets splashed with dry paint. "Rub the worst off you before you come in."

The boys took it in turn with the sheets, rubbing at the mud on their clothes and bodies. Meaty called out to Layla and took Reed's bag of meat from him.

"How'd you get on, kid?" Meaty asked.

Reed smiled. The café felt different, smaller, and the tangle of fear that always sat heavily in his gut was gone. Dan put his hand on Reed's shoulder.

"He did good," Dan said. "Real good."

Layla came into the kitchen, and smiled when she saw him. "Jeez," she said. "What have you boys been up to? Stick your hands in the sink."

Layla switched on the hose and blasted the mud from their hands and arms. Usually the sink would run red with the evidence of their activities, but tonight what the rain hadn't washed away was mingled with mud and invisible.

As Layla sprayed Reed's fingers, she looked at him and mouthed quietly, "You okay?"

He nodded and made a small smile.

"This is good food," Meaty said from behind them.

Reed dried his face and hair with a towel, then passed it to Dan. Wes got beers from the fridge for them all, and they sat around the table and drank and sighed and laughed. Steam rose from their clothes.

Reed felt transformed by the night's exertions. He felt bigger inside his clothes. If there were a mirror in Meaty's place, he imagined that he would look different to himself. Now that the excitement was slipping away, his muscles were beginning to ache, and a deep tiredness leaked out of his cells, making them bounce lazily against each other, dropping through his body like falling feathers.

Meaty prepared the food, and later, Dan and Troy worked the gate, letting in the stream of customers, swiping their credit cards and culling the penniless. Reed was teetering on the edge of something powerful, and he felt that if he had to deal with anything else tonight, he would topple over, and all his new confidence, and his new body, would fall away from him. He walked around in bare feet, as his shoes were sodden.

The old worlders shuffled about in the white room, bumping into each other and falling over, burying their faces into plates of neatly prepared flesh. Reed carried plates from the kitchen to the serving area of the café, and Layla took them from him to pass across the counter to the old worlders.

"What was it like today?" she asked.

"I think that if I think about it, I'll go mad, but while I'm not thinking, I actually feel great."

Layla nodded, the skin around her eyes tightening, her lips

shrinking with sympathy. She stroked his arm with the whole of her hand, then patted him on the chest, and the sensation lingered long after her hand had gone.

And then Reed heard an unfamiliar metallic click. In the far corner of the café, a corner too far from the serving counter for the old worlders to bother with usually, one of the zombies was pushing a coin into the jukebox. Reed had never really noticed the jukebox before. It hadn't been played in the time that he'd been there.

The old worlder pressed a soft finger against the buttons, and then the machine clicked again as a metal arm pulled a CD from its slot and moved it into the play deck. It took a few seconds of piano for Reed to recognise it, The Beatles' "Hey Jude."

The old worlder shuffled back over towards the food. Meaty stuck his flabby face round the door. His eyebrows rolled against each other, making confused arches in his forehead. Layla and Reed looked at each other and laughed. At one of the tables, an old worlder tapped his foot, and another nodded his head in time with the music, pink drool sliding from his lips.

Reed opened his arms, in a "dance with me" gesture. Layla grinned and looked down at her feet, then stepped forward and wrapped her arms around his neck. Reed held her round her waist.

"You're soaking," she said.

"I'm freezing."

Layla squeezed him towards her a little tighter, her body firm and warm. They shuffled from foot to foot, swaying round gently, stomachs pressed together. Hot tears stung his eyes and he laughed at the same time. He was at the edge again, and it was such a long drop down. Layla was the only thing he was clinging to. The only thing keeping him from falling, and he pulled her tighter and rested his face on her shoulder so she couldn't see the turmoil in it.

The old worlders groaned and slurped and burped, and somewhere in those cattle-like noises was a humming. One of them was humming to the music, and that was just too much for Reed, and he began to shake in Layla's arms.

"Are you okay?" she asked.

"I'm cold," he said. And she squeezed him until he was still.

ACKNOWLEDGEMENTS

Thanks so much to: everyone at ECW Press, you've been a delight to work with — Michael Holmes, Jennifer Knoch, Jenna Illies, Crissy Boylan and Erin Creasey; Ingrid Paulson for the super new cover; Ra Page, my editor at Comma Press; my agent Will Francis at Janklow & Nesbit; Maggie Gee, Alex Linklater, Alison MacLeod, Robert Shearman, Wena Poon and Clare Wigfall; Diana Reich at the Small Wonder Festival in Charleston, U.K.; Patrick Cotter at the Frank O'Connor International Short Story Festival in Cork, Ireland; my whole family, but especially my wife Naomi — when she reads my work, I hide round the corner, listening out for her giggles and shrieks of disgust to let me know I've done something right.

BackLit
INSIGHTS FOR
READERS

A Conversation with Adam Marek
225

Batman vs. The Minotaur
230

Tamagotchi
237

About the Author
252

A CONVERSATION WITH
ADAM MAREK

Senior Editor Michael Holmes was bowled over by Adam Marek's debut collection, passionate enough about the stories to break with ECW's convention of only acquiring Canadian fiction. Here he chats with the author about the surreal world of Instruction Manual for Swallowing.

◆ ◆ ◆

MICHAEL HOLMES: So many of your stories pit the grotesque or the monstrous against fragile, achingly real humanity. Giant talking centipedes, killer robots wasps, zombie-catering restaurateurs . . . in one case a man with cancer literally battles a Godzilla-like behemoth. What fascinates you most about confronting these kinds of extremes?

ADAM MAREK: I've always loved science fiction movies. I

grew up on them. So my imagination is filled with robots and monsters and mutations. But the books I like to read, and the stories I like to write, are always about real emotional moments of human interaction. When I sit down to write a story about something real, the pieces I pick up to build it with are most often fantastical. I get very excited about the creative possibilities of zombies and giant insects invading everyday human drama. It reveals something about the situation that a straight treatment couldn't reach. This absurdity versus mundanity is so much fun to write, but most of all, I hope it makes for an entertaining and unique experience for the reader.

MH: A real sense of play pulses through this book. It's there in each story, and in the way each story's told. At the beginning of one, "Cuckoo," the narrator offers this explanation of his fascination with the teenaged Alice: "She had an amazing power to make me see familiar things in a new way, as if for the first time." I wonder, can success as a writer of short fiction be measured in the same way? Why have you, formally, gravitated to the short story?

AM: You're right. The short story is the perfect form to attack familiar things from oblique angles. With novels, there's a huge amount of scaffolding that needs to be erected to keep the story aloft for a few hundred pages. There are conventions that have to be followed to hold the reader's interest. The short story form is not bounded by those same conventions. When I'm writing shorts, I feel an enormous sense of freedom, and yes, it is creative play. I pick up different images, themes, characters or situations and bang them together. When they make sparks, the writing is a real pleasure. I enjoy myself on the page, and I hope that translates to the person holding the printed book in their hand.

MH: When you're reading, who makes "sparks"? I wonder, who are your favourite writers, and what have they taught you?

AM: My favourite story writers are Haruki Murakami and Karen Russell — they both have a gift for dazzling mash-ups of absurdity and realism, which is my arena too. Also Etgar Keret, Will Self, J.G. Ballard. It was Kafka's story *The Metamorphosis* that first got me hooked on short stories, and it was this story that really opened my mind to the power of framing weird stuff within mundane settings. Salman Rushdie's *Midnight's Children* is one of my favourite novels for the same reason. William Burroughs was my hero when I was nineteen — you don't get much weirder than *Naked Lunch*. But I don't just like to read fiction that's like the stuff I write — I love George Orwell, Philip Roth, Margaret Atwood. And it's not just fiction that gives me those sparks. My first job out of university was working for a production company that made music videos and commercials — I got to watch showreels all day from directors such as Michel Gondry (my first job in film was moving a sofa into his new flat), Spike Jonze and Chris Cunningham, who all set a high benchmark for innovation.

MH: I'm curious: what makes you laugh? I ask, because for all that's absolutely terrifying in the worlds you create (Gilberts and Georges coming to life to battle giant slides in the Tate Modern, for some reason, scares the bejesus out of me — I've never trusted slides) I find myself frequently laughing out loud when I read these stories. Often I'm laughing at the very things that give me the creeps. Being funny's hard; being funny and scary at the same time seems almost impossible — how do you make it work?

AM: What makes me laugh? You know, I can't think of many books that I've read that make me laugh out loud. Maybe *Fear and Loathing in Las Vegas*. Larry David makes me laugh, and Woody Allen. I watch *The Simpsons* every night with my kids before they go to bed and that's still funny after goodness knows how many episodes. Oh, and Frankie Boyle — do you guys know Frankie Boyle over there? He's got a wicked imagination, and plays right on the very edge of bad taste. Sometimes he steps over it, but when he gets it right, there's no one funnier.

I'm glad *Instruction Manual* made you laugh and creeped out at the same time — that's what I was going for! When I was eight, my favourite author was Roald Dahl. He once said that when you're writing for children, you can make it as nasty as you like, as long as it's funny. I apply that to writing for adults. I guess I was trained from an early age to see the humour in ghoulish things.

MH: I wish I knew more about Boyle — I remember seeing his book *My Shit Life So Far* a couple years back and being intrigued. Dark Scottish humour is just one of the things I love about the family I've luckily married into. My seven-year-old has those genes — and that's probably why he loves Dahl-like books and shows too. Some day, when your kids are adults, what do you think they'll make of Adam Marek the writer and *Instruction Manual for Swallowing*? Will they recognize their father's voice instantly? And what do you hope they'll make of some of your book's most raw, emotional moments — the reaction of classmates to a young woman's suicide attempt, for example; or bad sushi kiboshing an affair and possibly teaching a man something about what he'd be giving up if he went through with the infidelity?

AM: Ha, I'd be amazed if my kids ever read anything I've written. By the time they're at an age where they can appreciate it, they'll be embarrassed by everything I do. And I'm okay with that. I'm fascinated by everything they do, but I'm not sure it works the other way round. When I'm writing, I've always got the end reader in mind — if I imagined that my boys might be among my readers, I would start to self-censor, write safer things. Maybe. When *Instruction Manual* was published in the U.K., my mum read it — she was proud, which was lovely, but if I'd imagined her among my readers while I was sitting at my desk, I wouldn't have been able to write opening lines like "Audrey wanted to play the bum rape game again last night." Blimey, I'm still cringing thinking about it now.

No, the reader I imagine is the person holding this book right now, somewhere in North America, whom I have never met, but who is delighted by the same odd things that fascinate me.

BATMAN VS. THE MINOTAUR

Casey ran through the leaves and light, skipping over tree roots and ducking under branches. He could win this game. He'd covered more ground than anyone else, venturing deeper into the forest than anyone else dared. His bag of rubbish was already bulging. His friends were all far behind.

A cloud snuffed out the sun. Casey looked up from the ground, just in time to stop himself before he ran right into a man who was just standing there, playing with the loose skin around his flabby throat. His leather shoes were broad and firmly rooted in the soft earth.

"What's the outfit for?" the stranger said.

Casey stared at the man for a long while before replying. "Batman."

The stranger raised his eyebrows and his head at the same time, like they were being pulled from behind. "What you got in the bag?"

Casey looked in the bag, even though he already knew that it was full of torn up envelopes. He didn't reply but looked sideways, hoping to see someone familiar nearby, but the woods were empty.

"Is it sweets?" the stranger said.

Casey looked at the leaves around his feet and shook his head. He felt compelled to linger in this man's shadow, as if to walk away would invite him to become angry. Casey opened the bag so that the stranger could see inside. He didn't know why he did this. The man was a big man. He dipped a hairy hand into the bag to open it wider, then knelt down in front of Casey and looked inside.

The light that had slipped between the trees earlier was gone, and Casey felt cold in his stomach. How long had he been? The party was far away and happening on fast-forward. Games were being played in the space between handclaps, and his friends were locusts at the buffet table, cleaning plates between blinks.

"What's that for?" he asked. "A game?"

Casey nodded. "I'd better get back," he said. "I'm late."

"You collecting rubbish or something?" the stranger said.

How could he have known this? Had he been at the party? Casey scanned through his memories of the last few hours, trying to remember if this man had been one of the adults there. But Casey only remembered two adults: his mum dropping him off, and Kelly's mum handing out the plastic bags.

"I'll help you," the stranger said. "I'll help you win the prize. There is a prize, isn't there?"

Casey nodded. "A *Finding Nemo* DVD," he said.

"Wow," the stranger smiled. "You could win that. How much rubbish do you have to collect?"

Casey shrugged his shoulders.

"Listen, there's a massive pile of old papers over there. I'll show you where they are; come on, follow me."

The stranger walked on a few steps, then turned and seemed confused when Casey didn't follow. "Come on," he said. "I'll help you win that DVD. The rubbish is just over here. You'll have more than all the other kids."

Casey took a few steps towards the stranger. His feet took three paces, but his body moved ten, as if on a conveyor belt beneath the early autumn rot. The space between him and the edge of the wood, which butted up against Kelly's garden fence, swelled, filling up with frosty air, becoming thick and slowing down movement. This dense air pushed against Casey's back, nudging him towards the stranger and the steep bank of earth at which the stranger was gesturing. Casey's cheeks prickled and he felt a little sick. He didn't want to upset the strange man, who was now walking towards him with his hand outstretched, reaching to take his own hand, to lead him to the bank. To help him gain his prize.

The stranger's hand moved around Casey's small fingers. His palm was hot and slippery. He pulled Casey towards the bank. Casey felt the tug at his elbow and shoulder. The stranger wasn't looking at him, but at the brow of the mound.

The bank was steep, and Casey tripped. His hand flew out to break his fall, slapping his bag of rubbish against his cape, but the stranger lifted him up by his arm before his bag even hit the ground. His feet levitated, and when they came down again, the stranger didn't give him time to find his balance.

From the top of the bank, Casey saw a steep drop and a hollow like the imprint of an enormous fist.

"I can't see any papers," Casey said.

The man's fingers tangled as they sought to renew their grip on Casey's hand. Casey snatched his hand back. Pain shot up his arm as the man's fingernail raked the top of Casey's thumb.

The boy ran, his mouth open with a soundless sob. Fear stampeded around his body. His legs felt weak stumbling down the bank. He had to fight to move through the dense air that had filled the forest. He'd moved so far away from the house. His body was too light. The gentlest breeze was blowing against it, but he was tissue paper and it lifted him back through the air where the stranger was waiting to catch him. His breath burned in his chest and throat.

He glanced back, long enough to see the man charging through the forest, steam pouring from his nostrils. His face was bloated and red, the eyes invisible because the brows had sunk so low over them. The ground shook as his feet pounded. He was so fast and strong, ripping through the air. His arms were long enough to almost touch the back of Casey's neck. He was burning up the forest with the heat of his rage, dead leaves flying up at his feet.

And then Kelly's gate was there.

But as Casey thundered towards it, pistons exploding, the edges of the gate began to melt into the surrounding fence. The handle shrank into the wood, as if retreating from a cold touch. With a terrible sucking sound, the gate became fence.

Casey bounced off it, bashing his elbows, his Batman helmet sliding over one of his eyes. He scrambled up and smacked the fence where the gate had been with his fists. His face grew sore with screaming for Kelly's mum to let him in.

Gravity changed. The earth pulled him to the ground, and he knew that the stranger was behind him. The man was engorged, his grotesque inflating muscles splitting the seams of his clothes. Two great horns sprouted from his forehead, curling as they lengthened. His eyes filled with black ink. His shoes disintegrated as his now-cloven feet split the leather. His whole body went rigid and his bones cracked as they set into new positions. He roared again, hot air and spit firing from his mouth.

When the transformation was complete, the minotaur stomped the ground. The shockwave knocked Casey down. The monster was right over him, its enormous balls swinging between its legs.

Casey scrambled in the leaves to stand up, but the minotaur cuffed him with the bottom of its fist. The strike sent Casey sprawling. He closed his eyes against the pain and put his arms over his head, expecting another blow. A weight pushed into the centre of his back, pinning him to the ground. Casey tore a fingernail off scratching at the dirt to escape. He couldn't twist to his side. His feet kicked at the ground but were useless. The minotaur's breath was hot on the back of his head.

And then Casey remembered his utility belt. He flicked open one of the small yellow pouches and pulled out a penknife. He drew the knife out of the handle with his teeth then slashed it about at his side, hoping to get lucky.

The minotaur pushed so hard against his back that Casey thought his spine would snap. The blade caught something and the minotaur yelped. Casey aimed for this spot again and the knife sank into the beast's ankle. The minotaur stepped back to avoid another stab, and Casey rolled over and backed up against the fence, panting for breath.

The minotaur threw its head back and bellowed. Casey went into his utility belt again. Of course, the samurai sword.

The forest was ash grey, spots of rain dripping down through the branches and turning to steam on the minotaur's back. Tiny lights from fireflies made grottoes of the dying bracken. Casey gripped the samurai sword with both hands and held it before him. A security light in the garden behind him flicked on, and the light bounced off the blade, stunning the monster for a second.

Casey ran between the minotaur's legs and slashed the blade along the inside of its red thigh. He didn't stop to see the damage but continued round to the minotaur's back and swept the blade diagonally across its calf muscle. The muscle unravelled like fistfuls of string, spraying dark blood over the ground.

The minotaur swung round and its howl knocked Casey off his feet. It lunged forward, thrusting its horns at the boy. But the gouges in the beast's legs slowed it down, and Casey leapt to the side. The minotaur's horns thumped into the ground where Casey had been, and while the monster struggled to pull them out, Casey swung the samurai sword down on its neck.

He felt the blade cutting through the air, could see the exposed neck, could feel victory thumping in his arms, but the sword hit the minotaur's shoulder, slicing off a neat cutlet of flesh. The cut was enough to show the beast how close it had come to defeat, and it went crazy, fists on the ground, bucking its back legs up off the ground like a bull. Casey ducked to the left as the minotaur charged at him. The tree he had been standing in front of splintered beneath the minotaur's shoulder. Casey leapt backwards and the hoof that was aimed for his head sank deep into a rotted tree trunk.

Fear filled the monster's face for the first time as it struggled to pull its stuck hoof from the trunk. Casey saw his opportunity. He ran to the side and drew the blade back, winding himself up. He leapt into the air and uncoiled, the blade spinning around, streetlight glinting on its bloodied surface. He slashed the blade through the bull's penis and blood erupted everywhere. The minotaur's scream was so loud that Casey only heard it for a fraction of a second before he went deaf beneath the sound.

The beast writhed on the ground, a red fountain spewing from between its legs.

Casey ran along the fence, occasionally glancing back to make sure the minotaur wasn't following. The trees came to a stop at a path that was lined with amber lights. A car moved past, leaving an orange vapour trail on the inside of Casey's eyelids. Casey wiped his sword on the tufty grass growing at the base of a concrete post, then slipped it back into his utility belt. He wiped the minotaur's dark blood from his face with his cape.

Stumbling along the street, Casey soon came to a junction that led onto Kelly's road. Kelly's windows were lit, and two balloons dangled from the front door. The sound of laughter spilled out of the mail slot.

Casey turned away, skipping homewards, keeping to the shadows. Fireworks exploded overhead, muffling the sound of his footsteps.

TAMAGOTCHI

My son's Tamagotchi had AIDS. The virtual pet was rendered on the little LCD screen with no more than thirty pixels, but the sickness was obvious. It had that AIDS look, you know? It was thinner than it had been. Some of its pixels were faded, and the pupils of its huge eyes were smaller, giving it an empty stare.

I had bought the Tamagotchi, named Meemoo, for Luke just a couple of weeks ago. He had really wanted a kitten, but Gabby did not want a cat in the house. "A cat will bring in dead birds and toxoplasmosis," she said, her fingers spread protectively over her bulging stomach.

A Tamagotchi had seemed like the perfect compromise — something for Luke to empathise with and to care for, to teach him the rudiments of pet care for a time after the baby had been born. Empathy is one of the things that the book said Luke would struggle with. He would have difficulty reading facial expressions. The Tamagotchi had only three different faces, so it would be good practice for him.

Together, Luke and I watched Meemoo curled up in the corner of its screen. Sometimes, Meemoo would get up, limp to the opposite corner, and produce a pile of something. I don't know what this something was, or which orifice it came from — the resolution was not good enough to tell.

"You're feeding it too much," I told Luke. He said that he wasn't, but he'd been sitting on the sofa thumbing the buttons for hours at a time, so I'm sure he must have been. There's not much else to do with a Tamagotchi.

I read the instruction manual that came with Meemoo. Its needs were simple: food, water, sleep, play — much like Luke's. Meemoo was supposed to give signals when it required one of these things. Luke's job as Meemoo's carer was to press the appropriate button at the appropriate time. The manual said that overfeeding, underfeeding, lack of exercise and unhappiness could all make a Tamagotchi sick. A little black skull and cross-bones should appear on the screen when this happens, and by pressing button A twice, then B, one could administer medicine. The instructions said that sometimes it might take two or three shots of medicine, depending on how sick your Tamagotchi is.

I checked Meemoo's screen again and there was no skull and crossbones.

The instructions said that if the Tamagotchi dies, you have to stick a pencil into the hole in its back to reset it. A new creature would then be born.

When Luke had finally gone to sleep and could not see me molesting his virtual pet, I found the hole on Meemoo's back and jabbed a sharpened pencil into it. But when I turned it back over, Meemoo was still there, as sick as ever. I jabbed a few more times and tried it with a pin too, in case I wasn't getting deep enough. But it wouldn't reset.

I wondered what happened if Meemoo died, knowing that the reset button didn't work. Was there a malfunction that had robbed Luke's Tamagotchi of its immortality? Did it have just one shot at life? I guess that made it a lot more special, and in a small way, it made me more determined to find a cure for Meemoo.

I plugged Meemoo into my PC — a new feature in this generation of Tamagotchis. I hoped that some kind of diagnostics wizard would pop up and sort it out.

A Tamagotchi screen blinked into life on my PC. There were many big-eyed mutant creatures jiggling for attention, including another Meemoo, looking like its picture on the box, before it got sick. One of the options on the screen was "Sync your Tamagotchi."

When I did this, Meemoo's limited world of square grey pixels was transformed into a full colour three-dimensional animation on my screen. The blank room in which it lived was revealed as a conservatory filled with impossible plants growing under the pale-pink Tamagotchi sun. And in the middle of this world, lying on the carpet, was Meemoo.

It looked awful. In this fully realised version of the Tamagotchi's room, Meemoo was a shrivelled thing. The skin on its feet was dry and peeling. Its eyes, once bright white with crisp highlights, were yellow and unreflective. There were scabs around the base of its nose. I wondered what kind of demented mind would create a child's toy that was capable of reaching such abject deterioration.

I clicked through every button available until I found the medical kit. From this you could drag and drop pills onto the Tamagotchi. I guess Meemoo was supposed to eat or absorb these, but they just hovered in front of it, as if Meemoo was refusing to take its medicine.

I tried the same trick with Meemoo that I do with Luke to get him to take his medicine. I mixed it with food. I dragged a chicken drumstick from the food store and put it on top of the medicine, hoping that Meemoo would get up and eat them both. But it just lay there, looking at me, its mouth slightly open. Its look of sickness was so convincing that I could practically smell its foul breath coming from the screen.

I sent Meemoo's makers a sarcastic email describing his condition and asking what needed to be done to restore its health.

A week later, I had received no reply and Meemoo was getting even worse. There were pale grey dots appearing on it. When I synced Meemoo to my computer, these dots were revealed as deep red sores. And the way the light from the Tamagotchi sun reflected off them, you could tell they were wet.

I went to a toy shop and showed them the Tamagotchi. "I've not seen one do that before," the girl behind the counter said. "Must be something the new ones do."

I came home from work one day to find Luke had a friend over for a playdate. The friend was called Becky, and she had a Tamagotchi too. Gabby was trying to organise at least one playdate a week to help Luke socialise.

Becky's Tamagotchi gave me an idea.

This generation of Tamagotchis had the ability to connect to other Tamagotchis. By getting your Tamagotchi within a metre of a friend's, your virtual pets could play games or dance together. Maybe if I connected the two Tamagotchis, the medicine button in Becky's would cure Meemoo.

At first, Luke violently resisted giving Meemoo to me, despite me saying I only wanted to help it. But when I bribed Luke and Becky with chocolate biscuits and a packet of crisps, they agreed to hand them over.

When Gabby came in from hanging up the washing, she was furious.

"Why did you give the kids crisps and chocolate?" she said, slamming the empty basket on the ground. "I'm just about to give them dinner."

"Leave me alone for a minute," I said.

I didn't have time to explain. I had only a few minutes before the kids would demand their toys back, and I was having trouble getting the Tamagotchis to find each other — maybe Meemoo's Bluetooth connection had been compromised by the virus.

Eventually though, when I put their connectors right next to each other, they made a synchronous pinging sound, and both characters appeared on both screens. It's amazing how satisfying that was.

Meemoo looked sick on Becky's screen too. I pressed A twice and then B to administer medicine.

Nothing happened.

I tried again. But the Tamagotchis just stood there. One healthy, one sick. Doing nothing.

Luke and Becky came back, their fingers oily and their faces brown with chocolate. I told them to wipe their hands on their trousers before they played with their Tamagotchis. I was about to disconnect them from each other, but when they saw that they had each other's characters on their screen, they got excited and sat at the kitchen table to play together.

I poured myself a beer and half a glass of wine for Gabby (her daily limit), then, seeing the crisps out on the side, helped myself to a bag.

Later, when my beer was gone and it was time for Becky's mum to pick her up, Becky handed me her Tamagotchi.

"Can you fix Weebee?" she asked. "I don't think she's feeling well."

Becky's pink Tamagotchi was already presenting the first symptoms of Meemoo's disease: the thinning and greying of features, the stoop, the lethargy.

I heard Becky's mum pull up in the car as I began to press the medicine buttons, knowing already that they would not work. "There," I said. "It just needs some rest. Leave it alone until tomorrow, and it should be okay."

Luke had been invited to a birthday party. Usually Gabby took Luke to parties, but she was feeling rough — she was having a particularly unpleasant first trimester this time. So she persuaded me to go, even though I hate kids' parties.

I noticed that lots of other kids at the party had Tamagotchis. They were fastened to the belt loops of their skirts and trousers. The kids stopped every few minutes during their games to lift up their Tamagotchis and check they were okay, occasionally pressing a button to satisfy one of their needs.

"These Tamagotchis are insane, aren't they?" I remarked to another dad who was standing at the edge of the garden with his arms folded across his chest.

"Yeah," he smiled.

"Yeah," I said. "My kid's one got sick. One of its arms fell off this morning. Can you believe that?"

The dad turned to me, his face suddenly serious. "You're not Luke's dad, are you?" he asked.

"Yes," I said.

"I had to buy a new Tamagotchi thanks to you."

I frowned and smirked, thinking that he couldn't be serious, but my expression seemed to piss him off.

"You had Becky Willis over at your house, didn't you?" he continued. "Her pet got Matty's pet sick 'cause she sits next to him in class. My boy's pet died. I've half a mind to charge you for the new one."

I stared right into his eyes, looking for an indication that he was joking, but there was none. "I don't know what to say," I said. And truly, I didn't. I thought he was crazy, especially the way he referred to the Tamagotchis as "pets," like they were real pets, not just thirty pixels on an LCD screen with only a little more functionality than my alarm clock. "Maybe there was something else wrong with yours. Luke's didn't die."

The other dad shook his head and blew out, and then turned sideways to look at me, making a crease in his fat neck. "You didn't bring it here, did you?" he said.

"Well, Luke takes it everywhere with him," I said.

"Jesus," he said, and then he literally ran across a game of Twister that some of the kids were playing to grab his son's Tamagotchi and check that it was okay. He had an argument with his son as he detached it from the boy's belt loop, saying he was going to put it in the car for safety. They were making so much noise that the mother of the kid having the birthday came over to calm them. The dad leaned in close to her to whisper, and she looked at the ground while he spoke, then up at me, then at Luke.

And then she headed across the garden towards me.

"Hi, there. We've not met before," she said, offering her hand with a smile. "I'm Lillian, Jake's mum." We shook hands and I said that it was nice to meet her. The precision of her hair and the delicateness of her thin white cardigan made her seem fragile, but this was just a front. "We're just about to play pass the parcel."

"Oh right. "

"Yes, and I'm concerned about the other children catching . . ." She opened her mouth, showing that her teeth were clenched together, and she nodded, hoping that I understood, that she wouldn't need to suffer the embarrassment of spelling it out.

"It's just a toy," I said.

"Still, I'd prefer . . ."

"You make it sound like . . ."

"If you wouldn't mind . . ."

I shook my head at the lunacy of the situation, but agreed to take care of it.

When I told Luke I had to take Meemoo away for a minute he went apeshit. He stamped and he made his hand into the shape of a claw and yelled, "Sky badger!"

When Luke does sky badger, anyone in a two-metre radius gets hurt. Sky badger is vicious. He rakes his long fingernails along forearms. He goes for the eyes.

"Okay, okay," I said, backing away and putting my hands up defensively. "You can keep hold of Meemoo, but I'll have to take you home then."

Luke screwed up his nose and frowned so deeply that I could barely see his dark eyes.

"You'll miss out on the birthday cake," I added.

Luke relaxed his talons and handed Meemoo to me, making a growl as he did so. Meemoo was hot, and I wondered whether it was from Luke's sweaty hands or if the Tamagotchi had a fever.

I held Luke's hand and took him over to where the pass-the-parcel ring was being straightened out by some of the mums, stashing Meemoo out of sight in my pocket. I sat Luke down and explained to him what would happen and what he was expected to do. A skinny kid with two front teeth missing looked at me and Luke, wondering what our deal was.

When we got home, Gabby was pissed off. "There's something wrong with the computer," she said.

"Oh great," I said. "What were you doing when it broke?"

"I didn't do anything! I hate the way you always blame me!"

I showed her my palms, backing away. After the party, I didn't have the strength for an argument.

The computer was in the dining room and switched off. While it booted up, I forked cold pesto penne into my mouth. After I'd tapped in my password, the computer got so far into its boot-up sequence and then made a frightening buzz. The screen went black with a wordy error message that didn't stay up long enough for me to read it. With a final electronic pulse, and a wheeze as the cooling fan slowed, it died.

"That's what it keeps doing," Gabby said.

"Were you on the Internet when it happened?"

"For God's sake!" Gabby spat. "It wasn't anything I did."

In my frustration, I jabbed the forkful of penne into my lip, making a cut that by the following morning had turned into an ulcer.

I had to wait until Monday to check my emails at work. There was still nothing from the makers of Tamagotchi. At lunch, while I splashed Bolognese sauce over my keyboard, I Googled "Tamagotchi" along with every synonym for "virus." I could find nothing other than the standard instructions to give it medicine when the skull and crossbones appeared.

Halfway through the afternoon, while I was in my penultimate meeting of the day, a PA announcement asked me to call reception. When a PA message goes out, everyone knows it's an emergency, and because it was for me, everyone knew it was something to do with Luke. I stepped out of the meeting room and ran back to my desk, trying hard not to look at all the heads turning towards me.

Gabby was on hold. When reception put her through, she was crying. Luke had had one of his fits. A short one this time, for him, just eight minutes, but since he'd come round, the right side of his body was paralysed. This happened the last time too, but it had got better after half an hour. I hated the thought that his fits were changing, that it seemed to be developing in some way. I told Gabby to stay calm and that I would leave right away.

When I got home, Luke's paralysis was over and he was moving normally again, except for a limpness at the edge of his mouth that made him slur his words. I hoped that this wrinkle would smooth out again soon, as it had last time.

I hugged Luke, burying my lips into his thick hair and kissing the side of his head, wishing that we lived in a world where kisses could fix brains. I stroked his back and hoped that maybe I would find a little reset button there, sunk into a hole, something I could prod that would let us start over, that would wipe all the scribbles from the slate and leave it blank again.

Gabby was sitting on the edge of the armchair holding her stomach, like she was in pain.

"Are you okay?" I asked.

She wiped her nose with the back of her hand and nodded. Gabby's biggest fear was that Luke's problems weren't just part of him, but part of the factory that had made him — what if every kid we produced together had the same design fault?

The doctors had all said that the chances of it happening twice were tiny, but I don't think we'd ever be able to fully relax. I knew that long after our second kid was born, we'd both be looking out for the diagnostic signs that had seemed so innocuous at first with Luke.

This fit wasn't long enough to call out an ambulance, but because the paralysis was still new, our GP came round to the house to check Luke over. Luke hated the rubber hammer that the doc used to check his reflexes. The only way he would allow him to do it was if he could hit me with the hammer first.

"Daddy doesn't have reflexes in his head," Gabby said as Luke whacked me.

"Not anymore, I don't," I laughed.

Luke has a firm swing.

A letter came home from school banning Tamagotchis. I knew this was my fault. Another three kids' Tamagotchis had died and could not be resurrected.

"People are blanking me when I drop Luke off in the morning," Gabby said. She was rubbing her fingers into her temples because she had a headache. It felt like everything in the house was breaking down.

"You're probably just being a bit sensitive," I said.

"Don't you dare say it's my hormones."

The situation had gone too far. Meemoo would have to go.

I was surprised at how hard it was to tell Luke that he'd have to say goodbye to Meemoo. He was sitting on the edge of the sand pit jabbing a straw of grass into it, like a needle.

"No!" he barked at me and made that frown-face of his. He gripped Meemoo hard and folded his arms across his chest.

"Help me out, will you?" I asked Gabby when she came outside with her book.

"You can handle this for a change," she said.

I tried bribing Luke, but he wouldn't fall for it, and just got angrier. I tried lying to him, saying that I was going to take Meemoo to hospital to make him better, but I had lost his trust. Eventually, I had only one option left. I told Luke that he had to tidy up his toys in the garden or I'd have to confiscate Meemoo for two whole days. I knew that Luke would never clean up his toys. The bit of his brain in charge of tidying up must have been within the damaged area. But I went through the drama of asking him a few times, and, as he got more irate, stamping and kicking things, I began to count.

"Don't count!" he said, knowing the finality of a countdown.

"Come on," I said. "You've got four seconds left. Just pick up your toys and you can keep Meemoo."

If he'd actually picked up his toys then, it would have been such a miracle that I would have let him keep Meemoo, AIDS and all.

"Three . . . two . . ."

"Stop counting!" Luke screamed, and then the dreaded, "Sky badger!"

Luke's fingers curled into that familiar and frightening shape and he came after me. I skipped away from him, tripping over a bucket.

"One and a half . . . one . . . come on, you've only got half a second left." A part of me must have been enjoying this, because I was giggling.

"Stop it," Gabby said. "You're being cruel."

"He's got to learn," I said. "Come on, Luke, you've only got a fraction of a second left. Start picking up your toys now and you can keep Meemoo."

Luke roared and swung his sky badger at me, at my arms, at my face. I grabbed him round the waist and turned him so that his back was towards me. Sky badger sunk his claws into my knuckles while I wrestled Meemoo out of his other hand.

By the time I'd got Meemoo away, there were three crescent-shaped gouges out of my knuckles, and they were stinging like crazy.

"I HATE YOU!" Luke screamed, crying, and stormed inside, slamming the door behind him.

"You deserved that," Gabby said, looking over the top of her sunglasses.

I couldn't just throw Meemoo away. Luke would never forgive me for that. It might be one of those formative moments that forever warped him and gave him all kinds of trust issues in later life. Instead, I planned to euthanize Meemoo.

. If I locked Meemoo in a cupboard, taking away the things that were helping it survive: food, play, petting and the toilet, the AIDS would get stronger as it got weaker and surrounded by more of its effluence. The AIDS would win. And when Meemoo was dead, it would either reset itself as a healthy Tamagotchi, or it would die. If it was healthy, Luke could have it back; if it died, then Luke would learn a valuable lesson about mortality and I would buy him a new one to cheer him up.

It was tempting while Meemoo was in the cupboard to sneak a peek, to watch for his final moments, but the Tamagotchi had sensors that picked up movement. It might interpret my attention as caring and gain some extra power to resist the virus destroying it. No, I had to leave it alone, despite the temptation.

Meemoo's presence seemed to transform the cupboard's outward appearance. It went from being an ordinary medicine cabinet to being something else, something . . . other.

After two whole days, I could resist no longer. I was certain that Meemoo must have perished by now. I was so confident that I even let Luke come along when I went to the cupboard to retrieve it.

"Okay," I said. "So have you learned your lesson about tidying up?"

"Give it back," Luke said, pouting.

"Good boy." I patted him on the head, then opened the cupboard and took out the Tamagotchi.

Meemoo was alive.

It had now lost three of its limbs, having just one arm left, which was stretched out under its head. One of its eyes had closed up to a small unseeing dot. Its pixellated circumference was broken in places, wide open pores through which invisible things must surely be escaping and entering.

"This is ridiculous," I said. "Luke, I'm sorry. But we're going to have to throw him away."

Luke snatched the Tamagotchi from me and ran to Gabby, screaming. He was actually shaking, his face red and sweaty.

"What have you done now?" Gabby scowled at me.

I held my forehead with both hands. I puffed out big lung-fuls of air. "I give up," I said and stomped up the stairs to the bedroom.

I put on the TV and watched a cookery show, and there was something soothing in the way the chef was searing the tuna in the pan that let my heartbeats soften by degrees.

Gabby called me from downstairs. "Can you come and get Luke in? Dinner's almost ready."

I let my feet slip over the edge of each step, enjoying the pressure against the soles of my feet. I went outside in my socks. Luke was burying a football in the sandpit.

"Time to come in, little man," I said. "Dinner's ready."

"Come in, Luke," Gabby called through the open window, and at the sound of his mum's voice, Luke got up, brushed the sand from his jeans and went inside, giving me a wide berth as he ran past.

A spot of rain hit the tip of my nose. The clouds above were low and heavy. The ragged kind that can take days to drain. As I turned to go inside, I noticed Meemoo on the edge of the sandpit. Luke had left it there. I started to reach down for it, but then stopped, stood up and went inside, closing the door behind me.

After dinner, it was Gabby's turn to take Luke to bed. I made tea and leaned over the back of the sofa, resting my cup on the windowsill and inhaling the hot steam. Outside, the rain was pounding the grass, digging craters in the sandpit, and bouncing off the Tamagotchi. I thought how ridiculous it was that I was feeling guilty, but out of some strange duty I continued to watch it, until the rain had washed all the light out of the sky.

ABOUT THE AUTHOR

ADAM MAREK'S prize-winning stories have appeared in many anthologies and magazines. He won the 2010 Arts Foundation Short Story Fellowship and was shortlisted for the inaugural Sunday Times EFG Private Bank Short Story Award. This story collection was nominated for the Frank O'Connor Prize. Visit him online at AdamMarek.co.uk.